WELL TRAVELED

WELL TRAVELED

JEN DELUCA

THORNDIKE PRESS
A part of Gale, a Cengage Company

**LIBRARY OF CONGRESS CIP DATA ON FILE.
CATALOGUING IN PUBLICATION FOR THIS BOOK
IS AVAILABLE FROM THE LIBRARY OF CONGRESS.**

ISBN-13: 979-8-88578-629-4 (hardcover alk. paper)

Published in 2023 by arrangement with Berkley, an imprint of Penguin Publishing Group, a division of Penguin Random House, LLC.

Printed in Mexico
Print Number: 1   Print Year: 2023

I dedicate this book to me.
We did it, Jen.

year." The glass ceiling in the firm had been broken only once, as far as I could tell: by Imogen Dunbrowski, one of the founding partners. I'd worked on exactly one project for her when I first got to the firm, and she'd never asked for me again, so that's how well that went. Rumor was she ate law clerks for breakfast. I had yet to break through my own personal glass ceiling, and at this point I wasn't sure what it would take.

But that wasn't my concern today. And my grandmother wanted to make sure I remembered that. "Go have some fun," she said. "Drink some wine, look at some kilts. That's what I'd do."

"Don't I know it." We hung up, and as I fumbled my phone into the back pocket of my jeans and my wallet back into my bag, I spied the brochure I'd found in my hotel room last night, next to the room service menu. *Spend a day in the past!* it said in bright, eye-catching yellow. The large photo in the middle depicted two knights on horseback charging toward each other, lances trained on their opponent. The audience was out of focus in the background, but I could still make out their waving hands and wide smiles.

When was the last time I'd smiled like that?

When I came across that brochure last night, I'd remembered the sunshine at the Willow Creek Faire. The music and the laughter. Everything inside of me had ached with memory, so this morning instead of ordering a room service breakfast and opening my laptop, I'd jumped in my rental car and come here.

But now that I'd arrived, it wasn't what I'd expected. I'd been looking for the coziness of a wooded setting, a feeling of getting lost in the trees. This place was . . . not that. It was a settlement hidden behind large gates, with buildings that lined wide gravel streets — it made the small Faire in Willow Creek look like a fly-by-night operation. I felt anonymous here: the medieval equivalent of being a nobody in the middle of Times Square.

I'd been handed a map at the entrance, and I checked it now as I walked, doing my best to dodge other people on the path. The late-May morning was warm and I already regretted the jeans I had on, but I hadn't planned for a day out in the sun when I'd packed for my out-of-town trip. It was either this or the gray pantsuit I'd worn for twelve hours yesterday. At least my silk tank was weather appropriate, and the purple matched my weekend Converse sneakers. Green probably would have looked better against my strawberry-blond hair, but I liked purple better. Sue me.

I let out a little "aha!" as I found what I was looking for on the map. The Dueling Kilts — those were Grandma's kilt boys. First show at eleven fifteen. I got lost once on the way, so the show had started by the time I got there. They attracted a good-size crowd and most of the benches in the audience were full, so I lingered in the back.

Now that I was here, the full memory of this band came flooding back. There were three of them, playing folk standards and drinking songs — your typical Renaissance Faire playlist — on an acoustic guitar, a fiddle, and a hand drum. I pulled out my phone — ignoring the texts that had piled up during the ten minutes it had been in my pocket — and started snapping photos to send to Grandma later. I still felt guilty about forgetting to call her, and pictures of hot men should do the trick.

"Get any good ones?" While I hadn't been looking, a costumed woman had sidled up next to me. She was short and round, with long blond hair and a sunny smile. Her off-the-shoulder dress was the color of a blazing sunset, worn under a brown-and-green bodice that turned her body into soft curves everywhere. Over that, her brown skirt was hiked up on the sides, setting off that sunset-colored dress.

Something about her tickled the back of my brain. She looked familiar, but I couldn't place it. Who would I know around here anyway?

"I don't know." I looked at my phone, but the sun glared off the screen and I could barely see the pictures I'd taken. "Just taking some shots for my grandmother. She has a thing for kilts."

"What is it with grandmothers and kilts?" Her smile widened as she shook her head. "My friend's grandma is the same way. She came to see us at my old hometown Faire, up in Maryland. This small town called Willow Creek. Anyway, she was —"

"Willow Creek?" I cut her off as my heart skipped a beat and pieces clicked into place. Blond hair, big smile. Hanging out with the musical group I'd just been taking pictures of . . . Now I knew her. "You don't mean Mitch's grandmother, do you?"

Her brown eyes flew wide. "You know Mitch?"

"Yeah. I . . . uh, I think we may be talking about the same grandmother."

16

"Wait. Yes!" Now her eyes lit up with recognition. "I remember you! You're Mitch's cousin, right? Um . . . Lolo?"

"Lulu," I corrected. Who the hell would name their kid Lolo? "Louisa, actually. Mitch couldn't say my name right as a kid, so he called me Lulu instead. It kind of stuck."

She laughed. "That sounds like Mitch. He has a nickname for everyone."

"Always has." My smile widened to match hers. It felt so comfortable, so right, to be talking about my cousin in a place like this. "I'm sorry, I forgot your name."

"Stacey." She offered me her hand and I clasped it. "It's so great to see you again! And how random that you're here. Do you live around here?"

I shook my head. "I'm here for work." And right on cue, my phone buzzed in my hand. Probably another text. "See?" I waved it in illustration. It didn't stop buzzing, though, so this was an actual phone call. "Ah, crap. I should probably take this." I pointed away from the stage, back toward the main part of the Faire.

Stacey waved me on. "Go ahead, don't let me interrupt! Do you want to grab a drink or something when you're done?"

"I'd love that." I glanced at the screen,

which flashed a Boston area code. Someone from national counsel's office. Great. "This should just take a second." I answered the call as I walked toward the relative quiet of the main thoroughfare teeming with people. Yeah, there was no quiet at a place like this.

But I heard Jacob Arnold's voice loud and clear. "How are you coming on that summary?"

"Oh. Hi, Jake." He never used a nickname, so I gave him one anyway. I was more like my cousin than I thought. "Working on a Saturday, huh?"

"Always am." His clipped voice brought our small talk to an abrupt end. "And so should you. Didn't you say you were up for partner?"

"Perpetually." I kept my voice pleasant while I bit back a sigh. "What do you need?"

"I need that summary."

That didn't take long. All those good feelings I'd had while talking to Stacey were gone. Crushed like a peasant uprising. Tension gripped the back of my neck. "Like I said in the email I sent at four this morning, the transcript won't be available till Monday, so there's nothing I can do now. Unless you'd like me to go stand over the court reporter's shoulder while she works on it." I shouldn't have said that. He'd think it was an option.

The Dueling Kilts' show must have ended while we were talking, because patrons came streaming out of the entrance to the stage. I stepped to the side of the path, covering my ear while people walked around me. They ignored me the way water in a fast-moving stream ignores a rock. I was jealous of their laughter. Of the carefree day they were having. I'd come for that too, but I sure wasn't getting it.

On the phone, Jacob was still talking, though I'd stopped listening. I could barely hear him anyway. "I'm going to have to call you back," I said. "I'm in a crowd, can't hear you too well right now." I hung up before he could answer and swam upstream toward the entrance of the stage, shoving my phone back in my pocket. I'd pay for that later, but I couldn't find it in me to care.

Stacey was behind a table off to the side, selling all kinds of merchandise with the band's logo: shirts, CDs, those little things you put over your beer can for some reason. I reached her table just as the last patron left, and her smile chased some of the tension from the morning.

"Everything okay?"

No, but she didn't need to hear about

that. I forced a smile I didn't feel. "All good." I picked up a CD and turned it over in my hand. Would Grandma like one of these, or was she just in it for their outfits?

There was a rustle at my feet, and I looked down to see a tuxedo cat secured to one of the table legs by a long lead. He was currently mid-battle with a leaf, paying no attention to me.

I glanced up at Stacey. "Friend of yours?"

She laughed. "This is Benedick." She bent to scoop the cat up in her arms, which he tolerated without protest. The lead was plenty long enough for her to give him a snuggle and a kiss before setting him down again. "He's part of the group." She tapped a finger on a tank top that featured a logo I hadn't noticed on the others: a winged dragon that was actually a little tuxedo cat.

"You should get that," a voice said to my left. "It's our bestseller." I turned to see one of the band members — the tall fiddle player — next to me. But his attention didn't stay on me; instead he plunked a small wicker basket of cash down on the table. My eyes went wide as a confusing thought ricocheted through my brain: Was he buying all the merch?

But Stacey collected the basket and scooped out the cash within, stacking the bills with quick, practiced fingers. "Not bad, huh?"

"And that was just the morning crowd," he said. "This is looking like a good day."

"We could use some of those. Oh, Todd, this is Louisa. She's Mitch's cousin." She stowed the cash in a lockbox before taking it to the backstage area, out of sight. "You remember Mitch, right?" Her voice floated from a few feet away. "From back home?"

"Malone?" His eyebrows shot up and he turned back to me, a smile of recognition breaking across his face. Apparently my cousin's name opened doors on the Renaissance Faire circuit. "Aw, man, he's great! He's your cousin? I'd love to know what he was like as a kid."

"Shorter," I said. "His biceps were a little smaller. But otherwise pretty much the same."

He chuckled and shook his head. "That sounds about right." He touched my shoulder in a familiar gesture, something between a tap and a squeeze. "Nice to meet you." With that he was gone.

Stacey rolled her eyes as she emerged. "Todd's not terribly chatty. Anyway, how about that drink? There's a tavern right over here."

"It's noon somewhere, right?" God, I loved Renaissance Faires. "Lead the way."

TWO

Stacey and I strolled through a wooded glen dotted with merchants and tourists. Everything around us was a riot of color and sound. Music and merriment, swirling skirts and elaborate hats. Cloaks and leather, despite the heat of the late-spring day.

I took a good deep breath, letting the surrounding trees feed oxygen directly into my lungs and push away any negative thoughts. Now I could understand why people would want to come here, to immerse themselves in a world that's nothing like their normal day-to-day. I was getting sick of my own day-to-day myself.

Before long we made it to the tavern, which was little more than an open-sided tent, yet it managed to feel like a cozy, hole-in-the-wall place you'd happen across without looking for it. At one end of a makeshift bar an older man dressed as a pirate, complete with an eyepatch over one eye, held court. He had a growly kind of voice that made it hard to eavesdrop on, but he finished his story with a guffaw that made others around him join in, and my smile was involuntary, enjoying the atmosphere without knowing the words being said.

As we emerged with our plastic cups — white wine for Stacey, cider for me — we heard a shout from down the lane.

"Advice!" the woman called out, in that general *hear ye, hear ye!*–style voice that addressed everyone and nobody all at once. She was dressed in green, from the feathers in her dark hair to the toes of her leather boots peeking out under her long skirts. "Advice!" she called out again, pointing to the sign that she carried in one hand, suspended over her head. ADVICE, it read, predictably, with an arrow pointing down at her head. "Do you need advice?" She directed her question to a young couple, walking hand in hand. "Because I am very, very good at giving it."

The woman giggled while the man looked wary. "Uh . . . well . . ."

While Stacey and I shared a smile and watched the impromptu show, the woman peppered them with questions: How old were they? How long had they been together? My phone buzzed in my pocket, because five minutes to myself was the legal limit. I swore under my breath as I reached for it. It was my assistant, Cheryl: **Mr. Stone says you're sending me something to type up soon. What's the ETA on that?**

I sighed a very long sigh. I hadn't said anything of the sort. Not to Mr. Stone, not to anyone. I pictured Cheryl sitting there at her desk on a Saturday, spinning her chair in lazy circles, waiting for a dictation file that wasn't coming because I was drinking cider at a Renaissance Faire.

"Everything okay?" My sigh must have carried, because Stacey's smile slipped a little, and she looked at me with concerned eyes.

"Yeah. Just . . . just a work thing. Again." I held my plastic cup of cider between my teeth while I texted back. **I'm not sending anything. Tell Mr. Stone I said you can go home.** I blew out a breath as I hit Send. That wasn't going to go over well.

I stuck my phone back in my pocket and took another sip of my drink as the advice lady finished up with the couple. ". . . And that's why I think marriage is a great idea! For you. Because you're already married. Otherwise I might think differently. Who knows?" The couple laughed, and I felt a smile come to my own lips.

"Excellent advice."

"Isn't it, though? And so specific." Stacey laughed and we toasted with our plastic cups. We were a strange-looking duo, me in my modern-day street clothes and Stacey dressed like she belonged here.

She nodded toward my hip. "Everything okay with work?"

"Oh. Yeah." But of course my phone buzzed again, reminding me that while Stacey belonged here, I didn't. My life was in the real world. Maybe the advice lady could tell me how to get away from my job for a few hours. That was all I wanted.

The text was from my boss. **Cheryl said you sent her home. Want to tell me why?**

There's nothing for her to do, and there's no sense in paying her to wait around. Maybe making it sound like a fiscally responsible move would work well in my favor.

"My advice to you is to chuck that thing in the lake," Advice Lady said, pausing as she passed me. "It's too nice a day to be dealing with work."

Stacey laughed and nodded in agreement, while I blinked at her. "How do you know I'm dealing with work?"

She pointed to her forehead, at the space between her eyebrows. "You're all furrowed

26

here," she said. "That's the stressed-out-about-work furrow. I'm telling you." She mimed an overhead throw with the hand not holding her Advice sign. "Right in the lake."

"Hmmm." Maybe it was the half glass of cider I'd had on an empty stomach, but that didn't seem like a bad idea. "Any lakes around here?"

"No idea. But if you find one, you know. Advice still stands." Then she gave me a big smile and was on her way.

She wasn't wrong, was she? I'd thought coming here would make me feel better. When I'd visited Mitch at his Renaissance Faire, I'd remembered it as a special kind of day, where my soul had lightened and things had seemed . . . better. I'd been seeking that feeling today. But instead, I was juggling my drink and my phone, hardly paying attention to anyone or anything around me. Stacey had been nothing but nice to me, and I was all but blowing her off.

If Stacey noticed my rudeness, she didn't say. Instead she tugged on my arm. "Come on. The laundry wench show is just up ahead. That's always a fun one."

"The what?" But I followed her gentle pull, and as we rounded a bend I heard a shriek, followed by audience laughter like a distant roll of thunder. We approached the stage, where two women performed for a large crowd seated on long rows of benches in front of the stage. Their costumes were your typical tavern wench fare: simple dresses with comically patched skirts and lace-up bodices, and their braided hair stuck up in ways that couldn't be natural. On either side of the stage, outlandishly large shirts and bloomers were hung on a washing line, and words scrawled on a sheet behind them proclaimed them to be laundry wenches. There was my answer: now I knew what a laundry wench show was.

As we slipped onto a bench in the back, the wenches onstage slapped clothes into a large tub of water situated between them, creating a splash zone out of the first couple of rows. If a joke they told didn't get enough laughter, they'd slap a shirt into the tub and threaten individual audience members with the soaked garment. Before long I was laughing along with them, texts from work forgotten as the laundry wenches flirted shamelessly with the men in the audience, threatening them with wet clothing if they didn't reciprocate. Their act was just on the safe side of risqué, that type of humor that parents got but flew over the heads of their kids.

As the show ended, the performers threaded their way through the outgoing crowd, collecting tips and doing some more flirting. I remembered the guy in Stacey's band with his basket of cash, and it all made sense. I dug into my bag for my wallet.

"What did you think?" Stacey bumped her shoulder against mine. "Good, right?"

"Definitely." Cash in hand, I moved through the departing crowd, Stacey on my heels. One of the laundry wenches was by the stage with a basket for collecting tips, and she grinned at me in thanks when I put a five in there. One of her teeth was blacked out, and I took a moment to wonder how she got the braids on either side of her head to stick up like that. Was there wire involved? "You were great," I said.

"Thank you, milady!" She dipped her head at me in an approximation of a curtsy. "And are you enjoying your day here at the Faire?"

"Ummm . . ." I had no idea how to answer that question. I'd been here for a couple hours now, and what had I really enjoyed? The cider in my hand — which was mostly medicinal — and about a show and a half I'd barely been able to pay attention to with my phone constantly going off.

Of course, just then my phone buzzed. "It's been great." I reached into my back pocket for my phone. "Except I should have left this in the car." I waved my phone at her, and she laughed.

"Terrible things, those." And with one more dip of her head she was gone, working her way through the thinning crowd. Alone now at the front of the stage, I glanced down at my phone. My office number: this wasn't good.

Sure enough, it was William Stone. One of the four names on the outside of the building. Everyone called him "Bud" for some damn reason, but I called him Mr. Stone because he was my boss.

"Where are you?" His voice barked through the line, and my spine straightened by instinct. "Are you *outside*? Am I hearing *bagpipes*? That doesn't sound like a hotel room."

"That's because it's not." I worked to keep my voice as nondefensive as I could. "I needed to get some air." There. It sounded like I was out for a walk, on a brief break, bagpipes notwithstanding.

"Listen, you need to get this done. The Boston office is depending on us."

"I know that." Now I was defensive. "But,

Mr. Stone, this isn't that important a witness. You were copied on the initial summary I sent. He was the car behind them in the crash and he didn't see much. I don't think his testimony is going to make or break anything."

"That's not for you to decide." The bark was still in his voice, making the hair on the back of my neck stand up. "That's for the lead attorney on the case to determine once he's reviewed your detailed summary. Your job is to provide that summary in a timely manner."

"And I'm doing that." My voice dripped patience and professionalism, but all I heard was what was unspoken. *You're not the lead attorney. Your opinion doesn't matter. Your years of law school and litigation experience don't matter.* My opinion didn't matter because I wasn't a partner. Not yet.

Not ever. It all suddenly snapped into very clear focus. No matter how hard I worked, no matter how many late nights or out-of-town trips I took, I was never going to make partner. Not when some mediocre white man was in the running. And there was always a mediocre white man in the running.

But Mr. Stone was oblivious of my revelation. "Jacob Arnold says you're giving him excuses, and now I call you and you're not even in the office, or your room, or anywhere in front of your work. What are you —"

"Bud." I'd never called him that before. I'd never interrupted him before. But something inside of me had just broken, and broken people did those things. "It's not going to happen, is it?"

The non sequitur shut him up. Silence stretched out for a good ten seconds. I let that silence stretch. "What?" he finally said. "What's not going to happen?"

"Me. Making partner." My breath shook on my next inhale, and something scary swirled in the pit of my stomach. But I also felt very, very awake. Maybe for the first time in years. "You've said *maybe next year* for five years now. And instead of getting put on any real track to making partner, to being allowed to prove my worth, I'm here in Bullshitville, North Carolina, taking a deposition that could have been farmed out to a first-year associate." Oh boy. This was *really* how not to make partner. But the words were out of my mouth now; may as well forge ahead. "It's not going to happen for me, is it?"

Silence greeted my outburst. I half expected the next words out of his mouth to be that I was fired. To instruct me to come into the office on Monday long enough to clean out my broom closet of an office, and of course turn in that detailed deposition summary on my way out the door.

Instead Mr. Stone — Bud — sighed, and oh, God. I knew that sigh. I heard it every year, every time I wasn't on the list for a promotion. It was going to be followed by my name, said very seriously, very kindly. The same verbal pat on the head. The one that said *maybe next year.* The one that kept me going, that kept me working harder, that kept me billing more hours and missing more family functions. The one that kept me chained to a job and chasing a dream that I wasn't even sure I wanted, but that my family wouldn't let me leave behind. Grandma was right. I worked too much. And for what?

"Louisa . . ." There it was. The pat on the head. The kind words. But this time I couldn't hear them. All I could hear was the sound of my blood pounding, whooshing in my ears. All I could see was the advice lady in the green dress, miming throwing my phone in the lake.

There wasn't a lake anywhere around here. But there was a giant tub of water on the stage, not five feet away. And that was close enough.

"I'm done," I said, cutting off whatever platitudes Bud had chosen to placate me with this time. "I quit."

I didn't do what happened next. Someone else lowered the phone from my ear, not even disconnecting the call. I watched a hand that looked like mine toss the phone sideways, like you might skip a stone across a still pond. It bounced once, twice, across the surface of the laundry wenches' tub before sinking with a plop. How long did it take for the phone to die? What did Bud hear on his end of the line as the phone hit the bottom of the washing tub?

In the space between heartbeats I was back in my body, my phone ruined at the bottom of the tub, my career similarly trashed. I turned around to see Stacey just behind me, her brown eyes wide. She opened her mouth, closed it, opened it again.

"I think . . ." She cleared her throat. "I think we need to get you another drink."

THREE

"I quit my job," I said to my third glass of cider that morning. It didn't respond.

But Stacey did. "It's going to be okay." Her voice was overly calm, like she was talking me out of jumping off a bridge. Didn't she see it was too late for that? I'd already jumped, and the impact was going to hurt like hell.

"I don't see how." I shook my head and took another gulp of cider, oblivious to the revelry around me. We were back in the tavern, the drink in front of me served by a barmaid in a cinched-up corset and a huge smile. Next to us a frat boy in chain mail chugged a light beer, his friends in variously elaborate costumes cheering him on. A faint melody from those goddamn distant bagpipes floated by on the breeze. I should have been enjoying this day at the Faire the way everyone around me was. But I was too numb to enjoy anything.

"You don't know my family. They want . . ." They want perfection. They want excellence. My stomach clenched, and the cider threatened to come right back up. Sure, I was in my late thirties, but judgment from your parents was eternal. They'd been so proud of my upward trajectory with the law firm. This was going to kill them.

"Here. Take this." Stacey took away my cider and pushed a bottle of water into my hands. "Our next show starts in a few minutes. Why don't you stick with me for a bit."

I was out of options and my brain was offline, so I followed her like an obedient child. We dodged costumed Faire-goers and kids with fake swords until we reached the stage. She ushered me to a bench at the back of the audience, where words echoed in my head to the rhythm of my heartbeat.

I quit my job. I quit my *job.* I *quit* my *job.*

It was midday and the sun was high, the heat making those three ciders hit even harder. As the Dueling Kilts took the stage, I uncapped the bottle of water Stacey had given me, forcing myself to take measured sips and calm down. During their earlier show, I'd been so focused on taking pictures for Grandma that I hadn't paid much attention to the act itself. I could rectify that now. Focus on the stage in front of me.

Time for a confession here: kilts have never been my thing. Men had many attractive qualities, but knees weren't one of them. My cousin in his kilt looked like bad Catholic schoolgirl cosplay as far as I was concerned. Whatever fetish Grandma Malone had didn't make its way down to my generation.

But with these guys in front of me I could let myself enjoy kilts for a change. And let me tell you, it was an easy thing to do.

I'd already forgotten the name of the fiddle player I'd met earlier, but a lot had happened since then. He was tall and lean, his trimmed beard a shade or two lighter than his long, dark auburn hair tied back in a queue. The other two were dark-haired and looked closely related to each other. The one on the hand drum was shorter and boyish looking, slender with close-cropped hair, but the guitarist . . . there was nothing boyish about him. Talk about a man who didn't skip leg day, set off to great effect by his red kilt. He was the most muscular of the three, with dark hair tied carelessly back from a face that boasted sharp cheekbones and a sharper jawline, framed by just enough stubble to be called a beard. If this were a boy band from my childhood, the

drummer would be the cute, nonthreaten-
ing lead singer, while the part in me that
coveted bad boys would have gone straight
for the guitar player.

Good thing I was over my bad-boy phase.

Stacey was on to something, bringing me
here, because watching this band was doing
wonders to stave off my panic attack. The
tall one closed his eyes sometimes while he
played his fiddle, sun glinting off his long
auburn hair. He didn't sing, though; that
duty seemed to fall to the bad-boy guitar
player, whose growly baritone seemed to be
perfectly made for the drinking songs and
shanties they featured. Sometimes the
drummer backed him up, in a clear tenor
that made for a perfect counterpoint.

I wasn't usually one for folk music, but
something about the rawness of the acoustic
instruments spoke to my soul, even ampli-
fied by wireless mics and unobtrusive speak-
ers on either side of the stage. Instruments
and voices combined in rich harmonies, the
music feeling greater than the sum of its
parts.

The trio bantered and joked with the
audience members, raising wooden tankards
in toasts before, after, and even during the
songs. I wasn't familiar with most of the
songs in their set — sea shanties weren't my

usual thing — but eventually they swung into "Drunken Sailor," putting me on more familiar territory. Except their version seemed to be a million years long, as the verses deviated from the original, obviously made up by the band and becoming more and more silly. Eventually they started taking requests from the audience of things that could be done to said poor sailor, and laughter rippled through the crowd.

"Whoa!" The guitar player pointed to someone in the second row, who had called out something I hadn't heard from my seat. "You want him to do *what* with a socket wrench? You're a sick man!" A laugh bubbled out of me, louder than I'd intended, and I clapped a hand over my mouth. But the sound carried, and he turned his head in my direction. Our gazes locked, he smiled, and *whew*. There was a long moment where the world stopped, and all that existed was this ridiculously hot man in a man bun with a day's worth of scruff, smiling at me like I had his full attention. Suddenly the world wasn't such a bad place. Kilts were a little more attractive.

The singer's gaze swept over me in a quick up-and-down, and his smile widened as he inclined his head in acknowledgment. I couldn't imagine what he saw in me that looked appealing, but then again maybe he liked half-drunk women on the verge of a breakdown.

The drummer broke in then, realizing that the guitar player had been distracted. "Okay!" He clapped his hands together, and I blinked hard as though waking up. "I think we've abused this poor sailor long enough. Some of y'all are just plain sadistic."

"You're right." The guitar player turned to his compatriot, shaking off the remnants of whatever moment we'd just shared. But his smile looked different now, more performative, not quite the same one he'd shown me. "How about a little 'Whiskey in the Jar' next?"

I knew this one too. As the music started I closed my eyes and leaned back on my hands, tipping my face toward the sun. I could practically feel the freckles erupting over the bridge of my nose, but I didn't care. While the breeze teased some of my hair out of my ponytail and danced reddish-blond strands across my cheek, the notes of the song flowed over me, carried on the air from their guitar, fiddle, and hand drum. Hard cider hummed through my bloodstream, and music surrounded me, soothed me. For a blissful few minutes nothing could touch me.

But far too soon the show came to an end and reality came crashing back, along with the beginnings of the panic attack I'd seen coming. I needed to get out of there. Out of the sun. Out of this Faire. Out of this whole damn day. I had to update my résumé. I had to find another job. Was there a market for slightly unstable attorneys with a penchant for the dramatic? Because that would be perfect for me right about now.

Oh, God, what was I going to do?

White static crept in the edges of my vision. Standing up was impossible, walking out of here even more so. I bent forward, putting my head between my knees and breathing deeply. Tears pricked my eyes as the panic attack took hold. All my life I'd been on this path, and now the path was gone. I was alone, lost in the woods.

"Is she all right?" A man's voice spoke over my head, and I chanced a look up. While I'd been freaking out, the audience had mostly gone — a couple stragglers took pictures with the band up by the stage. The man near me was tall, dressed in black jeans and T-shirt, a baseball cap eclipsing his vivid red hair. He wasn't dressed for a day in the sunshine, but he acted like he belonged here. His attention was on Stacey, threading her way through the maze of benches toward us.

"She's fine." Stacey waved him off.

"Are you sure? She doesn't look so good. Do we need to call someone for her?" The redhead's eyes flicked from me to Stacey, a question in them. By "someone" I had a feeling he meant "paramedics."

"I already did." Stacey brandished her phone like it had all the answers. "Here." She sat down next to me, handing me her phone. "It's for you."

"Me?" But when I looked down at the screen, relief swept through me in a cool wave. God bless Stacey, she'd called in reinforcements. "Hey, Mitch." The words were a sigh, directed at my cousin at the other end of the video call. My favorite cousin. He was five years younger, but I loved him more than my own brothers. Mostly because my brothers were dicks, and Mitch was awesome.

"Hey, Lulu." He looked as happy to see me as ever. "What the hell are you doing in North Carolina? Stace says you're making a scene there."

"You know me," I said weakly. "Always a troublemaker." I finished off my water, and Stacey took the empty bottle from me, replacing it with a fresh one. I watched as she took the arm of the redhead in black, pulling him away to give me privacy. His head bent toward hers as they talked intently.

Mitch snorted. "Yeah, right. We both know that's my job." His brow furrowed, and his voice gentled. "Seriously. What's going on, Lu?"

I pressed the heel of my hand to my forehead, staving off more tears. "I was here for work, and . . ."

"Work?" Mitch blinked. "Who needs lawyers at a Renaissance Faire?"

The ghost of a smile tugged at my lips. "North Carolina, you weirdo. I'm in *North Carolina* for work, and then I got one phone call too many from my boss and . . ."

"Yeah, Stacey filled me in on that part. You wanna tell me why you made your phone part of the laundry wenches' show?"

"Okay, technically the show was over." He acknowledged my joke with a smile, but I knew I wasn't getting off that easy. "I'd just had enough, you know? All this time I've been 'up for partner' " — I put down my water to make air quotes with one hand — "and my boss made it clear that no matter what I did, it was never going to happen, and I just . . . I lost it." The memory of that last phone call made my chest ache, but there was one part that had given me grim satisfaction. "Turns out phones don't skip like stones do."

That made Mitch laugh, and his boisterous laugh always made me feel better. I glanced up again. The guy in black had an arm around Stacey — so they were a couple — and they'd joined the rest of the band near the stage. They looked to be having a serious discussion, and when more than one of them threw a glance my way I had the sinking feeling the discussion was about me. Probably how to get the half-drunk, unemployed lady out of the audience and on her way.

The last thing I wanted to do was overstay my welcome. "I'll be fine. I just need to get home. Regroup. Get a new phone." I pushed to my feet. "Thanks for talking, Mitch, I really appreciate —"

"Oh, no, you don't." Mitch put out a hand like he could stop me from where he was. "I know you. You're gonna go right back to work on Monday."

I had to scoff at that. "I burned that bridge pretty well."

"Then you'll get another job. Same shit, different office. Is that really what you want?"

"I don't . . ." My mind went blank. I had

44

no answer for him. My goals had defined my life up till now, but were they really mine? High school valedictorian, summa cum laude at college, top percentile in law school, position with an established, high-profile firm, a partnership at said firm — they'd been my parents' goals, not mine. All laid out in front of me like landmarks, but no one had ever asked if I'd wanted any of them.

"I love you, Lu. And you know I'm proud of you. But this job has sucked out your soul. Don't think I haven't noticed. When's the last time you went out with friends? When's the last time you were happy?"

I didn't even have to think about that last one. "Just now. Today. Hanging out with your friend Stacey and listening to this music." My blood pressure momentarily lowered as I let myself relax into the memory, but I shook it off. "Doesn't matter. This isn't real life."

"Maybe not for you." Stacey had come back, and Mitch grinned at her through the phone.

"Damn straight. So what's the word?"

"About what?" But he wasn't addressing me, he was talking to Stacey, who nodded.

"As long as she's on board." She looked at me. "You are, aren't you?"

"On board with what?"

Stacey huffed. "You didn't tell her yet?"

"I was getting to it!" Mitch rolled his eyes as she huffed again, then he turned his attention back to me. "So, Lulu. Stacey and I were thinking. What if you disappeared for a little bit?"

"Disappeared?"

"Yeah. If you go home, our family of go-getters is gonna get in your head, the way they always do. You'll be back in that power suit, working for dickheads who don't appreciate you."

I clucked my tongue. "Don't hold back, Mitch. Tell me what you really think."

"You need a break," he shot back. "That's what I really think. Why not take one? Stacey said you can travel with the band."

I couldn't remember the last time I'd taken a vacation. The last time I'd had a day — weekend, holiday, didn't matter — where my phone hadn't rung or chimed with a text, with a fire at work that somehow only I could put out. I'd always told myself that when I made partner those days would end, but I'd been paying those dues for years with no return on investment.

But . . . "Let me get this straight. You're suggesting I run away and join the Renaissance Faire?" It sounded like a life plan made by a ten-year-old.

Stacey shrugged. "It worked for me," she said with a smile.

"Not forever," Mitch rushed to clarify. "Just till you clear your head. They'll be in Willow Creek for our Faire later this summer. Hitch a ride with them, and you can come stay with April and me in July. I'll get you home after that."

"July?" I was aghast. "You want me to do this till *July*?" It was the end of May; July seemed a lifetime away. I shook my head. "I have to find another job. I can't just . . ." But my mind whirled with possibilities. My rent and all my other bills were on autopay, and I had enough in savings to tide me over till I got back to real life. There was absolutely no reason for me not to do this. The thought of existing out here in the woods, not worrying about lawsuits or bosses barking orders . . . it seemed too good to be true.

Mitch must have seen me waver. "And *no phone*!" He pointed an accusatory finger at me. "That's part of the whole clearing-your-head thing. If you have a phone, you'll call your mom, and she'll fill your head with bullshit. You need to be bullshit free."

The idea of not having a phone — for weeks! months even! — was insane. It was like suggesting I leave one of my limbs behind. But I was nodding, going along with this whole plan. Until . . . "Grandma!"

Mitch's brow furrowed. "What about her? Is she okay?"

"She's fine. But can you call her? Once a week or so. She and Grandpa in that big house by themselves, I worry that they . . ."

"I got it." He waved a hand. "I'll call Grandma once a week. I'll call your mom too, tell her you're unavailable for a bit. Don't worry. I'll run interference with all of them, and we'll figure out the rest when you get here, okay?"

"Okay." I nodded, though I had no idea if I was really going to pull this off. Could I really live this life?

"Good." His expression softened. "I love you, Lu. You know that, right?"

My answering sigh took a lot of tension with it. He really was looking out for me, and maybe this was what I needed. "Love you too, big guy."

After disconnecting the call I handed the phone back to Stacey, a little dazed. I'd never been a "roll with it" kind of person, and I wasn't entirely sure what I'd just agreed to. But it had to be better than the life I'd been living up till now. "I don't suppose you're hiring?"

I was joking, but Stacey nodded. "We'll figure something out." She tugged me to my feet. "Come on. We still have time before the end of the day. Let's get you some garb so you'll be set up. Daniel's going to ask around tomorrow; someone always needs help with something around here." She hugged my arm with glee. "I love this! I've been the only girl in the group for too long now. You'll have fun, I promise."

"That sounds like a threat." But this was good. If I could make jokes, I was probably going to be okay.

But Stacey just laughed. "Lots of hair braiding and girl talk. Just don't let Dex flirt with you. He's bad news."

"I am not — how dare you." The voice came from behind us, a teasing growl. I turned to see one of the band members — the bad boy with the man bun and the wicked smile. My heart thumped in recognition. "Hey." He extended a hand to me in greeting. "Dex."

"Louisa." I slid my hand in his, giving him my best attorney handshake. Firm grip, firm eye contact, letting him know I wasn't going to take any shit.

And whoa, I needed that handshake to hide behind. I'd thought he'd been attractive onstage, but he was even more devastat-

49

ing close up. His hand in mine was strong, with a guitar player's calluses. That strength continued up corded forearms sprinkled with dark hair, with muscles that were barely hidden by the loose lace-up shirt he wore. My firm eye contact brought me into the depths of his eyes. Dark brown that, this close, glittered with slivers of amber.

But he had to ruin it by smirking. He had to ruin it by knowing the effect he had on women, and giving me an up-and-down appraisal.

"You're coming along with us, huh?" A slow smile traveled over his face. "This is gonna be fun." There was no question as to what kind of fun he meant.

I took my hand back, startled. Spell broken.

Stacey whacked him on the shoulder. "What did I just say? She's not here for you." She sighed a long-suffering sigh and turned to me. "Ignore him. Come on."

I followed Stacey out to the lanes leading to the clothing vendors, and even though I could feel those dark eyes still on me, I didn't look back. I was well over my bad-boy phase, and like Stacey said: I wasn't here for him. I was here for me.

FOUR

Turned out, it was easy to disappear.

After the final set of the day, Stacey's boyfriend, Daniel — the tall redhead in black — followed me back to my hotel. It didn't take long for me to pack up my stuff and check out, and before long I'd returned my rental car and tossed my weekend bag in the bed of Daniel's old rust-red pickup truck. The suit I'd worn on Friday for the deposition went in the trash in the hotel lobby — I wasn't going to need that where I was going.

I hadn't been this impulsive in years, and it was equal parts liberating and terrifying. But when Daniel swung into the entrance to a local campground, dread prickled at my scalp. What had I gotten myself into? There was changing my life in a radical way, and then there was sleeping on the ground when I'd just given up a perfectly good hotel room. I tried to turn my sigh of despair into a regular exhale so as not to appear ungrateful.

But he didn't pull up to a cluster of tents, like I'd imagined. He killed the engine in front of a 1970s-era motorhome, all beiges and browns with a single wide orange stripe wrapped around its snubbed nose. An awning stretched out from the vehicle's right side, over the open side door. Under the awning an outdoor carpet was laid out, with folding chairs grouped in a loose circle around a card table and a pair of lounge-style Adirondack chairs off to the side. Stacey sat in one of the lounge chairs, immersed in a book. Her corset and skirts had been exchanged for yoga pants and a loose top, her hair twisted into a messy bun on top of her head.

Stacey put her book down as I climbed out of the truck. "Hey, there you are!"

"Here I am." I tried to echo her enthusiasm, but I was quickly learning that being as enthusiastic as Stacey was a lost cause.

Daniel closed the door to his truck and looked around. "Where are the guys?"

"Back at the hotel." Stacey rolled her eyes with a smile. "Todd needed to call Michele. You know, get his long-distance goodnight kiss." She stretched up on her toes to give Daniel a quick kiss of his own, then turned back to me with a welcoming smile. "Come on in. Let's put your stuff inside."

It was close quarters inside the motorhome, and the seventies theme carried over to the interior. Lots of brown and burnt orange, but here and there was a sunny touch: white curtains printed with little sprigs of springtime flowers lined the windows over the sofa on one side and the counter and minuscule stovetop on the other. Through a short almost-hallway, past a bathroom that was little more than a closet, was a bed made up with a blue-and-yellow quilt, Benedick the cat already snoozing on top like a black-and-white circular throw pillow. All in all it gave the impression of a domain that no one had bothered to decorate in a long time, but had recently been taken over by a sunnier personality.

"I get the sofa?" I put my bag down on said sofa. It wasn't huge — nothing in this motorhome was — but it was better than a tent.

Stacey nodded. "I won't make you snuggle with Daniel and me. No promises about the cat, though. Hope you're not allergic."

"So, you and Daniel camp while the band stays at a hotel?" I followed her back outside, which felt wide open after the tiny motorhome. We got waters from the nearby

53

cooler, and I settled down next to her in the other Adirondack chair.

"We trade off, usually," she said. "Depending on what kind of accommodations we get from the Faire. The guys got the hotel rooms this stop."

"Some places provide housing, some don't," Daniel added. He cracked open a beer and claimed one of the folding chairs nearby.

"Oh," I said as the picture became clearer. "You're not always in the camper?"

He shook his head. "Sometimes we get a whole block of rooms. Other times it's just one or two, and then the rest of us take the RV. Or we spring for another room if we're sick of camping."

"At least you're not sleeping in the back of your truck anymore." Stacey's voice was teasing.

He huffed out a laugh as my eyes widened. "I'd never make you do that. Besides, once you hit your thirties that kind of thing stops being fun."

"God, I bet." My own over-thirties lower back twinged in sympathy.

"Anyway." Daniel clapped his hands to his thighs before standing up. "The couch in there folds out into a second bed, and there's an extra pillow and blanket for whoever uses it. Tonight that's you, so I'll set that up."

"And you're leaving us to do paperwork," Stacey said with an indulgent smile.

"And I'm leaving you to do paperwork," he confirmed. His smile echoed hers as he bent to kiss the top of her head.

"What paperwork?" I asked Stacey once Daniel had gone inside.

"He's the brains of all of this," she said. "Keeps the band employed. We're here for one more weekend, then off to the next stop. He's probably making sure accommodations are all set. There's also gigs at local bars during the week; that's some extra income. And then there's contracts and arrangements for stuff that's a few months down the road . . ." She shook her head. "His spreadsheets are intricate, and they make him happy. I find it better not to ask." She craned her head, looking in the window. I followed her gaze to see Daniel sitting at the small dinette table inside, illuminated by the glow of his open laptop, idly stroking the head of the cat, who'd come to help him out. It was a peaceful, oddly domestic scene.

"Don't worry," Stacey said, her dark eyes still on Daniel. "I know it's been a crappy day for you. Things will look better tomorrow after you get some sleep."

The bathroom inside the motorhome was laughably small. Showering while straddling a toilet wasn't the most comfortable experience, but the water was warm and it cleared away the rest of the alcohol from my brain. What a day this had been; crappy didn't even begin to cover it.

I'd packed a sleepshirt for my weekend away, and I paired it with my yoga pants to make the ensemble a little more decent for mixed company. Daniel had made up the pullout sofa for me as promised, and maybe it was the exhaustion talking, but it looked as cozy as a makeshift bed could look.

I settled down next to the pillows and pulled my laptop out of my bag. "Do you have Wi-Fi?"

Stacey clucked her tongue at me and shook her head. "None of that, now." She wagged her finger at me like I was a disobedient child. "Mitch told you to take a break, remember?"

I huffed out a breath. "I just want to send out a couple emails. I did quit my job kind of abruptly. I should let people know I'm okay and that I didn't have a breakdown."

"Maybe a little bit of a breakdown." Daniel raised his eyebrows as he took a sip from a mug of coffee — coffee? This late? The man was a machine.

"Maybe a little," I conceded with a smirk. The more distance I was getting from the whole phone-in-the-washtub thing, the funnier it became.

His eyes flicked from his laptop to me then, amusement in their green depths. "Pumpkin spice," he said. "All one word, capital *P*, capital *S*, exclamation points for both *i*'s."

"I don't know," Stacey protested while I punched in the password. "I still feel like it's cheating."

"I promise," I said as I logged into my work email account. "It's just for tonight and then . . ." My voice trailed off as an error message popped up. Huh. I typed in my email password again, but the same little error window popped up. "Or maybe not."

"Maybe not what?" Stacey dropped onto the sofa bed beside me, moving the pillows out of her way. "Don't you dare agree to do anything for those . . ."

"It's not that." A chill washed through me as I realized what had happened. My email had already been disabled. It hadn't even been twelve hours since I'd quit my job, but I'd been erased from the firm like I'd never existed. The devil worked fast, but law firms worked faster.

Stacey leaned over my shoulder, and we both stared at the error message for a few seconds before I closed my laptop. It was all but useless now. Keeping my work life and private life separate had always been a top priority; I'd never emailed any of my work colleagues from my personal email. There'd been a few numbers in my phone, but of course that was gone too. I'd cut myself off from everyone.

Stacey must have noticed my rising panic — my default state lately — because she slung an arm around me and I let my head fall onto her comforting shoulder. "It'll be okay." Her shoulder was soft, and her voice was soothing. I found myself almost believing her.

"You know what, you're right." I shoved the laptop back in its bag, zipped it up, and handed it to Stacey. "No laptop for me. Take it. Lock it up. Throw it in the lake for all I care."

"Throw it in the lake," she repeated. "That can't be your response to everything, you know."

"Right now it can."

"I'll just hold on to it." She took the bag to the back of the motorhome, stowing it in

58

the bedroom area. "Bring it with us to the hotel at the next stop. Remove the temptation."

"Good plan." But I already missed it, like I'd just cut off a hand or something. No laptop, no phone. How was I going to function? My hip had been vibrating on and off all afternoon with phantom notifications from a phone I didn't have anymore. Was it going to be like this all summer? Could I quit cold turkey, unplug from everything? Or would I be frantic in a convenience store in a couple weeks, grabbing for a prepaid phone, desperate for an online fix?

Man. I really did need to go off-grid.

It wasn't like I'd wanted my job back anyway, I thought later that night as I got into bed in the darkened motorhome. I'd just wanted to send a couple of goodbye emails, get some closure on the way out.

That lack of closure was the problem. I'd been the one to quit, but getting locked out of my email that fast made it feel like their decision, not mine.

I was mentally and physically exhausted, and despite the makeshift bed, I sank gratefully into the pillow with a relieved sigh. But I couldn't sleep. Everything was strange. My bed was about two inches too short, just barely keeping me from stretching out.

Outdoor lights only partially filtered by the flowered curtains. The sounds of the campground roughly six inches from my head, on the other side of the steel wall of the motorhome. Daniel and Stacey talking in their bed at the back, their low voices carrying but not the actual words, while I stared at the ceiling and hoped they weren't talking about me.

I couldn't stop thinking about my laptop. I pictured the emails piling up in my in-box on the other side of my password that no longer worked. The thought of those unread, unanswered emails made my blood pressure rise, and I reminded myself firmly that it wasn't my concern anymore. By Monday other attorneys would be assigned to my cases. I was nothing but a cog in that machine, and there were plenty of cogs to go around. I wouldn't be missed.

I'd given that career the best years of my life, not to mention a shitload of money in student loans that I was still paying back. Here I was in the latter half of my thirties, starting over at square one. All those years wasted, with nothing to show for it.

What the hell was I doing?

I didn't realize I was crying until the tears leaked from the outside corners of my eyes and ran into my ears. I swiped at them, risking a single sniffle while I hoped that Stacey and Daniel were asleep by now. The last thing I wanted to do was draw attention to myself. I'd done enough of that today.

There was a sudden dip in my mattress, followed by a deep rumbling sound that jerked me out of my half sleep. I blinked in the dim light as Benedick picked his way across the blanket, following a path beside my legs. He paused to climb onto my stomach, marching up and down in place on my belly. Little pinpricks of claws perforated my stomach.

I'd never been a cat person — my hectic work hours were a bad lifestyle to impose on any kind of pet — but now I curled my hand around his little head, scratching behind his ears. His purrs grew louder, and my heartbeat calmed as the cat's kneading paws slowed down and he settled to lie on my chest. Before I knew it, the hitch in my inhale had gone. The rumbling of his purrs sank into my chest, chasing away the last of my anxiety as we fell asleep together.

Two days ago, I'd taken a deposition wearing a gray pantsuit. I had six other pantsuits just like it at home, in neutral tones that ranged from navy to beige and, on the days when I was feeling spicy, taupe. Those pantsuits were my work uniform. They were my life.

But now I had a new work uniform. Benedick yawned in an early morning patch of sunlight while Stacey tugged a long, dark green skirt over my head, settling it at my waist over the wide-necked beige underdress I'd already put on. Then she handed me one of my newly purchased bodices in the same dark green.

"This is easier to wear than a corset, so let's start with that."

I scowled down at the garment while I tried to tug it together across my chest. "I knew I should have tried this on first. It's not going to fit." Did vendors at Ren Faires take returns?

"It'll fit. Here." She threaded a long string through the bottom holes before lacing it up like a sneaker. She was all business as she motioned for me to hike up my breasts while she tightened the lacing.

"It's a little tricky to do on your own," she said, "but once you've been doing it for a while you'll get the hang of it."

"Sure." Now it made sense. "Like a lace-up push-up bra."

"Exactly!" Stacey tugged at my under-dress, settling the now-ruffled edge in a mostly even line around my enhanced cleavage, and pulling the wide neckline down over my shoulders, leaving them bare against the straps of the dark green bodice. "This is good. These colors look great with your hair."

"You think?"

She nodded firmly. "Green with strawberry blond? Perfect. And the braid looks great." She gestured to my hair, and I patted the French braid I'd created that morning. I had a lot of hair and it was long, so it mostly lived in ponytails and braids when I wasn't at the office. And I was very much not at the office. "So now you've got the basics. We can get you a belt pouch, so you can stick your phone in there . . ."

"Phone?" I raised my eyebrows pointedly, and Stacey laughed.

"Okay, then money, your ID, stuff like that. And we might want to look into getting you some boots?" She looked dubiously down at my feet.

"You mean purple high-tops aren't period appropriate?" I tugged my skirt a quarter of an inch lower in a sad attempt to hide my Converse. All I had were these and my black heeled pumps, and neither choice was a good one.

"Not even a little bit. But don't worry about that today. There's a really great leatherworker at the next Faire, so we can get you some boots there."

The next Faire. That's right. I really had signed myself up for a few weeks of this. Now that it was happening, now that I was wearing an outfit that squeezed at my rib cage and inhibited my range of motion, I saw the future stretched out ahead of me like a road I didn't have a map to navigate. This wasn't like me; I always knew where I was going. I always had the next goal in mind. But not anymore. Now I was off the edge of the map. Here be dragons.

I should have been panicked. But now that I'd committed to this life the panic in my chest had morphed into an almost-giddy feeling. I really had run away and joined the Renaissance Faire, and I wanted to laugh at the absurd excitement of it all.

When we got to the grounds, it was early enough that the sun was still new in the sky, its light watery but still bright enough that I wished I'd worn sunglasses. The front gates of the Faire were deserted, making the place look like a ghost town. After we passed through those empty gates, Stacey gave Daniel a quick kiss and while he set off in one direction, she led me in another.

"Wait, where is he going?"

"There's a meeting most mornings for the

performers, where they talk about schedule changes, anything that needs to be looked out for. Mostly boring, businessy stuff. Daniel loves it." She waved a hand in dismissal as we walked down the path, and we were at the stage before we knew it. I followed her as she unlocked the black case backstage that contained their souvenir merchandise. Time to get the day started.

"What do you need me to do? Run the merchandise stand or something?" I could do that. Probably.

But Stacey shook her head. "Nah, I have that handled pretty well." She slipped her phone out of her belt pouch — now I saw what she meant by its usefulness — and took a quick glance at the time. "Help me get set up, though?"

"Of course."

"Think of today as orientation." She motioned to the folding table against the backstage wall, and I grabbed the other end of it. Together we carried it to the side of the performance area and set it up. "You know, when you start a new job, and you spend the first few days figuring out where the break room is, how the copier works . . ."

"Where the bathrooms are?"

She nodded emphatically. "The most important thing anywhere." She handed me the vinyl tablecloth, which I spread on the table while she dragged a box of T-shirts over.

"That's funny," I said. "I can't picture you working in an office."

"Not in this outfit." She grinned at me and hoisted Benedick in his carrier up onto the table. "I used to work the front desk at a dentist's office. Fewer corsets, more scrubs. More comfortable, but also more boring." She unzipped the carrier and hauled out the still-sleepy cat. Benedick wore his harness from yesterday, with little dragon's wings on the back. Everyone was in costume around here.

"Anyway," she continued. "Daniel said he'd ask around and see who needs help. There's always someone who's a little shorthanded." Stacey took a small round bed out of the carrier and placed it under the table for Benedick, securing one end of a leash to a table leg and clipping the other end to his harness. He woke up long enough to do a little sniffing around before settling down in his bed: a cat who was used to this life. Stacey crouched down to give him some chin scritches and smiled up at me. "But get acclimated today, and then you can really pitch in next weekend."

"I wouldn't mind that." Next weekend

seemed like a lifetime away.

"Heyyyyy."

I knew without turning around that Dex MacLean had joined us. No one else I knew around here would put at least four *y*'s into one syllable and make it sound so lecherous. I tried to sigh, but that was off the table with this bodice on. Instead I clamped my teeth together — I was tagging along with these people, should probably stay polite — and turned to spit out a good morning.

And then I immediately melted under the force of Dex's smile, because I was only human, and let's be honest: the dude was hot, with those dark eyes, chiseled cheekbones, and a wicked smile aimed directly at me. And there was something about where we were, how we were dressed, that made something more primal inside of me take over. I wasn't thinking about sexism or equality in the workplace. I didn't want to put him in his place with my handshake or my glare. With my shoulders bare and my legs hidden under layers of skirts, I felt more like someone who might find myself going for a guy like this.

That was startling. But I could roll with it. So instead of saying anything snarky, I bobbed a curtsy in his direction. "Good sir." I made my voice the best approximation of an Austen heroine that I could manage. Not quite the right period, but close enough.

His smile was half smirk; he'd probably gotten a good look down my dress while I was curtsying. "Nice. Fully assimilated already, huh?"

"Not quite." I twitched my skirts aside and pointed a toe, showing off my very modern footwear, and his smirk became an actual laugh.

"See, I think that looks great." That laugh was disarming, completely making me forget any defensiveness I'd felt toward him.

"Thanks. I don't think I'll get away with it for long, though."

"Eh." He shrugged. "Just keep your skirts over 'em. Nobody's gonna notice."

The thing about this outfit was that there were no pockets, so there was nowhere to put your hands. I settled for resting them on my suddenly smaller waist and I nodded toward Stacey. "She's gonna notice, believe me. I can wear them today, but I'm going to have to pick up something more authentic."

"Yeah, that sounds like her." His gaze flicked toward Stacey, then back to me. "You look good otherwise, though. Put together an outfit pretty quick." He propped his guitar case on the merchandise table we'd just set up, unlatching it and taking out his acoustic guitar. "Hold that?" He passed it to me, and I held it awkwardly by the neck while he closed the case up again and stowed it backstage. While he was doing this the other two-thirds of the band arrived, deep in conversation as they wound their way around the benches where their audience would sit later.

"Hi. Louisa, right?" The younger one smiled at me, his dark hair and brown eyes making him look like a more slender, kinder Dex.

"That's me . . ." I searched my memory for his name but was coming up empty. I'd been half-drunk and fully panicked when I'd met the rest of the band very briefly the day before, so I'd retained very little.

"Frederick." His handshake and smile were welcoming, and I felt everything inside of me smile in response.

"Todd." This was the tall redhead I'd spoken to yesterday. The one with the long-distance girlfriend, according to Stacey. The pieces were starting to come together. I could do this. "You joining the band?" He nodded toward the guitar, and the amusement in his eyes made a grin come to my own face.

"You know it," I said, fully aware that I

69

was holding a guitar the absolute wrong way in front of accomplished musicians. "Hope you like 'Freebird.' "

Frederick snorted out a laugh, and Todd's smile seemed to be the equivalent of a laugh on anyone else. Thankfully, Dex showed up then and I was able to pass him his guitar back. I joined Stacey behind the merchandise table with relief.

"You don't have to stay here if you don't want."

"I should probably . . ." I waved a hand toward the main path. "Go get oriented?"

Her smile was kind; I was probably doing a shit job of not looking completely lost. "You really should." She laid a hand on my arm, squeezing lightly. "I've always seen the Faire as a place to get away from real life for a while. Focus on that, okay?"

My breath escaped my lungs in a relieved sigh. "You're right. I'll go find the bathrooms. And . . . you know. The copier and all that."

"Good plan." She squeezed my arm once more before letting go and giving me a gentle push on the shoulder. "I'll give you a hint: the bathrooms at this Faire are painted orange, so they're easy to find."

"Oh, God." A thought occurred to me. "They're porta-potties, aren't they?"

70

"Yep." Her smile widened at the distressed look on my face. "Welcome to Faire life!"

Great.

FIVE

I didn't make it far.

I'd just made it to the path outside the stage area when I nearly collided with Daniel.

"Oh, good. You're still here." He glanced down at his phone, then back up at me. "If you're up for it, they could really use your help at the food stalls. Some of their volunteers aren't showing up."

I frowned. "That's not good."

"No kidding." He shook his head. "Some people . . . if you're not paying them, they consider it optional. Don't get me started. Anyway." He peered at me. "Are you sure you don't mind? It's not the most glamorous work."

I shrugged. "Is anything around here glamorous? I have it on good authority that I'll be using porta-potties for the foreseeable future."

Daniel huffed out a laugh. "You're not wrong."

"I don't mind, honest. If working the food stalls helps out the Faire, I'm your girl."

"Be careful who you say that to. We'll never let you leave." Daniel smiled as he checked his phone again. On anyone else this would look rude, but Daniel struck me as a guy who had checklists to keep track of his spreadsheets, which he used to organize his lists. And the master checklist probably lived on his phone, where he could refer to it at any given moment. "I have a few minutes. How about I walk you over there, so you can get situated."

"I'll do it." Dex had come up behind us while we were talking, and I started at his voice. He shrugged as we turned to him. "I was going to do a quick walk-around before things got busy. Gate just opened, right?" He nodded in response to Daniel's nod of confirmation. "There's an hour till the first show. I'll be back in plenty of time."

Daniel looked from Dex to me. "That okay with you?"

"Sure." I couldn't imagine why it wouldn't be.

"Cool. We'll take the long way around, and I'll give you the tour." Dex turned to me. "Ready?"

"Sure," I said again, with a bravado I didn't really feel. "Let's do this."

Dex wasn't one for small talk.

Silence stretched between us as we headed up the path. Although the gates were open and the day had officially started, the crowd was still thin. Patrons wandered here and there, mostly studying the maps in their hands and not looking where they were going. Yesterday all I'd seen were the gravel paths and the crowds of people. Today it didn't even feel like the same place. Today I noticed the slender, tall trees flanking our path, their tops waving in a breeze that didn't make it down here to ground level. This place felt like it was made of pure oxygen, and the breaths I took were clean and invigorating.

Finally Dex cleared his throat. "So. You're a lawyer, huh?" His expression was uncomfortable, but at least he was trying.

I made a hum of assent. "Until about twenty-four hours ago."

His laugh was more of a snort. "Yeah, but did you quit for good? Stacey said you were, like, taking a break. Clearing your head."

"I'm not sure." We passed vendors still setting up for the day, and I scanned the displays, looking for a leatherworker. No boots for sale, so I tugged my skirt down another inch or so to cover up my sneakers. "I realized yesterday that I've been doing what my family wants, you know? Like they've always told me I should be an attorney, so I went along with it. Making them happy. But I don't know if —"

"Heyyyy, Matt! What's up?" Dex stopped, both my story and our progress, to swing down a short side path that led to a small stage. A banner in red and yellow stretched across the top of the stage that read SPRING IN OUR STEP. Beneath it, a group of four acrobats in parti-colored costumes were scattered across the stage, stretching in ways that my mind couldn't even begin to contemplate. Sure, I went to yoga three times a week, more for the mental clarity than anything else, but there was no way I could put my leg behind my head like that. I was annoyed to have been silenced, but could I blame him? I'd been boring myself by rambling about my aborted career, and who cared when you could talk to bendy acrobats instead?

Two of them stopped their warm-up as we approached the stage, and one hopped up. He was tall and well muscled, and while I wasn't an expert on what kinds of things an acrobat might do during a show, I had a feeling he was the one who did the throwing and catching. The let-people-stand-on-his-shoulders-ing.

"Dex, how you been, man?" They did a fist bump followed by a handclasp kind of handshake. "How are the shows going?"

"Good." He nodded vigorously. "Can't complain, you know? Money's good, chicks are good. All good." Wow. Dex wasn't the most articulate, was he? And he came with a charming side of casual misogyny. I closed my eyes in a slow blink so I wouldn't be caught rolling my eyes.

"Hey, Dex." One of the girls limbering up onstage gripped her ankles, bending over her legs till her forehead touched her knees to hold the stretch.

"Hey, Delilah. Looking good." His eyes were appraising, and she looked up at him with a wicked grin. Hmm. Maybe misogyny was easy to overlook when you looked like Dex. There was something in the way they gave each other a once-over . . . I glanced from Delilah to Dex and back again. It wouldn't have surprised me in the least if they were an item.

I glanced over at the male acrobat — Matt? — expecting him to be protective of his cohort, but if he noticed or cared he didn't say. Instead he'd turned to me.

"Hey," he said. "You're new."

"I am." I wasn't sure what to expect next. Was he going to hit on me? Maybe that was how Ren Faire performers communicated with each other.

But Dex came to my rescue. "This is Lulu," he said. He touched my back between my shoulder blades, and a calloused fingertip brushed my bare skin above my underdress. His hand was warm, and I tried not to notice. "She's a friend of Stacey's. Traveling with us for a little bit."

"Louisa," I corrected, and almost winced at the sound of my own voice. I didn't sound like a performer, like someone who lived this life. I sounded like a lawyer meeting opposing counsel for the first time at a hearing. I stuck out my hand, trying for friendly but coming across as disappointingly professional.

"Matt." If he was amused while shaking my hand, it was easy to overlook. Then recognition sparked in his eyes. "Wait. You're the one with the phone, right?"

My stomach dropped all the way down to my not-period Converse. "What?"

"The phone." He looked from me to Dex for confirmation. "At the wench show yesterday, right?" He made a throwing motion with his arm. "I heard about you!"

77

Dex laughed, oblivious to my growing desire to hide under the stage over there. "That's her! We're so proud."

"Great," I muttered. I looked down, twitching imaginary lint off my skirts. "I'm Phone Girl now."

"There's worse things to be called, believe me." Matt's smile was kind. "Listen, it's a small world around here. And the wenches thought it was hilarious."

A layer of shame sloughed off, and I even felt a smile twitching at the corners of my lips. "As long as I provided some comic relief."

"That's the spirit." He gave my shoulder a friendly squeeze before turning back to Dex. "Y'all headed to Blue Ridge next?"

Dex nodded. "As always." Then his expression turned speculative. "Hey, do you know if Siren's Song is going to be there? They weren't there last summer."

"Yeah, because the soprano got married, remember?"

"Ah, shit, she did?" Dex's face fell, and Matt laughed.

"Yep. So cross that name out of your little black book."

Dex scoffed. "Like I ever write them down."

"Never change, man." Matt laughed again,

shaking his head. I'd been following this exchange like it was the world's most misogynistic tennis match. "Never change."

Dex shrugged, all wide-eyed innocence. "Any reason I should?"

"Not a one." Matt gave me a wave. "Nice to meet you, Lulu. See you around."

"Louisa," I corrected under my breath as we turned back toward the main path again.

"See you later, Dex?" Delilah called out as we left. I turned to see her sinking into a split as suggestively as possible. So blatant! Good Lord.

But Dex just smiled, a promise in his eyes. "Later, babe." Wow. Yeah. Those two were definitely banging.

We were silent again. I knew if I opened my mouth I was going to lecture him on being a sexist pig, and was that even my place? Delilah wasn't offended; she was hitting on him even while he was talking about his prospects at the next stop. I reminded myself that this was their world, not mine. I was just along for the ride.

But it was good to know this about Dex. It was easy to be swayed by his pretty face, the way he laughed. It was easy to find yourself wondering what it would be like to be with a guy like that. Now that I'd spent ten minutes alone with him, I knew; it would be empty sex while he had his eyes on the horizon, on who was next in line for him. Which, maybe that was fine for Delilah. But meaningless sex had never been my thing. I needed more out of relationships. Like, for one, an actual relationship.

Thankfully, there were no more detours on the way to the food stalls. We passed more stages, with performers in various phases of getting ready for a day of shows. Musicians tuned their instruments, and we passed one man doing something with a sword that I didn't want to think about too hard. Most of them called out hellos in our direction. Dex was a popular figure around here, and he greeted everyone with a smile. I'd never seen someone so comfortable before. Not just in their own skin, but in their life. He was exactly the kind of person he wanted to be, and it showed in everything he was. Maybe there was something to be learned from this. When was the last time I'd felt that at ease with who I was, with how I lived my life?

"Here we go." Dex's voice was cheerfully matter-of-fact as we arrived at a clearing that was filled with long, rough-hewn wooden picnic tables. Stalls and carts formed a corral around the tables, their signs advertising everything from period-appropriate turkey legs to less-period-appropriate cotton candy. It looked like a rustic, outdoor food court, and the air already smelled like anything and everything that could be deep-fried.

None of the workers behind the stalls and carts were in costume; they all wore the same dark blue T-shirt with a small logo on the left breast. Obviously a different kind of volunteer than I was. Most of them looked young — college age or early twenties. I was out of place in every way.

Dex walked a couple steps ahead of me while I trotted after him to keep up, approaching one of the people behind the counter. "Hey, Carmen," he said easily. "I brought you some help."

"Dex, you're a lifesaver," she said, even though I was the one bailing them out. He probably got credit for bringing me over. She wiped her hands on a dubious-looking rag and stuck one out toward me. "Carmen," she said. "So nice to meet you."

"Louisa." I concentrated on keeping my expression pleasant, neutral even, as I shook her hand. She looked a couple decades older than me, with the almost-leathery skin of someone who spent a lot of time chain-smoking in the outdoors. She wore the same staff T-shirt as everyone else, but she seemed to oversee everything going on in the food stalls.

"Glad to have you, Louisa. I'm sorry I didn't have time to get you a staff shirt, but what you're wearing should be fine." She waved a hand at me, like I wasn't wearing a ridiculous outfit to work a deep fryer. "Lends authenticity or whatever."

"I'm going to head back." Dex pointed over his shoulder toward the path we'd just been on. "First show's starting soon."

"Okay," I said. "I'll come find y'all at the end of the day."

"Cool. Have fun, Counselor."

I blinked at the nickname; he'd actually paid attention to my rambling earlier. "Thanks." I watched Dex walk away with a sense of loss. There were so few familiar faces in my life right now that losing one was hard. Even if it was Dex. But I took a deep breath and turned back to Carmen. "Where do you want me?"

To anyone else that would be an innuendo, and I expected at least a smirk. But Carmen was all business; she'd probably never made a that's-what-she-said joke in her life. She glanced around, and wherever her gaze hit, the people under her purview tried to look busier. I knew that look from working in the corporate world. Carmen commanded respect and would accept nothing less. Good for her.

"These guys have been working together for a few weeks now," she finally said. "Rather than train you on something too big, like food prep or cashing out, why don't you help back here, putting the orders together."

I nodded with only a small internal scream. I'd spent four years in college, and three years after that in law school. I was — or had been — a senior associate at one of the biggest law firms in the country. A seventy-hour workweek was a light load for me. But here, making change was too big a task for me to be trusted with.

"I think I can probably handle it." I tried not to smirk. Too much. "I worked fast food when I was a kid." I couldn't believe this. I was giving my résumé to someone to impress them enough to get promoted to the deep fryer. Enough. I moved back behind the tables, where a kid roughly ten years younger than me gave me the rundown. Plastic serving baskets were here, cardboard containers for fries were there, don't forget to wear gloves.

This was fine, I told myself as I snapped on a pair of latex gloves. I said I wanted to help out, and that's exactly what I was doing. Who cared if it wasn't glamorous. That had never been the point. The point had been to get away from my real life, right? So this was fine.

"We need you over at turkey legs."

This was a sentence that my thirty-seven years of life had not prepared me to hear.

"What? Why?" I turned back to my work while I talked, because there wasn't time to stop. No time spent under the employ of the golden arches could prepare you for the onslaught of Renaissance Faire patrons in various stages of drunkenness under the noontime sun on a Sunday. But I was a multitasker; I could portion out a fresh fry-basket's worth of fries while expressing utter confusion at the same time.

"Too many people at this table and we're drowning over there."

We were drowning here too, but a quick glance around showed me she had a point; we were a large group of worker bees here, swarming around one piece of honeycomb, while the booth across the way with the iconic turkey legs was almost impossible to see in the crowd around it.

"Okay." I shucked my gloves and followed my new supervisor across the way. I was immediately pressed into service as an order taker — not too hard since we served exactly one thing — and collected the money into the cashbox in front of me. It didn't take long for me to fall into the frenzied rhythm that came from serving as many people as possible as quickly as possible.

It felt like only a few minutes had gone by, but suddenly I looked up and the sun had started to dip in the sky. The crowd of patrons had finally, finally reduced to a trickle, and I was released from duty. I guzzled a bottle of water as I walked back toward the Dueling Kilts' performance stage, pitching the plastic bottle into a recycling barrel without slowing my stride. Not hard since my stride was more like a crawl. A limp. A hobble. My feet were killing me. My torso was killing me. My everything was killing me.

By the time I made it to the stage, the last show was just wrapping up, so I joined Stacey behind the merch table in case she needed help. Because helping was what I did.

But she waved me off. "I got this. You look like you've had a long day."

"That obvious, huh?" But I huffed a lock of hair out of my eyes and put a hand up to touch the back of my head. There was more hair escaping from my braid than was still left in it. I pulled out the elastic and shook my hair free. But it was way too long, and the day way too hot, to just leave it down like that. I finger-combed it out as best I could before plaiting it back into a loose braid that I flipped over the front of one shoulder.

Then I made a critical error: I sank down to sit on the ground. As soon as my ass hit the dirt I knew the mistake I'd made; the bodice made sitting like that awkward, and I had no idea how I was going to stand again. But that was Future Louisa's — like, Thirty-Minute-Future Louisa's — problem. I had no give-a-shits left.

As the show ended and Stacey buzzed around selling merchandise to the departing patrons, I stayed cross-legged in the dirt behind her with Benedick. We quickly devised a game of kill the leaf: I offered him a leaf, and he killed it. It was a simple game, but it was all I had the brainpower for, and he didn't seem to mind, so it worked for us.

The game was abandoned after a few minutes, and Benedick crawled into my lap. I scritched him on top of his head in that little fuzzy divot between his eyes. He purred in sleepy pleasure, and just like the night before his purr soothed me. I'd made more than one friend this weekend, and that felt nice. Nicer than selling turkey legs, at least.

"He really likes you!" Stacey beamed down at us between sales, not all fazed by the failed lawyer cuddling with her cat. Maybe things like this happened to her all the time. She lived a very different life than I did.

"He's pretty great," I said, a tired smile coming to my face.

"He is. You about ready?"

"Hmm?" I glanced up at Stacey in surprise. Benedick wasn't the only one dozing off around here; while I'd been lost in empty thought the performance space had emptied out.

"Come on." Stacey extended a hand down to me, and I let her haul me to my feet. "Help me put this stuff away and we'll get out of here."

"You got it." I sounded a lot more enthusiastic than I felt. I was one step removed from complete zombification. I'd thought a long day at the office was tiring, but I'd never ended the day smelling like a combination of dirt and smoked poultry. And a power suit had nothing on a bodice/long skirt combination for making it both hard to walk and to breathe.

What the hell had I signed up for? And how hard would it be to beg for my job back?

Six

At the end of a long day at work, some people dream of cracking open that first beer of the evening. But as I brought up the rear in a tired parade to Daniel's truck, all I wanted was to take off this outfit. The bodice was unlaced before we'd even left the grounds, and I heaved a sigh of relief as the laces gave way.

"Best part of the day," Stacey said, her fingers working at the laces in the front of her bodice, loosening the strings. "Congrats on surviving the day, by the way. You're one of us now."

"Great." I knew she meant it in a nice way, but all I could see was an exhausting future of serving turkey legs. Most people went on vacations when they needed to clear their heads. How had I signed on for the exact opposite?

But I had to admit it was working: I'd hardly thought about my failed career all day. Instead, all I could think about was a long hot shower and sleep. Maybe some food. Something that wasn't fried.

Of course, that long hot shower was off the menu, I remembered as we arrived back at the motorhome. I thought about the guys in the band, the hotel rooms they had while we lived at the campground, and tried my damnedest not to be jealous. Because they'd taken me in, were taking me on a ride-along of their lives, and it was the height of rudeness to criticize it.

But man, I could really go for starfishing on a king-size hotel bed right about now.

I made do with the motorhome shower, and once I was clean and back in my yoga pants my attitude perked up significantly. Stacey had changed out of her Faire costume, and she must have been craving fresh food as much as I was, because to my surprise the little countertop in the RV held the makings of a salad.

"It's not much." Stacey handed me a small fistful of carrots to peel and chop while she tore lettuce into a large bowl. "Sundays are for finishing up the produce before it goes bad."

"Is that what you're supposed to do with veggies?" I crunched on a piece of carrot. "I usually just toss them in the back of the fridge, then throw them out once they're mostly liquid."

"I hear you." Stacey giggled — she was one of those people who honest to God *giggled.* "That's one thing living on the road changed about me." She handed me a couple of tomatoes to slice once I was done with the carrots. "I used to live in a tiny place before, so this minimalism thing isn't a huge deal. But fridge space is at a premium here . . ." She opened the fridge to illustrate, and she wasn't wrong. It was barely bigger than a dorm fridge. The kind of fridge some of my friends from law school had in their first New York apartments. "You have to really think about what you want in here." She took some plastic bags of mostly depleted sliced deli meat and two hard-boiled eggs from the bottom shelf and bumped the door closed with her hip.

I nodded in understanding while Stacey made quick work of the protein, slicing it all up and adding it to the salad. "Probably not doing a lot of Costco runs, huh?"

She snorted. "Nary a one. We'll hit a grocery store tomorrow to stock up for the week." Salad finished, she reached into an upper cabinet for sturdy plastic plates and handed them to me. She carried the big bowl and I followed her outside, which had been transformed into the table and chairs setup I remembered from the night before. Strings of unlit white lights I hadn't noticed before lined the awning in looping swirls. The transformation was startling; none of that had been there when I'd gone inside to shower.

Then I spotted Daniel and Todd off to the side just outside the awning, arms crossed while they chatted. And here came Dex and Frederick carrying a large red chest cooler between them. So that's how this magic had happened. I'd been on the verge of annoyed at the backward idea of us women inside making dinner, but the men had been busy too. This life was a group effort.

"Oh, thank God, a vegetable," Daniel said as Stacey put the salad bowl on the table.

Dex rolled his eyes and snagged a beer from the cooler that he'd just set down. "We eat plenty of vegetables."

"We eat like five-year-olds," Frederick countered. "Chicken fingers and fries."

"Protein and carbs." Dex slapped the flat of his stomach with a dull *thwap,* obviously echoing off muscle beneath his shirt. "All I need." He caught my eye, and I didn't want to smile. I didn't. But I did anyway. Dammit. And to make matters worse, he saw it. His answering smile brightened his eyes and lightened up his expression. I reminded myself that Dex was a pig. It helped a little.

He bent over the cooler again, running a hand through the loose ice there. "Beer?" He glanced over his shoulder at me. "Or water? Soda?"

"Water's great," I said. "I didn't get much today."

"You gotta drink water." His hand was cold when he passed the bottle to me, a shock of relief against the heat of the day. "It's easy to get dehydrated when you're outside all day like this. It's not like working in an office, you know." He cocked an eyebrow at me, and I laughed despite myself.

"There is absolutely nothing about this that's like working in an office." I drank most of the bottle of water in one go; I really was dehydrated.

"Sounds like that's what you need." He passed me a second bottle of water.

"Thanks."

"No problem." He looked like he was about to say something else, but instead he turned to Stacey. "Is that all we've got? Salad? There's got to be some chips or something in there."

"Go look; I'm not your mom." Stacey shook her head, the messy bun on her head bobbing and threatening to tumble down into a blond tangle. "If it was up to you, we'd be eating Faire food all day every day."

"Good thing it's not up to me, then." Dex went into the RV, his boots clomping on the thin metal stairs.

Stacey watched him go, her lips pressed together, and rolled her eyes once he was safely out of sight. Then her smile was back, and she turned to me. "Hungry?"

"Starved." That was an understatement. I grabbed one of the plates and behind me the door to the motorhome slammed. Dex eschewed the stairs altogether, jumping to the ground in a swirl of kilt. He was the only one who hadn't changed out of his Faire attire. But on Dex, his performance outfit didn't look like a costume. No, this was what he threw on in the morning to start his day. Jeans and a T-shirt might look out of place on this guy. Then I told myself to stop mentally dressing him, like he was my own personal Ken doll to fantasize about. Because he wasn't.

Dinner around the card table was pleasant, made even more so by the sun going down, breaking the heat as night fell around us. It was obvious that, as an extra body, I made everything under that awning more crowded. But no one mentioned it, and while Daniel insisted I take a chair and that he was just fine to eat standing up, I moved to the rickety metal steps at the door of the motorhome. Perching there with a thick plastic plate on my knees was good enough. I let their conversation wash over me like ambient bedtime music while I sipped at a third bottle of water and figured out the group's dynamics.

Dex and Frederick were brothers — that much was obvious. They had similar builds, though Frederick was a little shorter and his shoulders were a little narrower. They both had a similar profile with dark hair and eyes, Frederick with a close-cropped haircut and Dex with his hair scooped out of his face in a messy man bun. But what really gave them away as brothers was the way they messed with each other, getting on each other's nerves like it was their job. At one point Dex put Frederick in a good-natured headlock while they argued about nothing important, and Todd and Daniel exchanged amused eye rolls. While those latter two were both very tall and lean with shades of red hair — Todd's closer to deep auburn while Daniel's was a much brighter ginger — that was where the resemblance ended with those two. But all four shared similar features — the line of the nose or shape of the jaw — that told me they were all related in some way.

And Stacey was the sun around which they all orbited. Her best smiles were saved for Daniel, but she was obviously an important part of their traveling family.

They were a *family.* Plus me: the stray they'd picked up along the way.

What was I doing here?

I took another long, slow sip of water and turned my eyes toward the sky. Sunset filled the horizon, and I calmed my now-racing heart by counting all the colors: purple, pink, tinges of orange, and dark blue. Eventually those colors faded, deepened to indigo and finally the blue-black of night. Daniel reached over my head and into the motorhome, flicking a switch, and fairy lights illuminated the awning, chasing away the darkest part of the night.

"Okay." Todd pushed to his feet. "Bus is leaving. I want to call Michele before it gets too much later."

Dex made a sound of disgust in the back of his throat but stood up too. "You're so whipped, man, I swear. She'd live if you didn't talk to her every damn night."

"She would, but she wouldn't be happy about it." He frowned. "This year is hard on her for some reason."

"Distance getting to her?" Stacey's voice was full of empathy.

Todd nodded slowly, his gaze fixed in the middle distance. "Something like that." He shook himself out of whatever reverie he was in and focused on Dex again. "Anyway, relationships are about compromise. You'll find that out someday when you grow up."

"Never!" Dex crowed to the sky, a kilted, beefy Peter Pan.

"Never what?" I asked before I could think better of speaking up. I didn't know these people; they didn't know me. What was I doing, butting into their lives? But if I was really going to do this thing, maybe butting in was okay. "Grow up or have a relationship?"

"Both." He actually shot me a wink; I didn't think people did that in real life. I shook my head in response; what had I expected? I'd seen him and Delilah this morning; there was no doubt they'd be warming a bed together tonight. "Life is good, why mess that up? Right, Freddy?"

Frederick rolled his eyes. "My name isn't Freddy," he said with the weary tone of someone who reminded Dex of that at least five times a day, probably for the past twenty years. He finished his beer in one quick swallow while Todd jangled his keys. "See you in the morning," Frederick said to the group in general, then they were off. And so was Daniel, back inside to do paperwork after brushing a kiss on top of Stacey's head.

"The morning?" I repeated. "Tomorrow's Monday. The Faire isn't open during the week, right?"

Stacey nodded. "Right. Still plenty to do, though. Errands and rehearsals and stuff. You'll see." Her smile widened. "Maybe you can help out?"

"Happy to," I said. "Whatever you need." Of course, the last time I said that I'd ended up slinging turkey legs. Despite my shower the smell of fry oil and smoke lingered in my hair, on my skin. Maybe this was part of my new life now.

Another part of my new life was Benedick. No sooner had I slid into my bed than he came creeping up to snuggle with me, marching his little body up my chest and purring us both to sleep. I fell asleep with one hand nestled in his fur, a perfect spot of calm in the chaos that my life had become.

Back at the law office, I didn't have a lot of weekends. Associates wanting to make partner didn't, as a general rule. But when I did, I fell victim to a phenomenon called

98

the "Sunday scaries." Wherein a perfectly good Sunday was wasted by that sense of impending doom because Monday was right around the corner. When things were especially bad, the Sunday scaries would start sometime around Saturday afternoon, thereby ruining the entire weekend. That awful feeling was such a regular part of my life that I hadn't questioned it in years. It was part of being an attorney, like the lack of free time and the student loans I paid every month.

But when I woke up that Monday morning, slightly cramped on the pullout couch in the camper with a warm, sleeping cat taking up most of the real estate on my pillow, the first thing I noticed was the lack of doom. Work was no longer a concern; the firm had quit me as firmly as I'd quit them. My biggest responsibility in life was to man the turkey leg stall at the Renaissance Faire, and it was another five days before I had to face that again. Sure, I didn't like the giant question mark that my life had become, but the absence of stress felt the same as unlacing my bodice yesterday evening. I could breathe for the first time in what felt like years.

The sun was shining, it was a gorgeous day, and for the first time in a long time I could just enjoy myself.

Of course, that didn't mean there was nothing to do. While the weekends were focused on performances, the week was for all the things that couldn't get done during those busy weekends. For the band that meant rehearsing, working on new songs, and finessing set lists. For Stacey and me it meant everything else. We had trips to the laundromat and grocery store to make, and a Target run was high on my list. My weekender bag had been packed for, well, a weekend. I needed more than one pair of yoga pants, a couple T-shirts, and three pairs of underwear if I was going to get through the summer.

The focus of my new wardrobe was comfort: loose sundresses and stretchy pants. Stacey cast a critical eye at a leggings-and-tank set I tossed into the cart. "I think those are actually pajamas."

I shrugged, unbothered, and after a beat she shrugged too, doubling back to snag a set of her own. But she frowned at the tag. "I think I'm too big for these."

I glanced at them, then at Stacey. I didn't like the dim look that had come into her normally bright eyes. "Pfft," I finally said. "More like they're too small for you. Here." I dug in the back of the rack till I found the next size up and tossed them in after the ones I'd chosen for myself. "I don't see Daniel complaining."

"True," she said with a giggle. "He'd probably prefer it on the tight side."

"See? There you go."

My digital detox was going well, though I did cast a longing look at the phones in the electronics section before Stacey steered me away. Instead I grabbed a hardback journal and a pack of the good pens I usually stole from the supply closet at work. I couldn't update my résumé online or apply for jobs this summer, but I could make to-do lists the old-fashioned way.

The motorhome was home base for everyone, not just the three of us who slept there at night. The guys showed up from the hotel around midmorning with the cooler full of ice, ready to rehearse in the shade of the awning. After a couple false starts, music began to drift through the open windows of the motorhome along with a warm breeze that ruffled the flowered curtains. Unaided by the microphones and amplifiers from the stage, the music sounded even more casual and raw. It was a better background than any streaming channel I could have chosen on the phone I no longer had. Daniel was mostly glued to either his laptop or his phone, and Stacey buzzed around, always busy with something.

I pitched in wherever I could, but I mostly found myself hanging out with the cat, trying to stay out of the way in a place where I was always in the way. I cracked open my new journal and pack of pens. Empty blank books intimidated me . . . all that potential, what if I ruined it with bad handwriting or jumbled thoughts? I turned to the first page and uncapped a pen. The best way to unjumble those thoughts was with a to-do list. Maybe I could start small. Write down everything I needed to do in the next week or so.

— Sell turkey legs.

Well. That hadn't taken long. Probably could expand my scope.

I wrote every day. It was hard to get my mind back on business in such an unbusinesslike setting, but I forced myself to focus. I started to-do lists — real ones this time. Ideas. Things I wanted to accomplish once I was off the road and home again. Rejoining a big law firm was out: I was pretty done with that endless grind. What if I went into business for myself? I'd need to downsize my life, probably. Get a smaller place. Could

I take out a small business loan? I'd never had a blank canvas for a future before, and while the prospect was terrifying, it was also exciting. So many possibilities.

When I wasn't journaling, I had my e-reader out, catching up on my reading for the first time in years. Stacey liked to read in her downtime too, I noticed, and Benedick was beside himself with the plethora of laps to choose from.

Thursday night the band had a gig at a local bar, and Daniel and Stacey took the opportunity to go out on their own. It was just me and the cat, and I relished the quiet of the evening. Until Dex and Frederick showed up, of course, when I'd already changed into my leggings-and-tank pajamas, interrupting my exciting night of reading with the cat.

"Nice outfit." Dex gave me a quick up-and-down glance.

I crossed my arms over my braless chest. I was certainly not dressed for company, but company was here nevertheless. "What are you doing here?" I sounded a little more snappish than I probably should have. I was a guest in their lives, after all.

"Out of beer at the hotel," was Dex's succinct yet effective reply. He headed straight for the fridge while Frederick lingered in the doorway of the motorhome.

"Where is everyone?" He glanced over his shoulder back to the outside, like there was someone out there he'd walked past without seeing.

"You mean Stacey and Daniel? Date night," I replied with a wiggle in my eyebrows. "They probably aren't getting much alone time with me around."

Frederick grinned, ready to play along. "Well, I hope they get lucky."

I considered that. "I should probably get earplugs, huh? And one of those sleeping mask things."

"At least." Dex straightened up, holding three longneck bottles. He passed one to Frederick and offered me the third. I wasn't much of a beer drinker, but I took it to be sociable.

"How was the show?" I scooted to the end of the sofa, making room, and Frederick took the spot next to me while Dex plopped down at the dinette table.

"Fine." Dex took a swig of beer. "If you like overcrowded bars and watered-down drinks."

I made a sarcastically appreciative noise around a mouthful of beer. "Sounds like heaven." He snorted a laugh, and I hated that I liked making him laugh.

"It was fine." But Frederick's voice was uncertain. His gaze dropped to the bottle in his hand, studying the label. "Probably telling Daniel not to book us there again, though."

"Not worth it?" I tucked my feet under me, curling up on the small sofa as I got more comfortable. It was nice, hanging out like this. Being part of the group. I hadn't had a lot of camaraderie at my old job. Then I noticed something. "Hey, aren't there usually three of you? What did y'all do with Todd?"

"He's back at the room . . ." Frederick started, before Dex cut him off.

"Pouting."

"Pouting?" I repeated. "Bad night at the show?"

Dex shook his head, taking a swig of beer. "His girl."

"Ohhhh." I took a sip of my own drink, warming up for gossip. "He was saying the other night that she's not happy about things, right?"

"That's putting it mildly." Frederick picked at the label on his beer bottle. "It sounds like they're talking marriage, kids, the whole thing. That's a hard future to plan when he's on the road most of the year."

I could see his point. "Yeah, that's tough."

A momentary silence settled as we sipped from our beers and I turned over some thoughts in my head. "What would that mean for all of you? The band?"

"I dunno," Frederick said. "Can you play fiddle?"

"About as well as I can play guitar."

Frederick laughed, and Dex made a noise that was somewhere between a sigh and a growl. I looked over at him. "You okay?"

His sigh was beleaguered. "Sure. Other than my brother trying to ruin my life, you mean?"

"Which one?" I asked. "Daniel or Todd?" Either one could be the case: Daniel for making them play at a shitty venue, or Todd considering quitting the band.

"Todd." He bit off the word as he slanted a grumpy look my way.

"Daniel's a cousin," Frederick supplied, and I nodded.

"Sorry," I said. "This gig didn't come with a family tree."

The edges of Dex's mouth kicked up at that. "It probably should."

Relieved that I'd deflected his ire, I got back on topic. "I don't think Todd's out to ruin your life. More like trying to keep his girlfriend happy."

"Sure." He sighed again. "But shouldn't

she want *him* to be happy too? Where's that part of the equation?"

He had a point. "He did say that relationships are about compromise," I said in agreement. "Has she ever come on tour with you all? Seen you all in action?"

They both shook their heads. "We do some local gigs up at home around the holidays," Frederick said. "Michele's been to some of those."

Dex rolled his eyes. "Shows at bars aren't nearly as fun. She needs to see us play at a Faire."

"Maybe we could take video or something." But even as I said the words I knew it wouldn't be the same. So much of the performance was about being out in the sun, the fresh air. The banter with the patrons, being part of the show. A recording couldn't capture that.

"Maybe." Dex looked as skeptical as I felt. "You're right, though. They've been together for, what, two years?" He looked over to Frederick for confirmation. "She should experience a Faire, see the show for herself before she pulls him off the road and fucks up everything." He thunked his bottle onto the table in punctuation. "We need to get back to the room. Unless you want us snuggling up with you." He raised an eyebrow in what could only be a joke, and I laughed in response.

"You kidding? This sofa's barely big enough for me and the cat."

"Just as well." Frederick levered to his feet. "No offense, Louisa, but you aren't my type."

"Not into redheads?" Calling myself a redhead was a stretch, but next to the blonds in my family my hair was practically aflame.

"Not into girls," Dex supplied, while Frederick gave an agreeable shrug. "Now me, on the other hand, I'm very much into . . ."

"Good night, guys!" I said loudly, cutting Dex off from whatever innuendo he was about to give me. Frederick snorted, and Dex met my eyes with a guileless grin. But he didn't push it, so clearly it was a joke. With a last wave on the way out the door they were gone, the side door banging closed behind them. That was how it was around here, apparently. The motorhome was everyone's touchstone, then at the end of the day people wandered off to their beds — or someone else's bed, I wasn't judging — when it was time to sleep.

Friday morning I woke up with a low-level

panic in my chest that only got worse as the day went on. I tried to trace the source — was I worried about the future of the band? The talk with Dex and Frederick last night had been concerning, and that concern increased when I saw Todd later that morning. A normally easygoing guy, he was quieter than usual, giving no input or opinions on any of the songs they worked on.

I wasn't the only one who noticed. Later that night, in the dubious privacy of their bedroom, I could hear Daniel and Stacey speaking in low tones.

"But what if he leaves?" Stacey was trying to whisper, but urgency turned her voice into a desperate squeak. "Fiddle is kind of important, you know."

"It'll work out." Daniel was, as always, a voice of calm, even pitched low like this where I wasn't supposed to hear. "We'll figure something out, okay? Don't worry."

"But . . ." Stacey's voice dropped further, a murmur that I couldn't make out, and I told myself it was none of my business. I shouldn't be listening in to their private conversations. I reached up to Benedick — hogging my pillow, as usual — to rub behind his ears and his purring increased. Unfortunately, so did my heart rate. Getting to sleep tonight was going to be hard.

That was when it hit me. Tomorrow was a Faire day. And I didn't want to go. I didn't want to put on that outfit — fresh from the laundry, bodice hand-washed and clean — and spend another ten hours on my feet selling turkey legs, ending the day smelling like smoked meat.

God, it was the Sunday scaries all over again. They were just on Friday now.

Now that I'd identified the source of the panic I could fall asleep. The familiar feeling of dreading work tomorrow was almost comforting: a sense of normalcy in a life that was nothing like normal.

SEVEN

I woke up the next morning resigned to my fate as a turkey leg slinger. I was going to be cool about it, I told myself as Stacey helped get me laced and buckled into my costume. We both sipped coffee, just two seventeenth-century girls getting ready for the day.

"This is so much easier with you here." Stacey grinned at me from the other end of the merchandise table that we'd just finished setting up. It was about time for me to set off for the food stalls when Daniel showed up, his face grim. The smile fell from Stacey's face and her eyebrows shot up, and even Dex, lounging at the lip of the stage, sat up straighter at his cousin's approach.

"Okay, so slight schedule change today." Daniel scrolled through the ever-present bullet-point list on his phone. "I know we're usually done after the three-fifteen show, but they're going to need us up front for pub sing."

"What?" Todd's eyes widened while Dex scoffed.

" 'We'? I don't see you wearing a kilt, Danny Boy."

Daniel closed his eyes in a long, slow blink that looked like he was gathering strength. "I am not an old folk song, so you can call me Daniel. And yes, I know it's cutting it close —"

"It's cutting it really close." Frederick sat down next to Dex at the edge of the stage, his hand drum next to him. "We finish at three forty-five, maybe three fifty, give us ten minutes for the tip basket, that's four o'clock. What time does pub sing start?"

"Four."

Silence. The trio of musicians stared at Daniel, and he stared right back.

"So. Uh." Todd scratched the back of his neck. "Are we running a four-minute mile here or have you figured out how to teleport?"

Dex huffed. "Why in the hell would you schedule us for —"

"It's not my fault," Daniel protested. "They drafted us — *you* — to fill in for Spring in Our Step."

"Wait, what?" Dex's gaze sharpened. "What happened to them?"

"Delilah didn't tell you?" Daniel raised his eyebrows, and I caught the meaning right away. Looked like I was right about Dex and the acrobat hooking up. Not that I was judging.

Frederick jumped in. "They were trying out some new stuff this week and Josh landed wrong. That was what, Wednesday?" He looked to Daniel for a confirming nod. "Last I heard they'd taken him to an urgent care for X-rays."

"Sounds like that didn't go well." Todd winced sympathetically.

"It didn't," Daniel said. "Sprained ankle. At least it's not broken, but he's out for a bit. Matt told me this morning they're still trying to rework the act, but they need another day."

"You really didn't know about it?" Frederick turned to Dex. "I saw you with Delilah Wednesday night. She didn't say anything?"

"Nope. Not a word." Dex's brows drew together as his gaze turned inward.

"Not a lot of pillow talk with you two, huh?" Todd nudged him with a shoulder, and Frederick snorted.

"She doesn't like him for his conversation." The two brothers chuckled, but I noticed a shadow pass over Dex's face. It was only there for a split second.

"You know me," he said in a cheerful voice that rang only slightly hollow. "I'm not there to talk." But the smile fell quickly from his face. As I watched a muscle jump inside his cheek, I realized I felt bad for him. Maybe he liked Delilah a little more than she liked him.

"Anyway." Daniel brought the conversation back on topic. "They should be fine by tomorrow, but today we're shorthanded, and they need us to pitch in."

Frederick frowned. "What if we skip the tip basket stuff? Maybe Stacey could do it while we go straight to pub sing." That last sentence trailed off as a question as Stacey shook her head.

"I'm already running the merch table," she said. "I can't leave that. I could . . . I dunno. Shake people down for tips while they're buying a T-shirt or something?"

"Yeah, that's not gonna work." Todd sighed a long sigh. "We'll haul ass with our stuff after the show and the tip basket, I guess. Or maybe we can cut our show down by a few minutes so I have time to —"

"I can do it." I heard my own voice chiming in, as though from far away. Why was my voice chiming in? I'd worked a Renaissance Faire show for zero minutes. I had no idea what I was volunteering for.

But they all turned to me, as though I had something to contribute to the conversation. "Do what?" Frederick asked.

"We really don't know 'Freebird,' " Todd added, a smile dancing around his mouth.

I rolled my eyes, a smile coming to my own lips. This was good; I already had in-jokes with the band. "I meant the tip basket. That's where you walk around afterward, right? Intercept the audience as they're leaving? Schmooze 'em for tips?" That was basically the one thing I'd seen around here that I had any confidence I could handle. "I can do that."

"You sure?" Frederick asked. "Not everyone's comfortable, you know, going up to people and demanding money."

Now it was my turn to scoff. "Please. I've been a lawyer for over a decade. If there's one thing I can do, it's schmooze."

Dex snorted, but the guys all nodded, turning back to Daniel for confirmation. He was the boss, after all — the one herding these cats. He looked unsure. "I suppose that would work . . ." He looked down at his phone, which was obviously his lifeline. "Carmen's going to be pissed, though. She was really looking forward to having you back —"

"Where was she working?" Frederick

looked from Daniel to me.

"Food stalls," Dex said, then he looked at me. "Right? That's where I dropped you off, but maybe she stuck you somewhere else?"

"Get your turkey legs here!" I called out in sarcastic confirmation.

A wave of shouts followed that announcement.

"That's where you put her?" Frederick looked outraged.

"Were you trying to get her to quit?" Todd turned to me. "Seriously, how did you not run away during the week?"

"Didn't have a ride," I quipped back, and he shook his head in sympathy.

"I would have given you one." His eyes sparkled with humor, but since I knew he was considering running away himself the joke didn't land as lightly as it could have.

"She's ours!" Dex protested, getting back on topic. And while I wanted to point out that I didn't belong to anyone, thank you *very* much, I felt a warm glow on the inside of my tight bodice to be considered part of the group.

"Come on, let her stay here," Dex continued. "At least for today. We're a lot more fun than food service."

"Just about anything's more fun than food service," Stacey said with a nod, and I had to say she wasn't wrong.

"Are you sure?" I looked from Stacey to Daniel, then back to the Kilts. "If they really need me I probably should . . ." But my protest was half-hearted. I didn't want to let anyone down, especially if I'd been volunteered to work elsewhere. But hope surged in my chest at getting out of turkey leg duty.

"Nah." Daniel's thumbs were already flying on his phone. "We need you more. All good," he said, already sending a text that I assumed said I was no longer available to work medieval fast food. "And Dex is right, you're ours." His eyes danced with amusement as he clicked his phone off, stowing it in his back pocket.

The relief I felt was palpable. I liked the Faire, and the costume wasn't even that bad, now that I was getting used to it. I wasn't a slacker; I liked being useful and pulling my weight. But damn if I didn't relish the chance to be useful somewhere that didn't involve turkey legs.

Before the first show I joined Stacey in the path near the entrance to the stage, the two of us acting like carnival barkers in our colorful costumes and loud voices, assuring passersby that they *really didn't want to miss*

117

what was about to happen inside. It was a frenzied few minutes, but once the show started it was our turn to breathe. We stood at the back, surveying the group we'd managed to usher inside, and Stacey bumped me with her shoulder.

"Much better than doing this by myself." She wrapped her arms around one of mine, giving me an affectionate squeeze. "I'm so glad you're here with us. Have I mentioned that?"

"Only a couple hundred times." I put a hand over hers with an answering squeeze.

"And I'll probably say it a couple hundred more. Do you have any idea what it's like to travel with all this testosterone?"

My eyebrows shot up. "I hadn't thought about that. That's gotta be hell. At least you and Daniel have some privacy, with the motorhome and all?"

"Oh, yeah. And it's about to get better: at the next stop we switch off, so we get a hotel room. I'm about to take so many bubble baths." She closed her eyes with a happy sigh, and I wasn't jealous. Nope. Not me.

Her eyes blinked open again, back to the present. "Anyway. Do you think you'll be okay sharing the RV with one of the guys?"

I shrugged. "Sure." But my mind went back to the other night, when Dex and

Frederick had dropped by. "Do I have to snuggle with someone on the pullout bed?"

Stacey giggled. "I think we can avoid that. The Faire is providing us with two rooms at a discount at this next stop. It'll be two of them in a room and one in the RV. Dex usually fights to get a room to himself. Better for his hookups, I think. So, he'll be disappointed." She rolled her eyes, looking amused, but there was an awkwardness to her levity. Something about it looked forced. There was a story there, and I wasn't sure what it was.

"I can handle Dex," I said, hoping that didn't sound like too much of an innuendo. I looked up to the trees, down to my feet, casting around desperately for a change in topic. My feet were a perfect solution. "Really should get some boots. Next stop, you said?"

Stacey nodded. "If you want the really good ones. But there's a leatherworker down that way . . ." She pointed off to our left, in a direction I hadn't explored yet. "He might have something that works. And you wanted to get a belt pouch anyway, right? You have time to go shopping, if you want."

"You sure?" I glanced back at the stage. Dex's jovial voice echoed out of the amplifiers, the same pre-song patter that I remembered from the weekend before.

"I'm sure. We don't need you till the end of the day, so you basically scored a day off." Her smile was mischievous, like your best friend convincing you to skip school.

She didn't have to tell me twice. "You're right," I said. "My bank account hasn't suffered enough yet." I'd stuffed my ID and credit card into my cleavage this morning when I'd gotten dressed. It turned out my hiked-up boobs made a pretty great wallet. But wasn't exactly sanitary. I needed a better solution, like a belt pouch.

"That's the spirit!" Her laugh followed me as I said goodbye with a wave and set off down the lane (not a *path,* Stacey had corrected me earlier; the terminology here was *lane*). This wasn't a useless souvenir I was after, I reminded myself. This was part of my new work wardrobe. If I was going to do this, I couldn't half-ass it. And wearing Converse under these skirts was definitely half-assing it.

The leatherworker didn't have boots, but he did have slippers that laced up the top of my foot. I wasn't sure how long they'd last, given how much time I spent on my feet, but they were a good stopgap until I could get something sturdier. His belt pouches, on the other hand, were perfect, and before long I had a dark green leather bag that matched my skirts, hanging from a new, wide brown belt that I cinched around my waist over my bodice. Then I gratefully moved my ID and credit card into the pouch and boom. Boob wallet no more.

"Excuse me, ma'am?"

It took a moment to realize someone was addressing me, and I turned in a whirl of skirts. A trio of women faced me, their sundresses short and their hair long. One of them held one of the maps they give out at the front, and the other two sipped beer from plastic cups. Last weekend that had been me. How things had changed.

"Hi. Yeah . . ." The one with the map pushed her sunglasses onto the top of her head and squinted at me. "I think we're a little lost. Where's the joust?"

Wow. What a good question. I opened my mouth, closed it again. I wasn't prepared for this. Was I supposed to be in character? Did I have a character?

"Sorry?" The word fell out of my mouth with a tinge of an accent, covering all my bases. "The joust?" I looked around, as though maybe it was on the other side of the lemonade stand. It wasn't.

One of the drinking girls bumped Map

Girl's shoulder. "She doesn't work here, Marianne. I think she's here like we are."

"Well, not exactly like we are." The other girl giggled into her drink. "She put in an effort. I told you we should have gotten outfits!"

Map Girl shook her head. "Too expensive."

I nodded firmly. "You're not wrong." I'd decided against an accent, or any pretense at character. It was too much all at once. "Anyway, the joust . . ." I looked over her shoulder at the map. "It's back there, in that big field . . ." I tapped a fingernail on the map. "And we're on this side of the food stalls . . ." If I never saw the food stalls again it would be too soon. I traced a line, following a lane that snaked down the left side of the grounds. "So . . . you'll want to go ahead and around to the left that way." I looked up and what did you know, there was a lane going in the exact direction I'd thought there would be. Go me.

"Thanks!" Map Girl folded up her map as her friends skipped on ahead. "Any other tips? Shows we should see?"

That was an easy answer. "Make sure you check out the Dueling Kilts; their last show is at three fifteen. Irish folk songs, men in kilts . . . what more do you need?" I laughed at her thumbs-up and we parted ways, her to catch up to her friends and me on the way back to said men in kilts. Eventually. I still had time to explore.

I followed snippets of music and sounds of cheers, lurking at the back of several audiences to catch the ends of shows before moving on. The variety of entertainment, now that I was sober and paying attention, was endless. Shows with interactive songs and magic tricks to enthrall children, and ones with fire-eating and whip-cracking to get the attention of adults.

And music. So much music. The Dueling Kilts weren't the only ones playing here, and while most of it seemed like variations on a theme (the theme mostly being acoustic and white European), those variations were striking. There was an all-woman group, singing with soaring harmonies over their instruments, voices and strings combining to form magic. Another group was made of tattooed men, their hair in elaborate braids or shaved off entirely, very Celtic-Viking looking. Their music was very drums-aggressive — Frederick would probably get a stroke if he played that hard — along with bagpipes that were frightening in their intensity. Not family-friendly music. This was music to pillage to.

One clearing was alive with activity, and I walked closer to see what the act was. Three small open-sided tents were set up in a rough circle in the middle of the lane. Inside each tent was a small table, with two people sitting on opposite sides. Patrons milled around outside the tents, impatiently checking the time on their phones. As I approached, two women stood from a table and emerged from one of the tents; the patron in modern street clothes left while the woman dressed not much differently than I was — typical Renaissance Faire garb — beckoned another patron over. I was close enough now that I could read the big yellow sandwich board–style sign in front of the tents: TAROT-PALMISTRY-RUNES.

Fortune-tellers, then. That made sense; a Renaissance Faire would be the perfect place for that particular brand of fantasy.

It was all bullshit to me. Woo-woo mystical stuff was never my thing. I didn't even check my horoscope. People made their own luck and were responsible for their own lives. No deck of cards was going to tell me what my future was going to be. And the only thing someone would get out of looking at my hand was my desperate need of a manicure.

By now my head was full of music and

colors and huzzahs, so I headed back to my assigned stage. When I got there Stacey looked delighted to see me, but I had a feeling that was just her face. "How is it out there?"

"Nice." I grabbed a bottle of water and took a seat on an empty bench. Sitting was . . . different in an outfit like this. The boning in the bodice kept my spine ramrod-straight, so slouching was out of the question.

It must have been later in the day than I realized, as patrons started trickling in. I abandoned my seat in the audience. "Time to start drawing 'em in, huh?"

"Last show of the day," she confirmed. "Today went by fast." That was putting it mildly.

I fell back into my new role as a barker, venturing out into the lanes with Stacey, approaching total strangers and promising them beautiful men in kilts, *right this way, sir*! Some patrons laughed. Some avoided us like we were offering them a timeshare, walking around us in an unnecessarily big circle.

One group of ladies stopped in their tracks. "Kilts? Did you say kilts?" They reminded me of the drinking girls from earlier that day: a trio in light cotton dresses and the beginnings of a sunburn.

"I did indeed!" My smile was wide and my accent was shaky, but I was doing my best impression of Stacey, which I figured was the way to go. "The kilts are hot, the legs are hotter, the music is questionable. But you should join us!"

Two of them looked excited, but the third chewed on her lip. "But we were going to the mud show . . ."

I shook my head emphatically. "Our guys are much better looking, trust me."

That sold her, and as they did an about-face toward our stage, I caught Stacey's eye. She was laughing, and I knew she'd heard the whole thing. Her laughter made my chest do that glowy thing again, like when Dex had said I was theirs. Like I belonged.

Once the show started, Stacey and I skirted the back of the audience to the merchandise table. She ducked down and pulled a small wicker basket from under the table and handed it to me, tossing in a couple of dollar bills from the cashbox so it didn't look empty. "You think that was fun," she said. "Now you get to talk those people into giving you money as they leave." Her gaze went to the stage, where Dex had a tankard hoisted high, encouraging the audience to drink along with him. "The good news is that a lot of the audience is pretty well lubricated by now."

"No problem." I tucked the handle of the basket into the crook of my elbow, nestling it against my side. "It'll be just like the charity galas we did at work." A hiccup of laughter escaped me as I thought about those galas. There, I wore dresses with crystal accents that cost as much as a month's rent, my hair done in an elaborate style that usually took an afternoon at a hairdresser's to achieve. Now the hems of my skirts were dusty and I didn't want to think about how much hair had escaped from my braid. So maybe not quite like a charity gala.

I tucked an errant strand behind my ear and shifted my weight from foot to foot as the guys swung into "Whiskey in the Jar." Now that I was standing still, the breeze from the treetops touched my face, teasing those errant strands of hair, and here came that same sense of peace that I'd felt the first time I'd listened to them play this song. It wasn't the song itself that did it, but it may as well have been. It was the primitiveness of it, the way the simple instruments the guys played wove around and through their voices in harmony, evoking a century that none of us had been alive for. It felt like an escape. Not only for the patrons listening, but for those of us who brought that escape to them.

Soon enough, the show came to an end. "Now, we hate to sing and run," Frederick said, his smile engaging. Offstage he was on the shy side, subordinate to his older brothers. But onstage his personality was completely different: the charming, nice boy. "But it seems that we are needed up front for pub sing."

"If you want to get your cardio in," Todd added, "feel free to join us as we do a little fun run up to the front stage to begin the end-of-the-day festivities."

"But before you do . . ." Dex picked up the thread of the narrative. They worked in a smooth patter that spoke of years of playing off each other, both literally and figuratively. "If you liked what you see, and you want to contribute to the Dueling Kilts' Drinking Fund . . ."

"It's not just about the drinking, Dex," Todd interrupted.

"Yeah," Frederick added. "We do like to eat on occasion too." Todd nodded in emphatic agreement.

Dex clucked his tongue in annoyance. "Fine. If you want to help us continue to do what we love to do, the lovely Lulu will

128

be right back there, accepting any and all financial contributions that will help us stay afloat. Never mandatory, always appreciated.

"Say hi to the nice audience, Lulu!" Dex threw his arm out, gesturing out toward the audience. Out toward me. The audience turned in their seats to look at me, and I cringed inwardly at the attention. I wasn't ready to be part of the show.

But that was too bad. I was here. Time to step up. "Hi to the nice audience!" My voice was clear as the afternoon sunshine as I swept my skirts in an exaggerated curtsy. As I held the basket over my head to emphasize Dex's words about financial contribution, I met his eyes across the sea of heads that made up the audience. He really did have a nice smile, and now that he was aiming it at me, I was a little breathless. Or maybe that was the bodice.

"There's our girl." His voice was pitched lower, but thanks to his headset mic it still carried across to where I stood, and whew. The eyes and the voice, both appraising and encouraging? *Whew.* We were in a crowd of easily fifty people, but he had a way of making you feel like it was just the two of you. Those dark eyes were hypnotic, and I wanted to step closer. I wanted to be nearer to him.

But I caught hold of myself, just as I felt myself starting to step forward, and I broke his gaze. What was I going to do, vault over the audience? And what was I going to do once I got to him? Ridiculous.

I turned my attention back to the audience, giving them a welcoming smile as the show ended, and they began to rise to their feet. I slipped through the crowd, beating them to the entrance/exit of our performance area so by the time they arrived I was there, basket in hand.

I thought that I'd have to work for it and really talk people into tipping us, but I was almost immediately surrounded. The bills in the basket must have done their job, priming the pump and encouraging people to toss in cash on their way out. The number of loose dollar bills was overwhelming, and I found myself holding them down with the flat of my hand so none flew out. Out of the corner of my eye I saw a flash of movement, as Todd, Dex, and Frederick slipped through the crowd with genial smiles and a couple of quick words. They stayed on the move, and after they cleared the bottleneck at the entrance, they dashed down the lane toward the front of the Faire grounds. Damn. Men should be required to run in kilts more often. You got a great view of those leg muscles.

This was the easiest job I'd ever had. I smiled and said thank you and curtsied as often as I could. It didn't take long to notice that sometimes a deep curtsy would encourage a stop and a look down my cleavage, followed by some cash in my basket. I wasn't above that if it meant another few bucks in the till. Use what talents I had, right?

As the crowd thinned out, I caught Stacey's eye over at the merch table. She'd been surrounded by patrons at the end of the show, needing Daniel to step in and help, and Benedick had hidden under the table until the worst of the crowd went away. Now she was down to her last few customers and Benedick had emerged again, rolling onto his back to catch some late afternoon sunshine on his belly. As she made change and smiled her thanks at the last patron, she beamed at me like a proud mother. Ready or not, I was part of the show now.

EIGHT

But the day wasn't over yet. Not if Stacey had anything to say about it.

"Come on. If we hurry we can catch some of pub sing." She collected my basket of cash and handed it to Daniel, who zipped said cash into a vinyl pouch that he then stuck into his backpack.

"What is a pub sing, anyway?" As we walked, hurrying along the lanes, I noticed how quiet it had become. The sun had started to dip in the sky, and there were more vendors on the lanes than patrons. The couple of stages we passed had sparse audiences — maybe five or ten people — for these late afternoon shows.

"It's a final show, up at the front stage. A bunch of the acts perform a number or two, we bid the patrons an official farewell and thank them for coming. That way everyone is mostly at the front near the gate at the end of the day."

"Strategic. I like it." Give the patrons a show they'd want to catch and then shove them out the exit when it was over. That made total sense.

We passed the fortune-tellers I'd seen earlier that day, and they were as busy as ever. Apparently finding out your future from a mountebank was more important than whatever variety show we were heading toward. Fools and their money and all that.

The Dueling Kilts had finished their mini-set by the time we got there, and the guys stood behind the audience benches, leaning back against some accommodating trees while a duo of juggling comedians took the stage. Which was . . . not my thing. But I laughed when prompted, because I was part of things now and the least I could do was support the other acts at the Faire.

"Everything go okay?" Stacey asked when we caught up to them.

Todd nodded. "Everything worked out great. We had to hustle a little, but the cardio's good for us."

Dex snorted. "Speak for yourself. I get plenty of cardio."

"Sex doesn't count as cardio." Frederick didn't even look at his brother as he delivered the put-down; his eyes were on the stage. I took in his smile and the brightness of his eyes, and questioned Frederick's taste in comedy until I noticed one of the jugglers drop a wink in our direction. Frederick's cheeks had reddened ever so slightly. Ah. He wasn't paying attention to the comedy. He was paying attention to the comedian.

"Sure, it does." Dex crossed his arms in front of his chest and bumped my shoulder with his. "Don't you think?"

"Depends. Am I wearing my Fitbit?" I fought against a smile, which would only encourage him.

But he laughed at my joke. "You got one? We could test it out." Wasn't it illegal for men's eyes to crinkle at the edges like that when they smiled? It should be.

"Alas." I extended my arm to showcase my bare wrist. "Another time, maybe."

"Oh, there's other ways of measuring heart rate." His gaze dipped down to my chest, as though he could see said heart through my layers of costume. Or maybe he was just checking out the way I filled out a bodice.

I gave my eyelashes a flutter. "I had no idea you were medically trained."

Frederick snorted from my other side, his eyes still on the stage in front of him, and

Dex's laugh this time seemed involuntary, bursting from a place deep in his chest.

"There's lots you don't know about me, Counselor." His smile this time was less predatory, more . . . friendly. He leaned against the tree at our backs, his posture casual and comfortable. The tree was plenty big enough for two so I joined him, enjoying the relief in not being entirely upright. Maybe he was right. Maybe there was more to him than I originally thought. I wasn't entirely convinced, but I was willing to give it a shot.

The jugglers gave way to a trio of women singing a cappella, and it didn't take long for Frederick to wander away from us. He wasn't subtle; I knew exactly where he was going, and I didn't bother to hide my smile. The whole thing reminded me of summer camp, and relationships that formed under the heady circumstances of summer heat and forced proximity. Did this kind of thing happen a lot? Were the guys at the mud show hooking up with the a cappella singers after the Faire closed for the day?

I glanced over at Todd. He was still talking to Stacey, but his eyes were restless. He didn't seem the type to stray, but what did I know? I'd just met the guy. Late-night phone calls could only do so much to keep the fire going. Unless you were Stacey and Daniel, joined at the hip and traveling together, this life was probably hell on relationships.

Meanwhile, Dex and I leaned together against that tree, our shoulders almost touching. I felt his eyes on me and looked up, only for him to look away. He seemed restless too, but probably for a different reason than Todd. I drew in a breath to ask him a question, when he straightened up from his casual lean. He bumped my shoulder again. "See you later."

So much for conversation. I watched as he threaded his way through the crowd, finally lighting on two belly dancers at the other end of the audience. They were close to the stage, waiting their turn to go on, but they quickly turned their attention to Dex with bright smiles, fluttering their hip scarves like plumage.

Yep. That made sense. Then why was I disappointed? I closed my eyes against the late afternoon sun. The music washed over me in a comforting flow, and I let it sink into my weary bones, chasing away the disappointment. It had been a long day, but I'd enjoyed myself. Better to concentrate on that instead.

Eventually I was drawn into Stacey and

Todd's conversation. "Thanks for helping out today." Stacey took up residence next to me against the tree, the spot that Dex had vacated. "Hopefully things will be normal tomorrow."

"Is anything really normal around here?"

"Nope," Todd answered immediately with a smile, but Stacey looked thoughtful.

"I guess it depends on your definition," she said. "At this point, an office job would be weirder for me than this."

I had to admit she had a point. "Not a lot of call for receptionists here, I guess."

The show up front continued, and while the acts onstage changed, the performers hanging out at the back of the audience changed too. While the belly dancers were on I spied Dex across the way, flirting with the mead seller. That bright red kilt and those legs were hard to miss. Frederick and the juggler had long since disappeared.

I was brought out of my reverie by a nudge on my left shoulder.

"If you're wanting your phone back, you're gonna need a hell of a lot of rice."

I turned to see the laundry wench from last weekend — was it only last weekend? — and I froze. How had she recognized me? But then I remembered what Matt the acrobat had said. Gossip traveled fast around here, and I was Phone Girl now. At least she was smiling.

"Keep it." I aimed for a breezy, unconcerned tone. "I'm going off-grid for a while."

Her laugh was almost a cackle, and she bumped my shoulder again, a little harder this time. I'd passed some kind of test. "Good for you!"

"Yeah, when I said chuck your phone in the lake, I didn't think you'd actually do it." Now Advice Lady had joined the party. She didn't have her sign with her, but otherwise she looked the same as last weekend, in her dark green dress and feathers in her hair. Her eyes were enormous with sincerity, but a smile played around her mouth.

I shrugged. "It was the closest thing I could manage."

She laughed. "I guess I need to be more careful about the advice I give out. I never expect anyone to take me literally." A look of horror dawned across her face. "God, I'm rethinking everything now."

"I'm sure you're fine," I said. "Believe me, your advice came at a good time, but the decision was all mine." I patted her on the shoulder. "Not a lot of people having mental breakdowns at a Renaissance Faire."

"You never know. May as well have it

somewhere, right?"

She had a point. All things considered, I'd picked a pretty good place to hit rock bottom.

Onstage the show ended, and we stopped talking to clap and cheer for the act that we hadn't been listening to. The whole shebang seemed to be coming to a close, as a man and woman in royal dress approached the stage to address the audience still gathered. While they spoke I scanned the crowd again, not looking for anything or anyone in particular, and my eyes landed on Dex. He'd moved on from the mead seller and was back with the belly dancers. Was he going home with one of them? All of them?

I must have said that last part out loud, because a reply came in the form of twin snorts, from the laundry wench and Advice Lady. "A chick at every stop, that guy," the wench said.

"At least," Advice Lady chimed in. "Sometimes more than one."

"No kidding. My sister wench Blossom — she does those winter Faires down in Florida — she was his hookup a couple times down there. Said it was worth it." She glanced over at me. "But I'm sure you know all about that, right? You're all caught up on *that*." As she said *that* she moved her hand around in a circle, encompassing Dex, the tree, the woman. Women. Whatever.

"She is," Todd confirmed from his place on my other side. His gaze followed ours, and he shook his head at his brother. "Believe me, she knows he's not relationship material."

"Definitely not." My voice was firm, but disappointment flickered back to life inside my chest. Something inside me remembered the way our eyes had met across the audience, the way his eyes crinkled when he smiled at me. But his flirting with me was always colored with humor; he was only joking when it came to me. I couldn't help but wonder what it would be like to be one of those belly dancers, getting the full force of his amorous attention.

Maybe it was better not to know. I wasn't here for that. Remember?

"Please." I couldn't believe I was begging for something so basic.

Stacey's mouth screwed up in a thoughtful scowl. "I still say it's cheating." But she drew her phone out of her belt pouch anyway, handing it over.

I seized it like a lifeline. "I'll give it right back, I promise." I scrolled through her contacts for the number I wanted and initiated the video call. I leaned back on the merchandise table we'd just set up as the call went through. It was early on a Sunday morning, but I knew he'd be up. Early morning workouts were part of Mitch's DNA.

Sure enough. "Lulu!" Mitch grinned at me through the screen. His hair was damp, and he looked relaxed, like someone who'd just had a post-workout shower.

"Hey, big guy." It had been a week since I'd talked to anyone in my family. I didn't realize how much I missed it till I saw my cousin's face. My heart swelled and tears washed my eyes. I missed him. I missed my home.

He laughed as he took in my appearance. "Damn, you look great! Blending in already, huh?"

I put a hand to my chest, my fingers skimming over the lacing up the front of my bodice. "Don't exactly have a choice, do I?" But a smile came to my face. This outfit already felt more like me than any of my myriad neutral-toned pantsuits.

"How's Faire life treating you?"

"It's not the law office, I'll tell you that."

His laugh was booming, despite the small speaker on the phone. "It's really not."

I moved on to the reason for my call.

"How's Grandma? You called her, right?"

He clucked his tongue. "I said I would, didn't I? It's like you don't trust me at all."

"I trust you, it's just . . ."

"That you can't let go of things? Yeah, I know." He shook his head ruefully at me. "That's what this is supposed to be about, remember? Letting go of real life. Clearing your head." His eyes narrowed. "I think this call is cheating. Did you steal Stacey's phone or what?"

"No, I didn't steal her phone!" But I cast guilty eyes in Stacey's direction. She laughed and shook her head.

Thankfully he took pity on me. "Grandma's fine," he said. "She seemed a little confused that I was calling her —"

"Then you should call her more," I shot back, and he rolled his eyes.

"Yeah, yeah. Anyway, she's a little worried about you, but when I explained that you were traveling with Stacey and the band she got really excited. Something about liking the kilt boys?" He raised his eyebrows, and I laughed.

"She was a big fan when she saw them last summer. I think she's their oldest groupie."

Mitch laughed. "We'll have to bring her up here when Faire starts this summer."

"I think she'd like that."

Mitch cleared his throat, his eyes darting off-screen momentarily. "Grandma said she heard from your mom."

There it was. "Great. And how pissed was she?" Were they already telling stories about me, the crazy member of the family, throwing her career away in one fell swoop? I closed my eyes, bracing for the onslaught. At least it wouldn't hurt as bad when delivered by Mitch, one of the few members of the family I could stand.

"I think she was more worried than anything." His voice was careful, and my eyes flew open in surprise.

"Worried?" I echoed. "Mom? You mean worried about my career, about her fall in the rankings as the one with the most successful kid?"

"She's not gonna lose that contest as long as I keep doing what I'm doing, you know? No worries there." His voice was light, with only a small tinge of bitterness creeping in along the edges. In a family of advanced degrees and advanced professionals, Mitch was the outlier. The gym teacher. The Renaissance Faire performer. And, now that he was settled down with his girlfriend, probably the happiest of us all.

"Stop that," I chided softly, before forcing

some cheer into my voice. "Besides, unemployed plummets me straight to the bottom. But that's okay. I'm coming up with a plan."

"A plan?" His brow furrowed.

"Yeah." I wished I had my notebook with me, so I could show him. "I'm making lists, you know? Things to do when I get back to reality. Plans. I want to —"

"Nope." Mitch shook his head vigorously. "Not listening to that. I want to hear about Ren Faire shenanigans. Drinking too much mead, dancing onstage with the Kilts. You need to be having fun for a change. You don't need to be working on your life plan."

I deflated, even as my heart soared at his suggestion. Dancing did sound like more fun than making lists. "But planning is what I do. I can't just . . . exist."

"Well, you're gonna have to. At least for a few more weeks. Get your head clear before you start filling it up with a business plan. Be a little less Louisa Malone, Corporate Attorney. A little more Lulu. I miss her."

He had a point; I missed her too. I sighed elaborately, something that was hard to do with my diminished lung capacity. "Fine." I glanced up to see the band had shown up while I'd been talking to Mitch; time to get the day started. "I have to go. Need to give

144

Stacey her phone back. Say hey to April for me."

"You got it. And Lulu? Seriously. Try to enjoy yourself. Turn that brain of yours off for a little bit. Try to just be."

When the hell had my cousin become a Zen master?

I waited until I'd disconnected the call to scoff. I hadn't turned my brain off since I'd started high school. Valedictorians didn't turn their brains off. Neither did law students. Or lawyers, for that matter. But I had to admit that not having work hanging over my head for the past few days had been nice. Like when you open the windows on the first day of spring and let the breeze flow in. Fresh air in my brain.

The front gate hadn't opened yet, so the lanes were empty of patrons as I left the stage. I meant to walk straight to the food stalls. Honest. I knew the way and everything.

But something I'd said yesterday was stuck in my brain. *Not a lot of call for receptionists here.* I wasn't totally right about that. Halfway to the food stalls I took a sharp left down a side path, and before I could really think about it I'd marched up to the fortune-tellers' camp like I had every right to be there.

It looked different in the early morning light. The three little tents were set up in a half circle, their canvas sides tied out of the way. Each tent held a pair of chairs with a table in between, but right now the chairs were pulled outside, and the occupants of the tents each sat on one with their feet up on the other. Judging from the fast-food bags on the ground next to them, they'd grabbed breakfast on the way in.

"You need help," I said without preamble, barging my way into their circle and interrupting their sleepy morning conversation.

They blinked at me for a few excruciating moments before one of them spoke. "We do?" She looked about my age, maybe a little older. Her dark curls were threaded with silver, and she wore a woven crown of greenery dotted with blue flowers, matching the rest of her outfit. She didn't wear any makeup, but her skin glowed with the look of someone who knew how to moisturize and wear sunscreen.

Another one of the fortune-tellers, a younger blonde dressed all in red and gold, finished chewing a bite of her egg sandwich before picking up her cardboard coffee cup from the ground next to her. She took a long swallow, her eyes on me the whole time. She had a heart-shaped face, wide blue eyes, and features like an angel. "Who the hell are you?" Her voice was throaty and matter-of-fact, not matching her angelic expression.

"Yeah. Wait . . ." The woman in blue squinted her eyes, peering at me. "I know you. You're the one who tossed your phone in the laundry wenches' tub."

Man, that whole thing was sticking to me like glue. "That's me. I'm Phone Girl."

The third fortune-teller laughed. She was a slender, reedlike girl whose costume was mostly yellow. She wore lots of crystals around her neck, strung on cords of various lengths. Rose quartz earrings peeked out from her long brown hair. "You're with the Dueling Kilts, right?"

"Ohhhhh." The girl in red nodded now. "She's with Dex."

"I'm not *with* Dex." Best to put that idea to bed as quickly as possible. *To bed.* Bad choice of words when thinking about Dex. "But yeah, I'm traveling with the Kilts."

"Tell me again how you're going to help us?" The older woman in blue kept the conversation on topic.

I'd never been a particularly shy person; whatever introversion I'd retained from my youth had been beaten out of me in law school. But this was bold, even for me. How long had they been traveling together, doing this work, living this life? And who was I to tell them they were doing it wrong? But I knew I was right in this, and more importantly I didn't want to spend another day selling turkey legs. "I saw y'all. Yesterday. You were slammed. Is it always like that?"

They glanced at each other, and I watched as silent communication flowed between them, less from any psychic ability they might possess and more from what was probably years of working and traveling together. "Yeah," the one wearing the blue flowers said with a sigh. "Pretty much. I mean, some days are busier than others . . ."

". . . But when we all get people wanting readings at the same time, it can get a little chaotic." The crystal-laden girl in yellow to my left crumpled the wrapper from her breakfast sandwich and shoved it into the paper bag at her feet. Then she wiped her hands on her napkin and disposed of it in the same place.

"We manage," said the girl in red. But the others shook their heads.

"Usually we do, but yeah, this Faire has been a mess."

"That's what I'm saying." I clapped my hands together, like we'd just worked out a settlement. "I want to help. I could take appointments for you, so you don't have a big crowd of people waiting around, getting pissed off in the heat. They can get set times to come back, and then you're more organized too."

"Appointments?" The one in red screwed up her face, like I'd suggested she trade her costume for a sensible pantsuit. "Like a doctor's office?"

"Or a salon." I thought fast. "I can tell them it's like a spa day for the psyche. Or something." Oh, I was good.

"What's going to make 'em come back after they make an appointment?" Red shook her head; I was having a hard time winning her over.

"She's got a point," Blue said. "People who say they're going to come back hardly ever do. It's all about impulse shopping in places like this. Out of sight, out of mind and all that."

"I make them pay in advance?" I shrugged. "Then if they don't come back, we — well, you — still have their money. Win-win." I thought about that. "Or, win-lose, for them. Whatever."

Blue laughed. "That's a really good point."

I was winning them over. This felt better than any closing argument I had ever made.

"I was thinking . . ." I kept going like I

149

had thought this all out in advance, instead of making it up on the fly. If there was something that lawyers knew how to do, it was bullshit their way through a situation. "There's a leather vendor up the hill there who sells journals. I'll go get one and be right back. That can be my appointment book, and then we can get started."

They all nodded, and I couldn't believe it. I'd insinuated myself into this band of fortune-tellers, and they were okay with it. But as I turned to go up the hill, Red called out to me.

"Wait a second. You never answered my question. Who *are* you?"

Good question, I thought as I turned back. But Mitch's suggestion stuck in my brain. A little less Louisa, a little more Lulu. That nickname was mostly reserved for family, my cousin Mitch especially, and I'd bristled yesterday when Dex had called me by that name. When Mitch used it I felt childlike, but in the best possible way. I felt carefree. I felt like someone who smiled a lot more than Louisa the Attorney did during her nine-to-five. Nine-to-nine. Nine-to-middle-of-the-night. Whatever.

"Lulu." Here came that carefree smile, lifting my face and my spirits. "My name's Lulu."

NINE

The summer after my second year of law school I interned at my first Big Law firm. A few weeks in, the receptionist went on maternity leave. While she was gone, it took three people to cover her job, at about half the efficiency. That was when I learned that the receptionist was the beating heart of an office. They were the one person you wanted to befriend; if the receptionist liked you, your job would be twenty-five percent easier. At minimum.

I may not have had a big mahogany desk with an ever-full candy dish on top, but I could do this. After a quick shopping trip for a leather-bound journal and a wooden pen from a nearby vendor, I was back to help them set up their sign: TAROT-PALMISTRY-RUNES, lettered in stark black on boards painted a bright yellow. And just in time: the first patrons of the day were trickling in from the front gate. I took what I'd learned from Stacey the day before and became the barker for my new employers.

"Limited spots available!" I called out, waving my book in emphasis. "Secure your time now, learn what's in store for your future!" It took only a few minutes for the three little tents to be full of customers. Time to start the waiting list, and I was ready.

I settled into a rhythm of scheduling readings and taking payment before sending patrons on their way, keeping a running waiting list. Everyone paid in advance and had a rough idea of when to come back. My leather belt pouch became a de facto cashbox, and I got good at tucking my little notebook into my bodice while I made change. As the day went on, I started planning improvements: tie a string from my journal to my pen to keep the two together. Get a watch. Could I get a hostess stand out here in the woods?

The two fortune-tellers who read tarot cards were the most popular. Once their appointment slots filled up, I steered prospective clients toward the third, the older woman in blue, who was a palm reader who also worked with runes. We were booked solid not long after noon, and while some patrons waited around in case there were no-shows, the whole vibe was a lot more "learn your future from these convenient mystics" and less "crowd in the middle of the woods for no damn reason." I considered that an improvement.

Don't get me wrong. It was still a long day on my feet dealing with the public, wearing a costume that made it hard to breathe. But at least I didn't smell like fried food anymore.

At the end of the day, I helped the older woman in blue, whose name was Sage, take down the big yellow sign. After that I handed her the wad of cash I'd collected in my belt bag during the day.

"That worked out great." She flipped through the cash, sorting the bills before stowing them away. Then to my utter astonishment she handed me a wad of cash of my own.

"What's this?"

"Your cut." Sage smiled. "It's not much, but we all chipped in some of our tips from today. We want you to know we appreciate your help."

"Oh." I glanced down at the cash in my hand. I wasn't going to be crass enough to count it in front of her, but I spotted some twenties in there. "You don't have to . . ." I hadn't anticipated making money doing this.

"Sure, we do." She nodded firmly. "You're working just as hard as we are. Don't think we haven't noticed."

"You did great." One of the tarot readers — Sasha — pulled her long blond hair up into a modern-looking messy bun, securing it with a red scrunchie that matched her outfit. "I hardly had a break all day." She reached into her belt pouch, drawing out a set of car keys that she flashed at us before heading off down the lane. Around me, the other two started breaking down their tents, folding up tables, and stowing tablecloths and tapestries. I jumped in to help.

"Sorry," I said. "I should have thought about making sure you had breaks. The patrons were pretty insistent, I'm sorry."

"No, it was great, are you kidding?" Sage rocked her head from side to side, cracking her neck. "It was the busiest I've been this whole Faire. Plus, people weren't standing around, breathing down our necks."

"That last part." Summer, the tarot reader in yellow, nodded emphatically. "The energy was so much less chaotic. The cards really liked that."

"Oh." I blinked once, very deliberately, so my eyes didn't roll back in my head. "Well, as long as I made the little pieces of cardboard happy, I can sleep well tonight."

Sage snorted, but Summer looked at me appraisingly. "Ah, you're one of those," she said with a knowing smile.

"One of what?"

"You think the cards are bullshit, right?"

"Um." I was usually good at diplomacy, but she had me here. "I think they're good for some people? Not my thing, though." That was putting it mildly.

"What's not your thing? Witchy stuff?" Sage bounced a handful of her rune stones in her hand before funneling them into a leather pouch hooked to her blue skirt.

I nodded. "I'm a lawyer. I'm used to thinking logically. Not relying on . . ." I gestured at her pouch of runes, at the deck of cards Summer had just put away. "All that. It's what, one step away from casting spells? I mean, none of that's real, right?"

"You'd be surprised." Sasha had returned with a largish Subaru hatchback in time to catch the end of our conversation. She popped the lift gate, and we started filling it with folded tents and tables. "You ever wish on birthday candles?"

"Sure," I said. "When I was a kid." And when I was an adult too, but I wasn't going to mention that. Who didn't wish on birthday candles? And then afterward kept that wish close to their heart, because speaking it out loud meant it wouldn't come true? That was what you did.

"What did you wish?" Sasha asked in that blunt, husky voice. "The last time you blew out a birthday candle. What did you wish for?"

I made an involuntary cluck of the tongue. "I can't tell you that!" I was only slightly scandalized.

"Why not?" Sasha raised her eyebrows.

"Because the wish won't come true. Everyone knows that."

"Hmmmm . . ." She looked thoughtful. "So you light a candle, make your intention known to the universe, then blow out the candle, sending your intention out with the smoke?" She trailed a hand through the air, imitating the smoke of a burned-out candle. "Sounds a lot like spellwork to me. Is that any weirder than reading cards and telling fortunes?"

"Yeah, but . . ." But the beginning of my retort had been an automatic thing, and now that I'd started it I realized she had a good point.

Sasha noted my silence with a smile and her trailing hand turned into a dismissive wave. "That's okay. Hang out with us long enough, you'll change your mind."

Good luck with that, I thought, but out loud I said, "We'll see."

"Speaking of," Sage cut in. "Are you sticking around with the Kilts? They're heading to the Blue Ridge Renaissance Faire after this one, right?"

Summer nodded before I could speak. "They're going to Blue Ridge. Dex was telling me that last weekend."

I tried not to raise my eyebrows and mostly succeeded. He really got around, didn't he? "I'll be there, then. I'm sticking around through the Willow Creek Faire, sometime in July." I loved the thought of this whole life being like a train, traveling slowly from destination to destination. Trains were slow-moving, romantic.

Sage looked thoughtful. "Willow Creek . . . oh, that's in Maryland, right? The little one?"

"Yeah." Summer nodded. "We don't do that one."

"Oh." I wasn't sure how to respond to that. Were they judging my cousin's Faire? I suddenly felt protective of the whole endeavor.

My displeasure must have shown on my face. "Oh, it's a great Faire!" Sasha hastened to add. "I've heard amazing things about it.

We just take a few weeks off around then. We have family in Delaware, so we hang there, recharge our batteries, you know?"

"Sure." My defensiveness still prickled as I tried to think of what kind of batteries they would need to recharge. They didn't play music, they didn't juggle or wrestle in mud. They sat in tents all day, looking at pictures printed on cards. How hard could that be?

But I told myself not to judge. They still dealt with the public all day, which in and of itself was draining on the soul. Even if this whole fortune-telling thing was bullshit, they still had to make it look real. They still had to spend the day looking people in the face and making up stories about their lives and what to expect in their futures. Mental energy was still energy. I should be painfully aware of that after years spent behind a desk typing legal briefs.

"Anyway," Sage continued, not noticing my mental turmoil. "You'll be back next weekend, right? Because you were right."

"I was?"

They all nodded as one. "We totally need you," Summer said, her face like the sun as she smiled, and I felt that warmth in my chest. It was nice to be needed. Not in a "break your back to make this multimillion-dollar law firm even more dollars and we'll never reward you" way, but in a "you genuinely helped us and we appreciate it" way.

And it beat medieval fast food any day of the damn week. "Of course," I said. "I'll be back." I tucked the money away. This was good. I could pass this along to Stacey, contribute to the grocery budget or gas money or something. Feel like less of a leech. "I'm glad to help."

"Good." Sage nodded firmly. "Because you're one of us now."

"Oh, no." I put up defensive hands. "I'm just your office manager. I don't know anything about any of that woo-woo stuff."

She shook her head, a smile cracking over her face. "Just like birthday candles, remember?"

As I started up the lane to meet up with Stacey and the rest of the gang, the Faire grounds seemed eerily quiet. Banners still lined the lanes, but the stages were empty, the clearings barren. Empty, as though nothing had ever been here. It was an odd feeling, for a place that had been so full of life and activity. Like the past couple of weekends had been a dream. It made me think of something out of Shakespeare — appropriate, considering the location. *That you have but slumber'd here while these visions did appear. And this weak and idle theme, no more yielding but a dream.* Leaving this place for the last time was starting to feel like waking up from a dream you didn't want to leave behind.

I could actually hear the light breeze in the trees now that the patrons were gone and the music was silenced. The sun had started to dip in the sky, and I was alone. In a rapidly darkening forest. That wasn't good.

I rounded a bend in the lane and almost ran smack into Stacey.

"Hey, there you are! I was worried when I didn't see you at turkey legs."

"Oh." Shit. I hadn't told anyone where I'd gone today. "No. Sorry. I ended up over at the fortune-tellers, helping them instead."

"Oh, cool!" Stacey didn't seem pissed that she'd had to hunt me down, but it would take a lot to dim her smile. I shouldn't push it like this. "People need all kinds of help. It's nice of you to be so flexible."

That wasn't exactly what had happened, but I decided to let her think that rather than correct her. "Sorry," I said again. "I was helping them break everything down, and I . . ." A terrible thought occurred to me. "I should have probably been helping you break down instead, huh?"

"Me?" Stacey made a *pfft* sound. "Are you kidding? I travel with four big strong guys . . ." She broke off and thought for a second. "Well, I travel with four guys, anyway." I snickered, and her smile widened. "Anyway, there's not much to break down. Daniel pulled his truck around, and they're getting it all loaded up now. So I came to look for you."

I winced. "Sorry. Again."

"Oh, it's no problem at all!" Her smile was as friendly as ever, but I could see some strain along the edges. Of course it was a problem. Not only was I a freeloader, but I was an irresponsible one.

I could solve one of those problems. "Here." I dug in my belt pouch for my share of the tips we'd gotten that day. I handed the wad of cash to her as we walked.

Stacey whistled as she sorted the cash. "Did you knock over the turkey leg stand?"

"Yep. That's my new career path: highwayman. Well, highwaywoman." I smirked as Stacey laughed. "That's period appropriate, right?"

"Maybe," she said. "I'll ask my friend Simon. He's good at all that historical stuff." She peeled off some bills and handed the rest back to me. I tried to protest, but she pushed the money into my hands until

161

it was either take the bills or let them fall to the forest floor. "You don't cost that much, believe me."

"I add to the grocery bill," I said. "And . . . I don't know. Gas money?"

She shook her head. "You don't eat as much as you think you do. I'll take this for the groceries —" She waved the bills she'd kept, then put them into her belt pouch. "But you hold on to the rest. This is a job, remember? There's no problem with you being paid to do it."

Well, when she put it that way . . .

It was a quiet Sunday evening, but the atmosphere felt different. The impending move made everything feel off-kilter. Dinner was scrounged-up deli meat and cheese sandwiches and whatever odds and ends were in the bottom of potato chip bags, as we cleaned out as many leftover groceries as possible. After the haphazard dinner, the band left to go back to the hotel, presumably to pack. I dug around in the back of the tiny fridge for the last container of yogurt, and I brought it out to the table for dessert. I cracked the lid and dug in my spoon. Peach. Yum.

I spooned the cool yogurt into my mouth, closing my eyes in tired pleasure. I'd been tired for most of my twenties and thirties, but this was a different kind of tired. It was the bone-deep weariness from a long day spent outside in fresh air, and I was sleeping better than I had in years. Maybe there was something to all of this unplugging.

My eyes were still closed against the glow of the fairy lights around the camper's awning when I sensed someone nearby. I frowned and opened my eyes to see Dex, sitting backwards in the chair across from me, a beer in one hand. "I thought you left."

"Trying to get rid of me, huh?" He took a sip from his bottle of beer. "I get that a lot."

I snorted. "That's not what I hear."

"You'd be surprised." But his voice was soft, his low energy matching mine. We were all tired tonight.

I took another bite of yogurt. "Don't you need to pack up? We're moving out tomorrow, right?"

He nodded. "Checkout isn't until eleven. Plenty of time to get my shit together. Besides, I'm helping out here." He lifted the beer bottle in illustration. "These beers aren't going to drink themselves."

"Ah." I smirked as he took another swig. "How altruistic of you."

"I'm a giver." The silence between us was companionable as we both stared lazily out into the night. I'd just let my eyes slide closed again when he next spoke. "So. Coming with us to the next one, huh?"

I opened my eyes to meet Dex's gaze squarely. Low energy aside, there was something different about him tonight, and it took a second for it to click. He wasn't flirting with me. He wasn't looking me up and down, making an appraisal. He was just talking to me.

If he'd approached me with an innuendo, my defensive hackles would have gone up. But those hackles lay dormant tonight. It was . . . nice.

"I thought I might." My plastic spoon scraped up another bite of yogurt. "That okay?"

"Sure." His eyes were on the motorhome, and I followed his gaze. The curtains were mostly opaque, but I could make out Daniel and Stacey inside, handing each other things to tuck away into corners.

"They're a well-oiled machine, aren't they?" I kept my voice low so it wouldn't travel through those flowered curtains. I knew how easy it was to hear outside conversation from in there.

"You have no idea." His eyes lingered on the oddly domestic scene inside before turning back to his beer. And to me. "No, I'm glad you're here. Stacey likes having you around."

"She's been great. I honestly don't know what I would have done without her that day."

A smile lifted his lips. "I wish I could have seen that. Did you really throw your phone into the laundry wenches' tub in the middle of their show?"

I covered my face with my hand as the mental image flooded my mind. "Oh, God, is that what they're saying now?" It was hard to laugh and cringe at the same time, but I managed it. "No. The show was over, I'd tipped her my five bucks, and . . ."

"That doesn't give you the right to use their prop as your personal trash can, you know." But his eyes flashed in amusement, inviting me to smile back.

"Eh, she said she didn't mind. As long as I don't do it again."

"So, did you, like . . ." He set down his beer and did an elaborate windup, miming a baseball pitcher about to throw a strike.

"Nah," I said. "It was more like . . ." I flicked my wrist, like skipping a stone across a lake. He grinned and picked up his beer.

"Nice." He tipped his head back, and I watched him swallow.

"So, um." I cleared my throat, not sure

how to broach the topic, not even sure if I should. "Is everything okay? Like with Todd and all."

"Todd?" Dex's eyebrows went up. "What about him?"

"You know . . ." I gestured with my plastic spoon at nothing. "The whole thing with his girlfriend." I hazarded a glance at the motorhome, but as far as I could tell no one was listening to us. "Are they going to be okay, do you think?"

"How the hell should I know? I'm not a relationship expert."

"It's none of my business." I ran my spoon around the inside of the yogurt container, but it was empty. I set both aside. "But Stacey seems worried. Like the band could break up."

Dex nodded. "She's right. It could." He moved his beer bottle from hand to hand.

"Aren't you worried?"

"Nope." He took a swig of beer, the green glass bottle glinting in the light. "I don't need to be."

I looked at him through narrowed eyes. "That doesn't seem likely."

"Believe it." He leaned forward in his chair, elbows resting easily on his knees. "Thirty-one years I've been alive, and you know how many times I've been asked what

I think?"

"How many?" I had a feeling the answer was a very low number.

Dex only responded with another shrug, his dark eyes looking out into the night. "I don't make the plans around here," he said finally. "It's not my job to think. I'm here to look good and sing songs. That's it." The cheerful tone had left his voice as he bit out the words.

"Dex . . ." My hand, my whole arm, itched to reach out. To give him comfort. I wasn't sure why. He was doing his best to mask whatever he was feeling, so the right thing to do was to let him think he'd fooled me.

But when he looked back at me, our eyes met in the dark and his gaze softened. For the space of a breath, of two, neither of us moved. Something happened there in the dark under the fairy lights. I let him know that I saw him, and he acknowledged it. Not the Ren Faire Lothario, but the man he was beneath the bluster. How many people knew that man?

"It's not my job," he said again. I'd never heard his voice like this. Low. Real. Not a joke, not a flirtation, not an innuendo in sight. "I don't plan the future. I leave that to the pros. They'll figure it out."

"Yeah, but . . ." I didn't have a retort for

him. It was foreign to me to not want to think. To plan. But that was the way Dex lived his life, wasn't it? Maybe he had something to teach me.

So I swallowed any argument I might have made and forced a smile. Looking at Dex, it wasn't hard to do. "Any beer left in that cooler?"

His lips lifted in an answering smile and he tilted his head back, finishing his before setting the bottle down with a thud. "Coming right up."

TEN

The next day was full of activity: packing things up and tucking them in place in preparation for a long day on the road. It was a convoy of cars and a truck and a motorhome, and after a long afternoon on the road, we arrived at dusk at . . . a campground that looked just like the one we'd left that morning.

Soon, it was like we'd never moved. The only difference was in my roommate: Stacey and Daniel had moved to the hotel and Frederick was in the motorhome with me. It was a very comfortable arrangement. He was quiet like I was, and sometimes we streamed baking competition shows on his tablet before bedtime.

This Faire was northwest of where we'd been before, in the Blue Ridge Mountains, and the change in altitude made the summer weather a little more temperate. On those slightly cooler, breezy days, Stacey and I kept the windows in the motorhome open as we sat inside at the small dinette table.

"How long did you say we're staying here?"

"I forget. Four weeks? No, five." She peered at her laptop screen and nodded slowly. "Five." She shook her head with a rueful smile. "See, Daniel can rattle that stuff off the top of his head."

"You have plenty of other talents." I smirked in response to her giggle, then looked down as a furry head bumped my calf. "What about Benedick?" I asked. "He's a great roommate, but am I going to need to give him a lift to work on the weekends?"

"Nah." Stacey leaned down, wiggling her fingers until Benedick came over to her for a scritch on the head. "He can take this Faire off. Just leave the air running in the motorhome during the day. He should be fine."

"He doesn't mind missing out?"

She shook her head. "I think he likes catching up on his sleep."

I snorted. "Makes sense. He works hard." Speaking of . . . I had work of my own, and I needed to get back to it. While Stacey worked on updating the band's website and arranging for orders of merchandise — the band did a decent business in the sales of things like CDs and digital downloads as well as shirts and other branded items — I poked away on my forbidden laptop. It had taken some hard negotiating with Stacey, but eventually she agreed to let me have it for a couple days so I could update my résumé. The laptop was going with her to the hotel on Friday, though, and I wouldn't get it back till Willow Creek. My ever-present notebook was at my elbow, and it was nice to have something to check off the massive to-do list that had taken shape in its pages.

I was doing my best to do as Mitch said: turn my brain off, escape from reality. But this escape was going to end in July, and when it did, I'd have to hit the ground running. Having an updated résumé was the first step. Did I do a little poking around on some legal recruitment websites too, while Stacey wasn't looking? Maybe. Mind your own business.

But we didn't work in silence. Outside, under our little canopy, the guys worked on their music. Over the course of the week they'd hashed out five new songs, which had originally sounded pretty rough. But today they finished running through them all with a minimum of stopping, and even less arguing. So that was going in the right direction.

Stacey obviously thought so too. "I liked that one!" she yelled out the window without getting out of her seat.

"Thanks!" Frederick yelled back. Or maybe it was Dex. Hard to identify a voice from yelling. I looked toward the window, as though I could see through the flowery cotton curtain and outside to where Dex was picking out a new melody on his guitar. My ponytail flipped over my shoulder, and I caught the ends with one hand, twirling some locks through my fingers.

The door to the motorhome slammed open, making us both jump.

"Why are you both stuck in here? It's too nice out." Dex squeezed past us to the minifridge, grabbing bottles of beer.

"I spend all my time outside." Stacey's retort was mild. "It's nice to be in the shade for a change."

He shrugged. "Suit yourself." He plucked the bottle opener from its spot on the magnetized backsplash, cracking open the bottles with a hiss of carbonation.

"Sounding great out there." Stacey had already turned back to her laptop, pecking away. "I think we'll do really well at this Faire."

"Again with the 'we.' " Dex shook his

head. "You and Daniel, I swear. I don't recall seeing either one of you onstage with us."

"Awwww." Stacey beamed up at him. "If you want me to sing with you, all you gotta do is ask."

He rolled his eyes. "We'll keep that in mind if Todd bails on us." He turned his attention toward me. "You sure you don't play the fiddle?"

I snorted a laugh. "Wouldn't that be something?"

"It would." He punctuated his words with one raised eyebrow and another swig of beer before he was gone, back out the door carrying the other beverages out to his brothers. I released my breath in what I hoped didn't sound like a sigh. The last thing I needed was to look like I was pining over the town bicycle of the Renaissance Faire circuit.

Outside, the music had stopped, and Daniel was holding a team meeting.

"I couldn't get us in anywhere this week, but that's fine since we're settling in, rehearsing, all that. But I have some calls in to some local places. There's this new Irish pub that opened up a few miles from here, so hopefully you can get in there on Wednesday or Thursday . . ."

"Not next week." There was no mistaking Dex's voice this time.

"What? Why not next week?" Daniel's authority wasn't challenged often, and he sounded more confused than pissed off.

"Because . . ." Dex's voice trailed off, like a kid trying to explain why his homework was late. "I'm tired, man," he finally said.

There was a bark of laughter. "You're *tired*?" Todd's voice was incredulous, and I was on Todd's side here. That made no sense.

Dex huffed. "I'm just saying. Can't we take a week off from side gigs once in a while?"

"The side gigs help keep us in the black." Daniel's voice was exaggeratingly patient.

"Are we in the black right now?"

"Well, yeah. But —"

"Then let's take a week off. Damn, dude, not all of us like to hustle as hard as you do, okay?"

The silence outside stretched for an uncomfortable amount of time, and I imagined the staring contest ensuing between Dex and Daniel — brown eyes boring into green. Finally there was a sigh.

"Sure. Fine. I won't put anything on the schedule next week. You can use the extra rehearsal time anyway. But I swear to God if this is because you're hooking up with someone out of town . . ."

"Not everything's about me and who I'm hooking up with." My eyebrows shot up at Dex's defensive tone. This whole argument was so unlike him. I met Stacey's eyes across the table. We exchanged puzzled looks, and she shrugged elaborately.

"Not touching that one." She bent back to her laptop, and after a moment I followed suit. None of my business anyway.

On Friday afternoon my laptop was safely back in Stacey's possession, and I was outside writing in my notebook. Dex was right — the weather was too nice lately to stay inside, and the picnic table was right out here, not being used. My to-do lists had morphed into journal entries, with each thing on the list getting a running commentary.

— Sell condo?? How much space do I really need? So many boxes at home I never unpacked.

— Job — am I going back to Big Law? Mitch is right, same old shit. Open my own practice? What would I specialize in???

I was contemplating adding a fourth question mark when the bench I was sitting on dipped with the weight of another person. I frowned and glanced over at Dex, sitting backwards beside me on the bench, his back against the table, a bottle of water in each hand. He offered one to me.

"You'll be at the shows this weekend, right? You were great with the tip basket."

"I don't think so. I have a job now." At least I hoped I did. I hadn't exactly made a plan with the fortune-tellers. I figured I'd just show up on Saturday wherever they were set up and see if they still wanted me. But now I was conflicted; I'd really enjoyed being the tip basket girl.

"Oh, right, the fortune-tellers. I heard about that. Well, you should come on Saturday, at least. To the first show. Check out the new stuff."

"Awwww." I rested my chin on my folded hands and batted my eyelashes. "You miss me that much? Why, Dexter, I'm flattered."

He clucked his tongue at me. "Declan."

"What?"

"My name's not Dexter." He finished his water and pitched the empty bottle toward a nearby trash can. To my utter annoyance it went in. "Dex is short for Declan."

That made more sense. Declan MacLean

was about as Celtic a name as you could get, wasn't it?

"Anyway." He stood up. "Come to the show Saturday. The first one. They won't miss you for that first hour of the day. And I think you'll want to see this one."

He was weirdly insistent, but I couldn't think of a reason to say no. "As long as y'all do 'Whiskey in the Jar.'"

"A classic. You have good taste." He rapped his knuckles on the table between us in farewell and left, moving across the campsite to where his brothers were waiting for him to rehearse. I watched him walk away, because I was only human and he looked as good in jeans as he did in a kilt. Which was criminally unfair.

That night, as I fluffed up my pillows and shook out my sheets on the pullout sofa, Frederick cleared his throat behind me. "So, I've been meaning to tell you something."

"Shit. Have we already hit the bread week episode?" I shook my head. "Those always stress me out."

"Oh God, me too. All that tension about whether or not it's going to rise the right way . . . but no, that's not it. It's . . ." He looked down toward the floor, rubbing the back of his neck. "Patrick's at this Faire. He texted me yesterday."

"Patrick?" It took a second for it to click. "Oh! The juggling comedy guy?"

"Yeah." His cheeks flushed as he smiled. "The juggling comedy guy. They got called at the last minute, so they're going to be performing here. For the full run."

"That's great!" I wondered why he still looked so uncomfortable. Did I look like a homophobe? I thought I'd telegraphed allyship as well as I could. There were a million coded ways I could ask him what the problem was, but coded wasn't really my way. Especially not these days. "Is he coming here? Do I need to clear out?" I thought fast. Was I going to have to move into Stacey and Daniel's hotel room with them? God, that was going to be awkward.

"Oh, no! The opposite, actually. He's staying with some friends in the area, and he . . ." Frederick cleared his throat, his cheeks going even redder. "He asked me to come stay with him." He glanced over his shoulder, and I couldn't believe it had taken me this long to notice the overnight bag sitting in the middle of the made-up bed in the back.

"Ohhhhhhh," I said in a sing-song voice.

"Yeah. He's picking me up in a few minutes." The redness faded from his face now, and his smile was more genuine. "I meant to tell you today, and I just forgot." He gestured behind him. "The bed's all yours from here on out, and you're welcome to borrow my tablet if you want to keep going on those baking shows."

"Yeah, but . . ." I tilted my head as I thought. "You'll be back during the week?"

He shrugged. "During the day, at least. For practice and all. Don't worry about it. I've slept on this sofa plenty of times. I don't mind taking it if I crash here sometimes during this Faire." The confidence in his voice told me that he wasn't planning to crash here a single night.

Good for him.

After the past few weeks of overwhelming togetherness, having an entire motorhome all to myself was luxurious. Decadent. The bed in the back wasn't even close to a king-size bed at a hotel, but it was big enough that I could do a little starfishing. Then I grabbed Frederick's tablet — another decadence. I'd only use it to watch videos. Nothing work or real life related — Stacey couldn't argue with that. Benedick joined me as I snuggled down among the pillows and cued up the baking competition.

"Just you and me, buddy." Benedick washed his ears while I clicked Play and swore under my breath. It was the bread week episode after all. I didn't need this kind of stress in my life.

Now, this was more like it.

The grounds of this smaller Faire reminded me of the one that I'd taken my grandparents to, the one where I'd watched my cousin wear a kilt and swing that impossibly large sword of his. Stepping onto these Faire grounds felt like coming home. This was what I had been looking for that first day.

The Dueling Kilts' first show was at ten thirty. That was an early start, and since they were featured at the closing-time pub sing as well, it was going to be a long day for everyone. I checked a map as the first patrons began milling around, hoping the fortune-tellers would be easy to find. I shouldn't have worried; this Faire had a whole section called Mystics' Glade, which sounded both romantic and esoteric. I wanted to run down and make sure they still needed me, but they were all the way at the other end of the site. Dex had been so insistent that I stick around for the first show that I helped Stacey get set up instead. If the fortune-tellers needed me, they'd still need me after the first Kilts show.

Once the show started, I skirted the back

of the audience to join Stacey. We stood together back there just like the day we met. Was it only two weeks ago? It felt like a lifetime. I could barely remember the law office anymore. That was a different person — Louisa. I felt more like Lulu now.

Stacey bumped my shoulder in greeting as the first song of their set ended. "Everything okay? I thought you were helping out the fortune-tellers again."

I nodded. "Dex wanted me to see this show. I'll go find them afterward."

Her brow furrowed. "Huh. I wonder why."

"No idea." I shrugged. "Maybe because it's a new set?" But my voice was doubtful; so far there wasn't anything new about this act. "Aren't they trying out some new material?"

"I think so, yeah. But . . ." She looked as confused as I felt. "I mean, you've seen their show. It's not going to be that different."

She had a point. They'd wedged a new song in after their opening number, and it came across seamlessly, like they'd always played it that way. But their between-song patter and jokes between the guys were the same. I smiled at jokes I'd heard a few times now; they felt comforting, like home.

The first change came a few songs in. "This one goes out to our darling Louisa,"

Dex announced, a smile playing across his mouth as he spotted me in the back. "Don't ask me why, but this is her favorite. Maybe she's into betrayal, I dunno."

I grinned at the first notes of "Whiskey in the Jar," and Stacey laughed beside me. "Is that why he wanted you here?"

"Maybe?" Mild irritation pricked at my smile. Did Dex expect me to show up four times a day for some light heckling? I'd told him I had a job of my own here, had that not sunk in?

Still, I really did like that song. I hummed along, and as the show continued I found myself half listening, half surveying the audience to see which of the new songs and jokes landed the best. I wasn't sure why Dex had been so insistent that I come to the show today, not to mention this show in particular. Nothing seemed especially . . . special.

Todd stepped forward then, adjusting the earpiece of his wireless mic. "This next one is new. Well, not new to the world, it's been around for a few hundred years, but we just started playing it a few days ago, so hopefully we can pull it off. It's called . . ." His voice faltered, bringing my attention back to him with a snap. His face had gone slack as he stared hard into the audience. "Michele?"

Eleven

"They don't have a song called 'Michele.' "
I turned to Stacey in confusion, but she
wasn't looking at me. She was looking into
the audience, and she suddenly gasped and
grabbed for my arm.

"Oh my *god*! That's . . ."

A woman in one of the middle rows stood
up. She wore casual shorts and a tank, and
her sunglasses up on top of her head pushed
her long blond hair back from her face. It
only took a moment, long enough to see the
way she smiled at Todd's stunned expression, to realize who she was. Todd's girlfriend was that effortless kind of gorgeous
that bordered on intimidating. But the way
she beamed at her man up on the stage
brought her down from intimidating to
relatable. Because who didn't love people in
love?

"Surprise." She barely got the word out
around her laugh, and while Todd stood on

the stage, unable to move, Dex and Frederick stepped forward to flank their brother. Dex took away Todd's fiddle, and Frederick grabbed the bow from his other hand. They both gave him a little nudge, and he stepped forward as his long-distance girlfriend made her way to meet him at the lip of the stage. He easily hopped the couple feet from the stage to the ground to envelop her in a hug as the audience applauded.

I joined the applause, clapping until my hands hurt, and when I glanced over at Stacey, she was blinking back tears. Onstage, Frederick laughed in delighted surprise, and as I glanced over to the side of the stage Daniel shook his head around a smile. But Dex . . . he was the only one who didn't look surprised. My smile shifted as realization dawned. This was why this show was special. He'd wanted me to see this.

I turned my attention back to Todd and Michele at the front near the stage. She'd pulled him down for a long kiss, which he returned with his whole heart, before they finally released each other to allow Todd to return to the stage and the show. He didn't keep his eyes off his girlfriend for the rest of the performance, and as I slipped from Stacey's side as they started the last song I wondered if he was going to be able to let her go.

How could a place I'd never been feel so familiar?

This Faire looked nothing like the one we'd just left. The lanes were hard-packed dirt instead of the semipaved gravel of the previous location. The vendors here had tents and makeshift stalls instead of permanent storefronts, so it had the air of a flea market instead of a medieval shopping center. The tents stood out from the lanes in pops of color, echoed by the banners hanging from the trees.

I'd studied the map enough to know the general area I was looking for, but I was surprised that Mystics' Glade wasn't just a name on a map. It was painted on a banner, strung overhead between two trees to form an archway to walk through in order to enter the glade. On this side of the banner, just off the lane itself, was the familiar TAROT-PALMISTRY-RUNES sign.

Entering the glade felt like walking into a new age shop out here in the woods. A vendor set up to the right of the entrance sold crystals, both loose in baskets on her table and strung on cords from nearby tree branches, where they caught the light with multicolored sparkles. Smoke and the heady smell of incense trickled from another setup to my left. I spotted the familiar trio of my fortune-tellers' tents toward the back of the glade, and thankfully they didn't look too busy yet. I hurried in their direction.

"Sorry!" I held up defensive hands when I got to the fortune-tellers. "I know I'm late, but —"

Two of them were engaged with patrons so they didn't acknowledge me, but Summer flashed a smile in my direction, as bright as her yellow costume. "There you are! So glad you could make it!"

"Sorry," I said again, even though I realized now that no one here was expecting an apology. "Got a little tied up with the Kilts."

She heaved a dramatic, swoony sigh. "Sounds like the perfect way to start the day. I wouldn't mind a little of that myself."

"Pervert." I batted her arm, and we both grinned. I really, really liked these girls. "Don't worry," I said. "I won't be late again."

She waved a hand. "Don't worry about it. I saw that y'all are on one of the stages up front; that's a long hike away."

"Y'all don't look nearly busy enough," I said. "Let me see what I can do about that."

Summer made a sweeping gesture with

her arm — *be my guest* — and I made note of the time on the watch I'd purchased during the week before grabbing for the little book in my pouch. Time to get this crew organized. "Right over here!" I called out to the handful of patrons milling around. "Make your reservation here to learn your future!" My carnival-barker voice attracted attention, and it didn't take long for our section of the glade to become crowded with patrons. That boded well for the rest of the day, and I relaxed into my role as receptionist for the otherworldly as I collected money and made appointments to the background sounds of the rattle of rune stones and the flip of cards.

The atmosphere at the motorhome that night was like a block party, as we all gathered to welcome Michele to the group. Stacey and Daniel had taken care of dinner, like they took care of so many things. Daniel backed his truck into the campsite, the bed full of food, turning the evening into a literal tailgate party. I ate way more pizza than was probably necessary, but it had been a long day out in the sun and I was starving.

As evening fell in earnest, I switched on the awning lights, lending even more of a party atmosphere. Michele was here for almost a week; her plan was to spend a few of the off days with Todd before she flew home to Michigan on Thursday. She and Todd were joined at the hip the way only a couple in a long-distance relationship could be. They held hands a little too tightly, as though they couldn't bear to be separated even long enough to get a drink. It would be a nauseating picture of romance if I didn't see the barely veiled desperation in Todd's eyes.

On a regular night, everyone would have headed back to their respective hotel rooms or hookups. But something about tonight felt different. While the guests of honor had left a while back for some well-deserved alone time, Frederick and Dex had lingered. The fire we'd built in the campsite's firepit for some after-dinner s'mores blazed merrily. I found Dex sitting in one of the Adirondack chairs, and without asking I took the other one.

"Nice job." I handed him a beer out of the cooler and passed him the bottle opener after I'd opened one of Stacey's hard lemonades that I'd stolen.

"Hmm?" Dex raised his eyebrows at me as he took a sip.

"Getting Michele here."

He shook his head, but I watched the spark in his eyes and the smile that played around his mouth. "I don't know what you're talking about."

"Oh, stop it." I set my bottle down on the wide arm of the chair. "You were the only one at that show, except Michele herself, that wasn't surprised. You had her come down here, didn't you?"

I could tell he wanted to deny it, and I was ready to fight. I'd dealt with combative witnesses who didn't want to tell the truth plenty of times — Dex would be a piece of cake. But he surprised me by not fighting. "Guilty." He didn't look guilty.

"And I assume that's why you wanted me at the show this morning? So I could witness your master plan in action?"

" 'Master plan,' " he repeated with a snort. "I made a phone call. Not exactly pulling off a bank heist here."

"Still . . ." I let my voice trail off. "Thanks. For making sure I was there. I'm glad I saw it."

"It was your idea." His voice was matter-of-fact. "You said she should see all this. See his life."

I nodded slowly, then another thought came to me. "And that's why you told Daniel not to schedule any extra shows this week. So Todd could spend more time with her."

He sighed a long sigh and let his head fall back on the chair. "He needed to see her," he finally said. "He's been a giant pain in the ass lately. There was no way he was gonna hold out till the holidays at this rate."

"Dex MacLean, I regret to inform you that you are a good person." I raised my lemonade to him in salute. "Even if you don't want to admit it."

The words took him by surprise, and he snorted through a mouthful of beer. "Thanks. I think."

I stared out toward the fire, mesmerized by the flames. "You did fuck up one thing, though."

"Only one? That's a good day for me." I glanced over to see him gazing at the fire too, smiling.

"I'm just saying . . . showing him what he's missing. Michele's going home in a few days. What if he wants to go with her?"

"He might." Dex's shrug was lazy. "But if that's what he wants to do I can't stop him, can I?"

"Don't you want him to stick around?"

"I want him to be happy. He's my brother." The words came out easy, but they had a weight to them that I wasn't used to hearing from Dex. "Besides," he continued, "Seamus plays fiddle. Next time I'm home maybe I'll see if he wants to join the band."

"Who's Seamus?"

"A cousin."

"Ah." I nodded, filing away yet another name in the MacLean family tree. "Daniel's brother?"

"Nope. Daniel's cousin too."

"How the hell many cousins do you people have?"

"Irish Catholic family? So many." He grinned in response to the laugh that barked out of me.

"Maybe Seamus and Todd could both do it part-time. Rotate in and out."

He tilted his head. "What do you mean?"

"You know, kind of like the laundry wenches do." A plan formed in my head even as I spoke. "They perform all over the country, right? Lots of wenches, doing basically the same show for lots of different Faires?"

"We're not laundry wenches."

"Nope. Your skirts are shorter." But I was serious. "What if, say, Seamus joins up with y'all, and he plays when you're in one part of the country, and then when you're up near home Todd switches out? Then if you ever wanted to take a break you could —"

Now he turned to face me, offense etched on his face. "Why would I want to take a break?"

I huffed. "Let's just *say you do,* don't argue with me. One of your cast of thousands of cousins could take your place too. I'm sure one of them plays guitar, right? Or you could teach 'em."

"Probably. If that was something I wanted to do. Which it isn't."

I thunked my head on the back of my chair. "It was just an example."

"Bad example." But his face had lost its thunder, and he shot me a smile. I rolled my eyes.

"Fine." We sipped at our drinks in silence for a few moments. "So, Seamus," I said. "Is he cute? Single?"

"He's seventeen."

I sighed. "Goddammit."

"I'm right here," he said. "I'm available if you ever . . . you know . . ."

"Need an itch scratched? I hear you provide that service around here." I took a thoughtful pull from my lemonade, finishing off the bottle. "How does that work? Like when you and Todd share a room? Kilt on the doorknob?"

He snorted. "Hard to hook up when you have a roommate. I like the gigs that give us more rooms." He shrugged. "But nah. I just go to her place. I'll sleep wherever."

"Classy."

"Hey, have toothbrush, will travel." He grinned at my involuntary laugh. "Or if I don't feel like staying the night, I'll head back to the room. Or here, if it's closer."

I didn't like the idea of that, but before I could say anything Frederick appeared next to me. "Hey, Stacey and Daniel are taking off."

"They are?" I turned around in my chair and gave them an awkward wave as they got into Daniel's truck.

"You good with the fire?" Frederick asked. "I can put it out for you, but if you want it going I could . . ."

"I can take care of it. Thanks." I gave him a knowing smile. "You out of here for the night?"

"I thought you were staying here, Freddy." Dex joined the conversation. "Or . . . ohhhhh." His wicked smile kicked up as understanding dawned. "I thought I saw Patrick this morning. You two hooking up?"

"Yeah." Now Frederick looked uncomfortable. Possibly he was annoyed — he looked like that a lot around Dex.

"This is great!" Dex clapped his hands together like some dilemma had been solved.

"I was worried someone was gonna have to snuggle, but that makes things a lot easier."

"Huh?" Frederick blinked at him.

"Huh?" So did I.

"Oh, I guess I didn't say. I'm crashing here tonight." He jerked a thumb over his shoulder. "Bag's in the car."

"The hell you are." I wasn't usually that rude, but I'd had a long day and it was getting late.

"You may not have noticed, but our two hotel rooms are filled with lovebirds. Should I bunk with Stacey and Daniel, or with Todd and Michele?" He raised his eyebrows.

"Ah," I said. "Shit." He had an excellent point. He'd done a really nice thing by calling Todd's girlfriend and having her meet us at this Faire, but he'd also given up his place to sleep. That was either unexpectedly generous, or he hadn't thought it through.

Frederick shook his head. "I'll let you kids fight this out. Patrick's expecting me." With a wave he took off down one of the winding gravel paths deeper into the campground, leaving Dex and me facing each other down. I was determined to not lose this staring contest, but then he kicked up an eyebrow, making me smirk in response.

"Fine," I said. "But the bed's mine. You get the sofa."

"Wouldn't be the first time," he said pleasantly. "Don't worry, Counselor, I'll behave myself." There went the eyebrow again. He needed to knock that shit off. "Unless, you know. You'd rather I didn't."

"I'd rather you put the fire out," I said primly. "I'm going to bed." I fled into the motorhome while applauding my quick thinking. By the time he'd closed down outside and locked the door behind him, I'd already changed into my pajamas and was snuggled down in bed with Benedick. I'd never wished for a door that I could close between us more than this moment. I made do by squeezing my eyes shut so I wouldn't see him get undressed, but the rustle of fabric and the sounds of water from the tiny bathroom next to my head set my imagination on fire.

He emerged from the bathroom in a pair of gym shorts that must have passed for his attempt at modesty, tossing his kilt and other performance gear into a careless pile on the dinette table. I didn't want to notice him, but it was hard. It was damn hard to not notice a back that muscled and legs that powerful. Not to mention the way his ass filled out that flimsy knit fabric. It occurred to me for the first time that maybe his kilt covered up too much. I wanted to bite my pillow. Scream into it.

He stopped about halfway to the sofa at the front, turning in my direction as though he could feel my eyes on him. I froze, caught on the precipice. Was he going to come back here? Make good on all that innuendo? How was I going to say no? Did I want to say no?

Instead he reached for the electric lantern on the countertop.

"Good night, Counselor." He flicked off the light, plunging the motorhome into darkness. I opened my mouth to reply, but my voice was inaudible, words choked out through a closed-up throat. My entire body tensed up, waiting. But all I heard was a rustling of blankets on the sofa and a couple of punches to the pillow. One long sigh as he settled into his makeshift bed, and within moments, his breathing deepened, evened out. He was already asleep.

Was I asleep? I was not. Was I likely to sleep at all that night? Also no.

TWELVE

Dex was gone when I woke up, the rumpled pillow and haphazardly folded blanket the only clue that he'd been here at all. On the one hand, it was nice to have the motorhome to myself again as I got ready for the day — the last thing I wanted was to hoist my boobs into this outfit while he looked on. But that relief faded as I tied off my bodice and a troubling thought occurred to me.

How was I going to get to Faire?

Stacey and Daniel had been my ride yesterday, but with Dex here they'd probably expected him to shuttle me around. Now he'd already left, and I didn't have a phone to call anyone for a ride. This could be a problem.

I procrastinated on my worry by puttering around inside the motorhome, finishing up my morning tasks. Benedick had the day off, still asleep on my hastily made bed, so I made sure he was set with food and water for the day. Just as I started to wonder if I too had a day off I heard the rumbling of an engine outside, pulling up to the motorhome and then cutting off. I peeked out the window to see Dex emerging from his black Dodge Challenger, a car that was almost as old and beat-up as Daniel's truck. These guys liked their classic vehicles. Almost weak with relief, I grabbed the rest of my things and practically leapt from the motorhome.

Dex leaned against the roof of his car, arms folded, and raised an amused eyebrow at my mad scramble. "You sleep late."

"I do not." I tugged on the passenger door, but it didn't give; Dex had to lean in and pop the manual lock for me. I flopped into the seat with a minimum of grace, adjusting my outfit to sit in the most comfortable and least revealing position possible. "What happened, did you get halfway to Faire before you realized you'd forgotten me?" My words trailed off, and I sniffed the air. Then I sniffed again and looked down. There in the cup holders were two identical takeout cups of coffee. Very large takeout cups, with those sippy-hole plugs in them to keep the coffee inside hot.

"Nope." Dex dropped into the driver's seat. "I know how long girls take to get ready —"

"Hey." I folded my arms and gave him my best withering feminist glare.

He met my stare, unbothered. "Because you've got, like, twice as many layers to put on as I do. Right?"

He had me there. I unfolded my arms. He nodded and continued. "I figured I had time to run down the street and grab us coffee. That coffee maker in the motorhome is shit." He indicated one of the coffees. "That one's yours. One sugar, three creams, right?"

All my indignation stuttered into oblivion. "Right." I took the plug out of the coffee and took a too-hot first sip. It burned my tongue but it was perfect. "Thank you." The words came out without a hint of sarcasm or irony, and his lips curved in a smile that warmed my insides more than the coffee did.

"You're welcome." He started the car, and we were Faire-bound. I relaxed into the passenger seat as much as my costume allowed.

"So." His hand on the wheel was casual as he made the turn out of the campground. "Any bets on how much sleep Todd got last night?"

My laugh sputtered out of me as I remembered the looks Todd and Michele had shared last night. "Can I place a bet for zero hours?"

"Yeah. He's gonna be fuckin' useless today." But Dex's complaint was made around a wide smile. He plucked a pair of sunglasses from the visor above his head, sliding them on against the glare of the early morning sun. "You could be right. Maybe this will bite me in the ass."

I shook my head in mock sympathy. "That's what you get for doing nice things for people."

He sighed. "I gotta stop doing that."

"I wouldn't go that far." I took a pointed sip of my coffee in illustration, and his smile became a grin.

Once at Faire I headed straight to Mystics' Glade, where the fortune-tellers greeted me like I was an old friend, not someone who'd forced their way into their lives last weekend, and I helped them set up their tables, put out their signs, and tie back the tent flaps.

They had a surprise for me too — my own receptionist's desk. Sage unveiled it with a flourish, as though it were the corner office of my dreams and not a tiny card table and folding chair out in the woods. It was perfect.

"We would have brought it yesterday," she said.

"But we weren't sure you were going to show up," Sasha added, her rebuke canceled out by her giggle.

I clucked my tongue. "Just try getting rid of me." I knew a good thing when I had it.

The table was too small for that endless bowl of candy that I remembered from my office days, but for the glade it was perfect. I situated it right beside the big TAROT-PALMISTRY-RUNES sign, so that any prospective patrons would have to go through me. I was ready.

Up until now my horning in on their business had felt invasive, and I'd worried that I was a haphazard addition, but today it all ran as smooth as the water in the creek out back of Grandma's house. I still spent a lot of time on my feet — I'd gotten good at that whole carnival-barker thing, luring people in — but as the morning went on and our schedule filled up, I sat in my little chair more and more. Soon we were so busy that I didn't need to do any luring. Once the schedule was full, all there was for me to do was check people in as they returned for their appointed readings, subtly let the girls know if they were going over their allotted time, and count the cash I'd collected.

Now that I had all their names down, I'd long since stopped thinking of them as the colors of their costumes anymore. Sasha — the blonde with the blunt tongue who wore red — interpreted her tarot cards like some people read children's books. She laid each card out methodically, leaning forward each time to study the picture on it as though it were brand new to her. The patron almost always leaned forward too, waiting to find out what Sasha saw in those cards. Her fingers danced from one card to the other, telling a sequential story that flowed in perfect order.

The older woman in blue was Sage, who cradled the hand of the patron in front of her, studying their palm with calm blue eyes, her voice low and assuring. She would tilt the palm of her patron this way and that, as though rolling a marble over the surface, pointing out significance in each line or crevice in the person's hand. More often than not I'd watch a patron leave Sage's little tent cradling their own hand, looking at it with new eyes.

Sage also worked with the runes, and the rattling of them sounded like a dice table in Vegas, just without the loud music and cocktail waitresses demanding tips. She examined the stones that her patron chose, finding meaning in each one as it related to the next. She asked more questions, I noticed, than the other fortune-tellers did, so the reading was more of a conversation. Not a one-sided proclamation of that person's future.

From even my limited experience, I could tell that Summer was a more chaotic reader than Sasha. She'd pull her deck from the pocket of her yellow skirt, shuffling them while she asked the patron questions. She didn't lay out a spread like Sasha did. Instead, she flipped the cards over in a pile, one on top of the other, glancing briefly at it, if at all, before flipping to the next one. Words flowed from her in a story while she flipped, her voice like a tinkle of bells, sweet and light, brimming with optimism with every turn of the cards. Occasionally she'd pause and linger on a specific card, as if stopped by an unseen hand. She'd tap a short fingernail on the card, elaborating on a detail of that card's meaning. Those pauses, those details, would be the most pertinent part of the reading. Those were the moments when she would say something that would make the patron sit back in their chair, jaw slack in astonishment. By the time the reading was done, roughly half the deck would be scattered in a haphazard pile on her table, and her breath came heavy like she'd been working hard. Which, let's face it, she had been.

It was fascinating to watch. And while I was too busy to linger every time they gave a reading, I found myself sneaking a look inside their tents whenever I dropped by to let them know time was up or to introduce a new patron. All three of them had stop-watches, mostly on their phones, which they kept tucked away, but sometimes they got carried away with a reading, or a patron got carried away asking questions. That's where I came in. I was tall, though not particularly muscular — Mitch had all of that in the family — and I was not only the reception-ist but the de facto bouncer around here. All I needed to do was use my Attorney Voice: the one that made witnesses tremble and opposing counsel reconsider their life choices. Attorney Voice worked almost as well as muscle — nothing like a command-ing woman's voice to tap into people's in-ner fear of their mom's authority.

As the day went on, I noticed something.

None of them ever gave out bad news. Which seemed weird, since some of those cards looked pretty damn dire. At one point

I glanced into Sasha's tent while she and her customer looked down at a couple of scary-looking cards. One had a skeleton riding a horse, and the word DEATH scrolled across the bottom. One next to it was labeled THE TOWER, and it depicted a circular structure that had been struck by lightning; it was actively in flames and people plummeted from the building to the earth. I sucked in my breath through my teeth. None of that looked good. At all.

But Sasha didn't look concerned. Not a furrow marred her brow. She tapped the creepy skeleton equestrian. "Transformation," she declared. "This is perfect for your situation, just perfect!" She beamed at the customer, and it was all I could do to not look at her like she had lost her mind. Then she tapped the tower on fire. "A dramatic upheaval in your life," she said, and *no shit,* I thought in response. That was putting it mildly. "But you're seeing the truth for what it is, maybe for the first time in your life. And this is great, because you can put it into practice. Out with the old, in with the new, do you follow?"

The customer nodded, and I went back to the front before I did something like laugh. Sasha should be in politics the way she spun things. There was no way that the flaming tower card could mean anything good.

For the rest of the day, I paid closer attention to the readings. And not a single one was negative. Not a *your partner doesn't really love you,* or a *you're stuck in a dead-end job.* It made me wonder what fabulous things they'd say about my career when I sat down across from one of them.

When? I was brought up short. I wasn't planning on getting a reading. That wasn't my thing. But the more I hung around them, the more getting career advice from a deck of cards, a handful of stones, or the already-existing lines on my hand seemed like a perfectly normal thing to do.

"It can't all be good news," I finally said, summoning my courage at the end of the day.

"What do you mean?" Summer raised her eyebrows in a question. She'd broken down her table and folding chairs, and I helped her tie down her tent, storing everything away for the week.

"I mean the cards. The runes." I gestured over to Sage, where her runes lived in her belt pouch. "I haven't heard a lick of bad news from any of you all weekend. Is that just a Faire thing, telling the customers what they want to hear?"

"Not at all," Sasha said from where she

lounged in her chair inside her still-open tent, drinking from an enormous water bottle. "The cards aren't good or bad, you know. It's about perception."

"Perception?"

She nodded. "Come here." She waved me over to her little table, nudging the second chair back with a stretched-out foot. "Sit down. I'll show you." She gestured me to sit down in the chair across from her while she took out her trusty deck, shuffling it in her hands.

"Oh. No." I remained standing. "You don't have to . . . I mean, it's been a long day. I'm sure y'all want to head out."

"Sit." It may not have been Attorney Voice, but Sasha could sound commanding when she wanted to. I sat like a well-trained puppy, my butt slamming into the seat.

"Perception," she said again. "Sure, there are some cards that have more dire meanings than others. That can look scary on the surface." She pushed the deck across to me. "Cut these into three piles, then put the deck back together. But those scary pictures don't mean something terrible is going to happen to you. I think of it like a phoenix, you know?"

"A phoenix?" I handed her the freshly cut deck, and she squared it in front of her.

"Something beautiful that comes from destruction. That's what the heavier cards mean sometimes." She laid out three cards, facedown, in slow succession. Then she turned over the first one and I sucked in a breath. Because there it was, that damn Death card again.

"See? Perfect example. It's like it knew we needed to talk about it." She tapped the gruesome image, but her smile was serene. "You know in movies, when there's a tarot card reader, she flips over the Death card, and there's usually a flash of lightning and a roll of thunder. It's a harbinger that someone's about to bite it, right?" She shook her head, her long blond hair flowing over her shoulders. "It doesn't mean that at all."

"It doesn't? It says *death* right there." I leaned forward like her customers always did, trying to see what she saw in the card. I had nothing.

"Nope. It's a great card, especially for someone who's seeking answers. Now, I'm doing a quick past/present/future spread for you, just as an example, and the Death card is in the past position. That signifies transition. The shedding of an old life, and the beginning of a new one." She met my eyes across the table and raised an eyebrow. She had me there. "Something's reached the end of its cycle — a job, a relationship — and it's time to transition to something else."

"You got all that from a skeleton riding a horse?"

"Yep." Her smile widened. "Neat, huh?" She flipped over the second card. Eight golden goblets were stacked in the foreground, but the figure on the card had his back to them, his stride and intent focused on the mountains in the background. "Oh, Eight of Cups, this is a good one. And it goes along with the Death card." She fell silent for a few moments as she examined the card, going over it minutely, like she'd never seen it before and needed to study it. "Wow," she said finally. "It is definitely time for you to move on."

"From what?"

She gestured at the card, as though it held all the answers, which maybe it did and I just couldn't see it. "From everything, basically." She peered up at me. "Which I guess you did when you threw your phone away. But see, look at this." She tapped a short fingernail on the stack of goblets. "You worked really hard to build a life, for a long time, right?" She continued, not even waiting or looking for my confirming nod. "And it meant a lot to you — financial stability, status, all that stuff. But it wasn't right for you. It wasn't letting you be who you really wanted to be. So you're walking away from it all." She leaned back in her chair and gave me a pleased smile. "Good for you."

"But what am I walking toward?" I pointed at the mountains on the card.

"Good question. This card also indicates a search for truth: spiritual, emotional . . . something to give your life real meaning. That could be what you're meant to do right now. Find that truth of yours."

"Huh." I sat back too, mirroring her stance. She wasn't wrong, was she? But it could still be all bullshit. She knew my situation: everyone at Faire knew I was Phone Girl. I'd created a massive change in my life when I'd thrown that phone in the washing tub, and it made sense that I was here, following the Renaissance Faire circuit because I didn't know what I wanted to do next. It wouldn't be hard to extrapolate my circumstances and apply them to these cards.

"Okay, so future." Sasha reached for the third card, flipping it over.

"Oh, good." I tried not to sound sarcastic. "Tell me my future."

She let out a small laugh. "I'm not predicting anything. That's not what the cards do. It's more like something to keep in mind as you move into whatever is coming your way." She looked down at the card. A king sat on a throne, looking as regal as a king should. He held a large stick in one hand — not a scepter, but more like a staff made of wood, small shoots growing from it. "Oh, yeah," Sasha said with a smile. "You got this."

"I do?"

She nodded firmly. "This is a card of strength. Leadership. Figuring out your goals and making them happen. Be yourself, your *true* self, and you're going to be just fine."

"So I'm the king?" My voice quavered with doubt, because if there was anything in the world that I did not feel, it was king-like.

"Could be. Or else there's . . ." She squinted at the card. "An elderly figure in your life? Someone important?"

My heart skipped a beat. "There's my grandma. We're pretty close." Was something going to happen to Grandma Malone? She and Grandpa were getting up there, but I wasn't ready to be without either of them yet.

"That might be it?" But she turned it into a question, her voice rising and her face screwing up in confusion. "This isn't feminine energy, though. It's more masculine, more businesslike. A mentor, maybe."

"Hey." I crossed my arms. "Women can't be businesslike?"

"Of course they can." She clucked her tongue at me. "I know, gender is a construct, and these terms are so antiquated. But for purposes of the cards, feminine energy is typically more nurturing, making things grow. Masculine is more about go-getters, you know?" She lifted one hand, brandishing an imaginary sword. "Argh."

"Argh," I repeated, trying not to laugh. But she caught my eye then, and we both dissolved into giggles. It had been a long day. A long weekend. We were both tired.

"Anyway." She looked at all three cards again before scooping them up and tapping them back into her deck. "You've gone through tremendous change lately, and you need to figure out what's next, so you can forge that path forward. There's something masculine and powerful in that future energy. Either a mentor figure in your life, or striking out on your own. Starting a business. Maybe becoming some sort of authority figure yourself."

"Running for office, maybe?" God, wouldn't that be a nightmare.

Sasha shuddered with a smile. "Better you

than me."

As she put her cards away, I looked at my watch. "Holy crap, I'm late." I'd missed pub sing completely, and Stacey or Dex, or whoever was giving me a ride home, was probably getting tired of waiting.

"We can give you a ride," Sage offered as we stowed my table and chair in Sasha's tent.

"I appreciate that," I said. "I'll let them know next time."

"Can't you let them know this . . . ohhhh." She sighed as realization dawned. "No phone."

I nodded in confirmation. "No phone."

Summer shook her head. "You're really taking the off-the-grid thing seriously."

"I can't be trusted," I said with an easy shrug and an easier smile, making them all laugh.

"Fine," Sage said. "But you better get going. It's getting late."

She wasn't wrong: it was long past time I headed up front. But I lingered in Mystics' Glade for just a little longer, my head full of the reading Sasha had just given me, and how she'd extrapolated so much from three little cards. A vendor near the front of the glade had a cart that was made up to look like a traveler's wagon, stocked with books and, now that I was up close, I could see that it was also stocked with decks and decks of tarot cards. My steps slowed and finally stopped as I looked over everything.

"Need anything?" The vendor had dropped her accent for the day as she counted out her cash. "I'm about to lock up, but I've got some time if you . . ."

"No, that's okay." But my voice was uncertain, and I bent to study the different decks. So many different kinds, with various designs to appeal to just about any aesthetic. My eyes skipped over the gothic ones — too scary, too not-me. I homed in quickly on a deck that looked like the one Sasha was using, my fingertips tracing the edge of the box. I wanted those cards. Sasha had said that the cards didn't predict the future, but I wanted more of the advice they'd offered.

"Ah, the Rider-Waite." The vendor smiled. "Classic. Great deck to learn on if you're wanting to try them out."

"I . . ." That hadn't been my intention, but my hand was still on the box, and before I knew it I was paying for the deck, as well as two books on how to read the cards that she swore would change my life. I stacked the purchases in my arms as I started up the hill to catch a ride back to the campground. It was Sunday evening, and there was a long week of non-Faire activities ahead. No time like the present to learn a new hobby, right?

My mind strayed then to my new roommate, and the way he looked in his gym shorts. Yeah. New hobby. Distraction was a good idea.

THIRTEEN

I had to ease into my new hobby. At first the deck, still in its plastic wrapper, sat on top of the two reference books I'd bought, all three together sitting at my elbow at the outdoor picnic table. I wasn't ignoring them, honest. I just wasn't ready for them yet.

Instead, while Dex noodled around on his guitar in the summer sunshine, Daniel frowned at his spreadsheets, and Stacey updated the group's website on her laptop, I turned to a fresh page in my notebook. First, I wrote down everything I could remember about the tarot reading Sasha had done for me. I was determined to crack the code on that third card, the one about my future. The only older male mentor I could think of was Bud Stone, and after our final phone call it was safe to say I'd burned that bridge.

Next, instead of my usual to-do lists or

action plans, I decided to go in a different direction. I emptied out my brain onto the page, writing down memories that I thought I'd long forgotten, with a hope that recounting the past would lead me to my future. I wrote about childhood days spent with my family. My grandparents. I wrote about my asshole brothers — Bryce was a dick even before he went to Cornell — and how family gatherings with my favorite cousin made things so much better. Mitch's smile and encouragement had always made me feel better, and I had always endeavored to be like him. To pass that encouraging smile on to others.

Instead I'd gone into law, and my smile had faded until it was almost nonexistent. I'd felt it start to sprout back lately, like a seedling under the summer sun. I needed to keep nurturing it.

But every time I looked up from my notebook that deck of cards sat there, mocking me. Finally, I heaved a big sigh and put down my pen.

"Okay, cards." I reached for the deck and broke the plastic wrap, pulling the string like I was cracking a fresh pack of cigarettes. "What do you have to tell me?" From the other side of the table, Stacey smiled at me briefly before going back to her laptop. If she thought it was weird that I was talking to a deck of cards, she had the grace to not say a word.

The cards spilled out of their box and into my hands. I'd played my share of gin rummy during study breaks in college, so I knew my way around a deck of cards. But these were different — bigger, and more cards in the deck than your typical pack of playing cards. Holding all of them was more awkward than I expected. The cards were stiff and hard to bend — they were going to take some breaking in if I was going to shuffle them properly.

The minuscule booklet that came with the cards was useless. All that small print did was remind me that it was almost time for reading glasses, and I wasn't ready to face that reality yet. So I set it aside in favor of the reference guides I'd gotten from the vendor. It didn't take long for me to get lost in the symbolism of the cards. Each one of those seventy-eight little pictures had so much meaning.

After a few minutes of reading, I turned to a fresh page in my notebook and began taking notes. Sasha was right; there was no predicting the future here, and there were no bad cards. Even cards that had what seemed to be dire warnings — the Death and Tower cards I saw last weekend, or the Nine of Swords that featured an anguished-looking person in bed with nine swords hung on the wall behind them — were more about taking stock and finding new directions.

When I wasn't taking notes, I practiced shuffling the cards, choosing a three-card spread to use as practice. The books showed me seven, ten, even twelve-card spreads that were overwhelming. Three was a good place to start. I closed my eyes while I shuffled, meditating on a question. One of the books talked about imbuing the cards with your energy, which made me raise my eyebrows. But it was also totally something that Sasha would say, so what the hell. I imbued the best I could.

I was so intent on laying out the cards that I hadn't noticed the music stopped until Dex dropped down onto the picnic bench next to me.

"You gonna tell me my future?" His grin was wicked, and I swear his dark eyes twinkled at me. Actually freaking twinkled.

"Hmmmm . . ." I swallowed my smile as I looked at the cards I'd just laid out. I didn't have a clue what any of them meant. Seventy-eight was a lot of cards to learn, and a tarot card reader wasn't built in a day.

But Dex didn't have to know that. I trailed a fingernail over the cards on the table, tracing the design. "I see music in your future," I said, making my voice as mysterious as I could. "And oh, what's this?" I tapped on a card where a man and a woman raised cups at each other. "Looks like you'll be picking up a girl. At a bar. Sometime very soon." I raised an eyebrow at him, and he laughed.

"Yeah, that sounds like me." He shrugged. "Not this week, though. We're not playing a bar, remember?"

"Oh, that's right." Michele was here until Thursday. Not that any of us had seen her. She and Todd had both stayed scarce, and we left them alone, let them have these days together as a romantic getaway.

From across the way, his laptop balanced on his knees while he sat in one of the Adirondack chairs, Daniel shook his head at Dex.

"You know, when you said that you didn't want to schedule any shows this week, you could have just told me that Michele was going to be here."

"Nah." A smile played around Dex's mouth. "It was more fun this way." He bent over his guitar again, testing chords and tuning. "You should have seen your face."

Daniel snorted and shook his head. "Fine.

I have a few options of places to book you guys next week. Wanna give me your opinion?"

Dex's hands froze in the middle of a chord and his eyes swiveled up toward Daniel again. "Why me?"

His cousin shrugged. "You're the only one here. Everyone else is out on a hot date." Daniel paused. "Kind of ironic."

"I don't do dates. You know that." Dex glanced over at us. There was an expression in his eyes that I couldn't place. He laid his guitar down flat on the table and walked over to Daniel. "Okay, let me see."

Stacey's eyes lingered on the men as they conferred before she turned back to me. "Everything going okay here?"

"Sure." I scooped up the tarot cards, tapping them into a neat stack. "I think working with the fortune-tellers has been better for me than I could have imagined. Broadening my horizons and all that."

"No." She clucked her tongue. "I mean, yay, that's great, but that's not what I meant. I mean, like . . ." Stacey glanced over at the guys again before lowering her voice, and I leaned closer to her in response. "I mean, like, here. Sharing the RV with Dex." She practically mouthed his name, putting no voice behind it.

Oh, *Dex*? I mouthed his name back, like we were teenagers talking about a crush in the high school cafeteria. "Yeah," I said, my voice a little more like normal. "That's all going great."

It wasn't a lie. Sure, there were some awkward moments. It was a really small motorhome, and squeezing around one another in there was a little more intimate than I'd anticipated getting with him. It was very, *very* hard to ignore a body like that when you were sliding past it to get to the fridge. Let's just say it was a good thing that the water in the shower didn't get very warm. Cold showers were working out well for me lately.

Stacey seemed surprised. "So he's behaving himself?" She sat back, telling-secrets-in-the-cafeteria time apparently over.

"Yeah." The question took me aback. "Of course he is. Why wouldn't he be?" Of course, this question wouldn't have surprised me a couple weeks ago. Back then, the thought of sharing a space this small with Dex would have garnered a hearty *hell no*! But I'd seen different sides to him now, and he wasn't just the Ren Faire bicycle. Sure, people were probably still lining up for a ride, but I'd talked to him enough one-on-one by now to see that there was more to him than that.

Which begged the question: why didn't Stacey see that? She'd traveled with him for much longer than I had. But she obviously *didn't* see that, because skepticism etched her face. She didn't argue the point any further, though, so neither did I.

After dinner, the air turned cool as the sun went down, but the heat of the day had settled into my bones. Stacey and Daniel had headed back to the hotel for the night, while Dex seemed content to hang around outside in front of the firepit, idly strumming through chords on his guitar. Before long those idle chords resolved themselves, coalescing into an actual melody that I didn't recognize.

"I like that," I said finally. "Something new?"

He shook his head. "Something old." He punctuated his sentence with an abrupt strum. "Irish drinking song from, like, the sixteenth century, I think. Not sure if it's ready to take to the rest of the guys yet. Still messing with it."

I shrugged. "I liked it."

"You barely heard it." He glanced at me under his lashes, and why was he smiling at me? He needed to knock that shit off. I tried to think of something to talk about, quick.

"Y'all play so many drinking songs," I

said. It wasn't much for topics, but close enough. "What's with that? Was everyone in the Renaissance a raging alcoholic?"

"Not much else to do." Dex turned his attention back to his guitar, muscles in his forearms flexing as his long fingers coaxed the melody from the strings. He was just showing off now. "It's not like they had cable, right? Drinking and fucking — that was pretty much it."

I tried to look thoughtful as I nodded. "So not so much 'Netflix and chill' as 'not dying of the plague and chill.' "

He laughed, and oh shit. It was getting easier and easier to understand why all the wenches at the Faire threw their bloomers at him or whatever.

I cleared my throat and finished my beer. "Anyway, I give you permission to add that song to your rotation. As long as you don't get rid of 'Whiskey in the Jar.' But I guess you can't. It's a drinking song, after all."

"We would never." Another couple of chords, another strum or two. "You're really into that song."

I shrugged. "There was this coffee shop I used to go to all the time in law school. It was a quiet place to study. Sometimes they had these open mic nights, which were usually pretty mellow. But this guy showed up one night and he was . . ." I trailed off, lost in thought. "Well, he was playing about half of your set list. You know, songs about drinking and fighting and winning over fair ladies."

Dex's chuckle was low, sending a shiver through my blood. "Yeah, that sounds like us."

"Anyway. He did 'Whiskey in the Jar' and . . . I don't know. Something about that song clicked with me. The woman in the song —"

"Molly." Dex nodded.

"In this guy's version it was Jenny. Not the point. The woman totally screws over the guy, right? Turns him in to the authorities, takes away his rapier, sabotages his guns. Probably kept the money he stole too." I felt my lips lift in a smile. "I liked that about her."

"That she fucked over her boyfriend?" His eyebrows shot up dramatically.

"That she was a woman in a man's world, doing what she had to do to survive." I dropped my gaze to the closed notebook in front of me, tracing patterns on its cover with my index finger. "Being an attorney is still an old white men's club, even in the twenty-first century. That song just hit me at the right time. Reminded me to kick ass and take names. Just like Jenny."

"Molly," Dex corrected.

I clucked my tongue at him. "Whoever." I waited for him to argue, but instead he just looked at me with an idle gaze. No up-and-down appraisal — this time he seemed thoughtful.

"So what do you want? After this. You going back to being a lawyer?"

That was the question, wasn't it? I tapped a fingernail on the notebook cover. "I think so. But not working for old white guys anymore. I got into law for certain reasons, but then I was so busy trying to prove myself it's like I forgot." I shook my head hard before looking back up at Dex. "I'm good at what I do. So if I go back to it, I want to do it on my own terms. You know?"

"Sounds like Molly. *Jenny.*" He corrected himself only a little sarcastically. I huffed a laugh in response, and a companionable silence settled over us. Any minute now, I figured, he was going to leave. Go hook up with his flavor of the week. But he seemed content to just be here, doing nothing. With me. Someone he wasn't actively sleeping with, and had even stopped hitting on. Hell, we'd just had a relatively innuendo-free conversation. That had to be some kind of record for him.

Eventually, I levered to my feet, gathering up my things. "I feel disgusting. Time for a shower."

"You need any help with that, let me know." Dex didn't even look at me, he just grinned down at his guitar.

And there it was. I knew he wouldn't be able to hold out too much longer. But there was hardly any heat in the offer; I couldn't take it seriously. "Aww, and I was just telling Stacey how nice you are," I teased. "You had to go and ruin it."

Dex stopped strumming, and the absence of music was suddenly very loud in the quiet evening. He blinked and looked up at me, his eyes flashing in the firelight. "Why would you tell Stacey that?"

I blinked too, confused. "Because it's the truth . . . ?"

He clucked his tongue. "Can't remember the last time someone's said that about me. Especially not Stacey. Bet she didn't buy it for a second."

My confusion didn't wane. "Why not? Are you and her not . . ." I ran out of words, waving one hand uselessly. "Not copacetic?" I finally finished the sentence.

He gave a one-shouldered shrug. "There's some history there. Not my story to tell."

"Not your . . ." That made no sense. If

there was some bad blood between him and Stacey, wouldn't that be his business as much as hers? But this was all venturing close to some family drama that I shouldn't be stepping into.

Before I could say anything else there was a shift in his expression, as though he also realized we shouldn't be going there. "Better take that shower," he said.

"Right." I turned to the motorhome. Taking a shower wasn't a big deal. It shouldn't be a big deal — it hadn't been these past few days that we'd been bunking together. But now as I got undressed I was hyper-aware that Dex was just on the other side of this very thin metal wall. I'd craved a long, luxurious shower — as long and luxurious as a shower in a camper could be, anyway. But now that I was naked inside this minuscule bathroom with Dex only a few feet away outside, I soaped up and rinsed down as fast as possible, throwing a sundress on over my still-damp skin. I stepped outside in my cheap Target flip-flops, sinking down onto the bench of the picnic table with a water bottle in one hand and comb in the other to untangle my hair. Dex hadn't moved from his spot in front of the fire, and now he watched as I combed out my hair, winding it into its usual braid.

Desperate to break the weird silence that had fallen between us, I waved my comb toward him. "Want me to do yours next? You'd look great with a French braid."

That did it. He laughed, and oh my. Something about that laugh, about his face lit by firelight, making his cheekbones stand out in stark relief, did something to me. I'd seen Dex laugh before, of course — the guy seemed to be made of merriment. But that was usually among other people, where his easygoing attitude was like a performance. In a life with very little privacy, we hadn't spent a lot of one-on-one time together before this week. Now, his smile made crinkles in the corners of his eyes, and his laughter was a little lower, a little more intimate. A little more just for me. I'd been right: the full force of his attention was a lot to take.

"I'm good," he said, a deliberate echo of me. He pulled the thick elastic band out of his hair, shaking it down. I hadn't seen him with his hair down before and it was a surprise. Longer than I'd expected, it fell just past his shoulders in dark brown waves, effortlessly gorgeous in a way that would take me an hour, a curling iron, and ton of product to achieve. He combed his fingers through those waves unselfconsciously before catching it up in his hands again, resecuring it at the back of his head with that thick elastic band.

Not a lot of guys could pull off a man bun unironically. It was a tricky look, and could fall very easily into the territory of a failed hipster who was trying too hard. But on Dex it looked less performative and more "get this damn hair out of my face." It reminded me of the way he wore a kilt: without artifice. For him none of this was a costume. It was the way he lived his life.

The rest of the night passed quietly, with Dex in front of the firepit and me at my place at the picnic table. After a little while, he ducked into the motorhome, returning with a beer and a bottle of water. He passed the latter to me before returning to his place by the fire. I sipped at it while I let myself be hypnotized by the flames.

It wasn't always going to be like this, I reminded myself. Soon enough he'd be out fulfilling my tarot card prophecy, choosing his Ren Faire hookup du jour. I was surprised he hadn't done so already, but maybe he was pickier than I gave him credit for. Maybe he just hadn't found the right one yet. But hey — have toothbrush, will travel, he'd said. Or if he didn't find himself a hookup right away, Michele was going back home to Michigan soon, so he'd have his spot with Todd back. Either way, it wouldn't be long before I'd be back in this motor-home solo.

FOURTEEN

But when I eventually brought up the idea of Dex returning to the hotel, he waved it off.

"Eh. I think Freddy beat me to it." His head was turned away from me as he checked for traffic before pulling out of the campsite.

"Freddy?" I was almost startled into a spit-take but managed to swallow my sip of coffee. Caffeine was precious and shouldn't be wasted. "What do you mean, Freddy?" I asked when I was once again able to speak. "He's with Patrick."

Dex shook his head. "Patrick left. I dunno, his contract was short or something." He shrugged. "That happens sometimes, especially if there's another Faire at the same time. Not everyone is here for the entire run."

"But . . ." My mind stuttered, and not just from being on my first cup of coffee.

"He had a one-week contract?" What was the point of that?

"Seems like it." He kept his eyes on the road when I most wanted to peer into them and see if he was fucking with me.

"Even so . . ." I took another sip of coffee. "It's Frederick's turn in the motorhome, right? I thought you'd rather be in the hotel."

"Nah. I'm good where I am. Unless you'd rather have Freddy back?" He cut his eyes over to me then, a quick glance. Assessing.

No. The thought was a knee-jerk reaction. But I swallowed it down with my coffee. "Doesn't matter to me," I said as airily as I could. "He used to watch TV with me, though. How do you feel about baking shows?"

A bark of laughter came out of him, widening my own smile. "You're on your own," he said. "But I promise I won't make fun while you're watching them."

Good enough. "Deal." I got to work, sucking down as much coffee as possible as he pulled into the Faire parking lot — well, parking field. It was going to be a long day, and this was the last coffee I was going to see until it was over.

The day was long, but not as exhausting as I'd anticipated — sometimes it worked that way, Sage told me at the end of the day when she handed me my much smaller cut of the day's tips.

"Middle of the summer," she said with a shrug. "Middle of the Faire too. Opening and closing weekends can be packed, but these ones in the middle . . . sometimes not as many people come."

"You're not worried?" I glanced down at the couple of bills she'd pressed into my hand. If my cut was this small, their total can't have been all that much.

But she shook her head, unconcerned. "People aren't in the mood for the unknown sometimes. Just the way it goes. It makes up for the days where we're so busy we can't see straight." She touched my shoulder, somewhere between a pat and a squeeze. "Don't read too much into it, okay?"

I squinted at her. "Was that some kind of fortune-telling joke?"

She smirked. "Maybe a little."

With it being such a slow day, not only was I able to catch up with the band to get a ride back to the campsite, but I could swing by the front stage on the way to check out pub sing. I hadn't had much of a chance to see the acts at this Faire, and now was my chance.

The first person I saw at pub sing was

Frederick, his slim frame leaning against a tree behind the audience. I bumped him with my shoulder.

"Hey!" He lit up with a smile when he saw me. "How's my old roomie?"

"Oh, you know. Same old grind." That was my idea of a joke — was there anything "same old, same old" about this life? "What about you, though? You holding up okay?" He sure didn't look like someone whose boyfriend had recently left the area and who was now forced to room with his brother.

"Yeah." The smile on his face slipped a fraction as he took in my expression. "Is there a reason I wouldn't be?"

"Well, Dex told me about . . ." Even as the words were coming out of my mouth, my ears took in what was happening on-stage. I turned my attention in that direction, letting my voice trail off. "Patrick," I finally said, because damn if that wasn't who was performing at that very minute. No wonder Frederick looked so happy.

"Oh, for God's sake." Frederick crossed his arms over his chest and huffed out a breath, leaning against the tree again. "Just because Dex doesn't have the brain cells to understand comedy . . ." He shook his head. "Patrick's act is fine, you know. I mean . . ." He pitched his voice lower, bending toward me. "Could it be funnier? Sure. Maybe. But I don't like him for his jokes." He shot me a wink, and I snorted.

"Not touching that one." But my mind churned. Why had Dex lied? About such a trivial thing that was easily disproven? It made no sense. I was going to have a little talk with Dex tonight about this.

Dex was, for all intents and purposes, my roommate; you'd think that if I wanted to have a talk with him it would be a simple endeavor. But not that night. It was Saturday night, and everyone decided to congregate at the motorhome, when I really wanted to corner Dex and find out why he lied.

For a family that played together, they hadn't had a lot of time all together lately, what with Todd's girlfriend being there most of the week. I'd thought that Todd would be more determined to leave the band to follow his girlfriend home, but I was wrong. Michele's visit seemed to have invigorated him instead. While he'd never been particularly grumpy, something about missing her had always tinged his smiles with melancholy. But now, as we sat around the fire, he recounted stories about some of the rowdier patrons they'd dealt with that day with an energy that was downright giddy. It was unnerving, even as it brought a smile to my face.

Stacey leaned into me at one point that evening. "We should get him laid more often."

I nodded thoughtfully. "How often do you think we can bring Michele down here? Probably not every weekend, huh?" Stacey shook her head, taking another sip of her wine with an amused chuckle.

As the hour grew later, it became obvious who among us had been at this whole life longer. Yawn after yawn began to split my face, and even though it felt incredibly rude, I had to bid good night to everyone. Conversation and laughter continued outside as I washed my face and got ready for bed. I expected it to keep me awake, but the murmur of familiar voices was peaceful white noise as I sank into the comfort of my pillow. A bark of laughter momentarily jerked me out of my half sleep, but it was so contagious that an answering smile lifted my mouth.

"Very silly out there, Benedick," I murmured as the cat marched up the bedsheets to his place by my head.

It wasn't until that last moment, when sleep swallowed me up in a slow slide, that I remembered that I'd wanted to confront

Dex about the whole Frederick thing. My sleepy brain decided it didn't matter. Was it really that big a deal who my roommate was? It certainly wasn't more important than sleep. That was my last thought before my whole world became my soft pillow and Benedick's softer purrs.

When the sun came up the next morning, it brought heat. Up until now, the summer had been bearable: warm days that were ameliorated by staying in the shade as much as possible. But when I opened the door of the motorhome that Sunday morning it was like opening the door to a preheated oven. It wasn't even eight in the morning yet; this was ridiculous.

"Hope you like iced coffee." Dex nodded toward the cup holders of the Challenger. He'd gone on what was quickly becoming our traditional coffee run. Seeing Dex in the bright morning sunshine reminded me that I was annoyed at him for lying about Frederick. But he'd provided me with caffeine. Yelling could wait.

"Thanks." I took a grateful sip. "I guess I should have known it would be this hot eventually, huh?"

"Yep." He gave a world-weary nod. "Every year about this time I'm glad we wear kilts, you know? Built-in air-conditioning and all that." He smirked in my direction as he turned onto the main road toward Faire. I tried not to think about the ventilation of whatever the hell he had going on under there. I didn't want any part of that. Instead, I took another sip of coffee and let it cool me off.

"Weird energy today." Sasha swiped at her forehead with the back of her hand as I took a break by her tent between patrons.

"I think it's just hot." That much was apparent. Sweat gathered at the small of my back and trickled down my spine, and I tried to ignore that. I could see it beading along Sasha's hairline too. The sun was bright overhead, unrelenting, without a breeze to break the heat. "Maybe it'll rain later." Heat like this had to break eventually.

She shook her head. "More than that. Like . . ." She paused and her gaze softened, like it was turning inward. She did that kind of thing a lot, and I was used to it by now. "Something's gonna give."

"Yeah," I deadpanned. "Like a thunderstorm."

Her gaze cleared and she shook herself out of whatever mood she'd slipped into. "Maybe that's all it is." She pushed up her sleeves, even though the worn elastic made them slip down again almost immediately. "Who's next?"

"Right this way." I motioned to a waiting patron and escorted her to Sasha's tent. Break was over, back to work.

But she had a point. The heat of the day was oppressive, sure. An aggressively hot morning that only got worse as the day went on. But it was more than that. It felt like . . . pressure. A kettle about to boil, a balloon about to pop. In between patrons at our little glade, I found myself peering up into the sky more than once, searching for storm clouds on this perfectly sunny day.

Something told me that when the storm finally came, it was going to be a big one.

"Hey, Lulu."

My attention was brought back from the sky and to the world in front of me by the group of acrobats walking by. One of them — the bendy one I remembered from one of my first days as a Faire person — greeted me with a smile. I was pleasantly surprised she remembered me; we'd met once a few weeks ago, and these performers met a lot of people.

But her name completely slipped my mind, and I was mortified. I used to be so good at that when I worked gala events.

"Hi . . . Delia, was it?" I shook my head almost immediately. That wasn't it.

"Delilah," she corrected with a pleasant smile. "Close enough." We shared a slightly awkward laugh, because was it really? Getting someone's name wrong was getting someone's name wrong; no matter how close you were it was still wrong.

"How's Josh?" I asked. "Wasn't he hurt?"

"He's good! It was a tricky few days there, but he healed up great." A pleased smile bloomed over her face, and I felt like I'd unlocked some kind of friendship code. "Thanks for asking." She glanced over her shoulder, where her fellow acrobats had left her behind, before turning back to me. "Between you and me, he was kind of a baby about it. You know how men are when they're hurt." We shared a snicker, all awkwardness between us now cleared up. "Anyway," she continued. "Have you seen Dex around?"

"Dex?" I looked up the hill toward the stage where the Kilts were playing, as though I could spot him from the other side of the grounds. "Not recently. He wanders around between shows, so he can be hard to catch. Maybe go by their stage at showtime?"

She shook her head with a laugh. "No, I

mean . . ." She shifted from foot to foot, and it was weird to see someone this graceful look uncomfortable. The awkwardness was back. "I mean after hours. You know." Her voice lowered, imbuing those last two words with way too much meaning.

"Ahhhh." I blew out a breath. I did indeed know. "I really can't help you there, sorry. He kind of does his own thing when it comes to extracurriculars." This wasn't a lie; I wasn't his schedule keeper. But he'd also spent all of his nights with me lately, seemingly content with our platonic arrangement. I kept waiting for him to get bored and go off to sleep with someone, but it hadn't happened yet. He was there every morning when I woke up, a cup of takeout coffee waiting for me. I had a feeling Delilah wouldn't believe me if I told her that.

Delilah nodded thoughtfully. "I keep trying to catch him. You know, see if he's up for . . ." She trailed off, and I knew exactly what she wanted him to be up for. The same thing that everyone else wanted him to be up for. I tamped down the possessive heat that surged up my throat as Delilah shook off the thought. "Anyway," she said again. "Can you let him know I stopped by? He has my number."

"You got it." Somehow my voice sounded

casual, pleasant even, although my jaw was clenched. I wasn't Dex's sex secretary — he could manage his own hookups. But Delilah didn't notice; she was already walking away, tossing a friendly wave over her shoulder, her slim hips swaying in her tight leotard. I swallowed hard before turning to the next patron waiting for her tarot reading, hoping my smile looked friendly and not like a shark waiting for prey.

FIFTEEN

The first roll of thunder came around four thirty. It was a low rumble literally out of the blue in a cloudless sky, the afternoon still hot as the fifth level of hell. All our gazes snapped up to the sky, almost in unison.

"Here it comes." Sasha's voice was an omen.

"Not yet." Summer put her hands on her hips, her eyes scanning the sky. "If we're lucky, it'll hold out till we get home."

"Home," I repeated under my breath. I hadn't been through a thunderstorm in the motorhome yet. Hopefully it wouldn't be too bad a storm: Weren't trailers the first thing to go in tornadoes?

You would think that a threatening storm would send patrons running for their cars, but not today. While the thunder continued to rumble in the distance, the sun still shone as brightly (and hotly) as ever, giving no

245

break from the heat. The patrons gave no break, either; my appointment book was filled to the brim, with people waiting outside our tents in case we could squeeze in another reading or two. The gates had long closed by the time we broke down for the day.

"Ah, hell." I looked out of the glade and up the hill. The rest of the vendors had closed up and were long gone; we were the only ones left. I could run up toward the Kilts' stage, but it was pretty likely they were already gone. Hadn't I told Stacey not to have anyone wait for me?

"Don't worry about it." Sasha looped her arm through mine. "Didn't we say we'd give you a ride if you needed one? Come on."

The thunder boomed louder on our heels as we headed to Sasha's beat-up Subaru hatchback in the employee section of the parking lot. We all piled in, the girls giving me the shotgun seat since I was getting dropped off first.

"Maybe it'll pass us by." Summer craned her neck to look out the back of the car. "It's still sunny."

"Too sunny." It was Sage's turn to sound like a portent of doom. "It's coming. Gonna be a big one."

"Great." But even as I said it, I realized I

was hoping for rain. I was hot, I was tired, my skin salt-crusty with dried sweat. All I wanted was to get clean and go to bed, all alone for the night except for the cat. But with an impending storm in the mix, I pictured the rain washing away the sweat of the day, more efficiently than the mediocre shower in the motorhome. How scandalized would the rest of the campground be if I stripped down naked in the rain? The thought of it made me snort.

But as Sasha pulled up to the campsite, all my laughter died in my throat.

"Ugh," I said. "Dex." Because there he was, sitting on the picnic table drinking a beer, his face tilted up toward the sky without a care in the goddamn world. My tired, sweaty, sun-exhausted brain had somehow forgotten that I had a roommate. Guess Delilah hadn't found him today after all. There would be no starfishing naked in the bed for me.

Sage giggled from the backseat. "Pretty sure you're the first person to have that reaction to him."

"True." Summer nodded emphatically. "I think half the Faire would be super happy to come home to that."

"I'm not half the Faire." My frown now felt etched on, and I made a concerted effort to smooth it away, replacing it with a grateful smile that I threw Sasha's way as I opened the door. "Thanks for the ride."

She waved a hand. "Anytime. You know that."

A sudden gust of wind helped me throw open the door, and as I grabbed for it, fat raindrops splatted against the windshield. "And here it comes." I hopped out of the car and slammed the door closed behind me, watching the Subaru peel out of the campsite as quickly as a Subaru could.

Dex looked up as I ran for the safety of the motorhome. "Hey," he said. "Storm's coming."

"No shit, storm's coming!" I turned to him with all the force of that oncoming thunderstorm. "What the hell are you doing here?" Why wasn't he at the hotel with Todd, that was the real question. Why had he lied to me about needing to stay here, that was the realer question. I was mad at him all over again.

He blinked at the unexpected question. "Last I checked I'm part owner of this RV. You?"

I stopped short. There was a fine line between cranky and bitchy, and I'd pole vaulted right over it. Had I overstepped? Probably. Adrenaline crawled up the back of my neck, accompanied by a lick of shame.

But then he cracked a grin. "Nah, just fucking with you. Want a beer?"

That asshole. Shame dissolved right back into cranky. "No, I don't want a beer! I want . . ." So many ways to finish that sentence. And most of them involved him not being there. Meanwhile, around us the wind picked up and the sun took on a desperately bright quality, as though it knew it was about to be swallowed up by the approaching storm. A fat raindrop hit me on the forehead as the outlier rain continued to fall. I swiped it from my face, furious.

"Doesn't matter what I want," I finished lamely. "You can go now."

He scoffed. "It's raining, in case you haven't noticed. And it's only going to get worse. Where should I go?"

"I don't care," I shot back. "Delilah was looking for you earlier, why don't you give her a call?"

"What?" His brows drew together, and it was his turn to stop short.

"Delilah. Remember her?" I waved my hand as though I could conjure her from thin air. "Acrobat? Super flexible? She misses you."

His expression darkened. "What the hell makes you say that? I haven't seen her since . . ."

"Well, I have. Ran into her today, so she could let me know that she has an itch for you to scratch." There. Message delivered. Probably nastier than intended, but that wasn't my problem.

Dex shook his head. "I don't want to go see Delilah."

Rage crept into the edges of my vision. Dex was not a deep guy; there was no way he was being this obtuse on purpose. "Then pick someone else! Isn't that what you're supposed to do, hook up with someone at every Faire? Quit dragging your feet and go fuck a belly dancer already!" Why was I so angry about this? Sure, his sexual habits smacked of misogyny, but it wasn't as if he was forcing any of his partners. If they were all like Delilah, they knew the score when it came to Dex and still sought him out. They were welcome to him.

"That's not . . . I don't want . . ." He looked puzzled as he shook his head. Too many options, probably; the boy was overwhelmed with choice.

"Then you could, I don't know, go back to your hotel room!" A rumble of thunder rolled by, and the rain fell harder now. I was getting the outdoor shower I'd craved, but it wasn't making me feel better. My skin was hot and angry, making the raindrops practically sizzle as they hit.

He faltered, just long enough for me to see the discomfort in his eyes, but he rallied. "I can't, I told you. Frederick —"

"— isn't staying at the hotel with Todd. You know that I know that, right?"

His shoulders slumped a fraction, but righteous anger darkened his expression. "Of course you do. You know fuckin' everything, don't you?" He paced away from me, then came right back. "Maybe I don't want to stay with Todd. Maybe I'd rather hang with you." He didn't look happy. He looked furious. Which made no sense. Why the hell was he mad at me?

Then his words registered. He wanted to stay here. With me. "You . . . what? Why?" Apparently when my mind went blank I could only communicate in interrogatives. I settled for glaring at him before asking him *when, where,* or *who.*

"I want to stay here." He looked less angry about it this time. "I don't want Delilah, or a belly dancer or whoever. I don't want to bunk with my boring-ass brother. I want to stay here. With you."

"With me." I repeated the two words as though they were in a language I had never bothered to learn.

"Yeah." His dark eyes bored into mine, intense, daring me to dispute him. He raked a hand through the soaking strands of hair that had fallen out of its tie during the last few minutes as we stood here, yelling at each other in the rain.

A clap of thunder, closer now, made me jump. But Dex didn't react, his dark eyes trained on me. His gaze made me feel vulnerable, almost naked — how many women did he look at like that? I wrapped my arms around myself, ineffectually shielding myself both from the thunderstorm that was getting worse by the minute and from the heat in his eyes. He didn't seem seductive, though, or particularly lustful. He seemed livid. I shook my head, making pieces of wet hair stick to my cheek in a very unsexy way. "That doesn't make any sense."

"No shit, it doesn't make any sense!" His voice was still raised, hell, mine was too, to be heard over the rain. But did we go inside, like sensible people? We did not. He threw up his hands. "The thing is, Lulu, I'd rather hang out with you. You know, just *talking*!" He spit out the last word as though it was something unthinkable. Ridiculous. "Do you know how long it's been since I just talked to someone? Night after fucking night?"

I snorted. "Oh wow, don't make it sound like such a chore."

"It's not! That's the fucked-up thing. It's the best fucking part of my goddamn day, when everyone else goes away and it's just you and me here." He must have been pissed; his swearing was turned up to eleven. "You *talk* to me, you know how messed up that is?" He scoffed, because obviously that notion was ridiculous. "And I know that's all you want from me, so I'll take it. Just to spend time with you!"

It was probably one of the most romantic things I've ever heard someone say, but Dex sounded utterly furious as he said it. All I could do was gape at him like a freshly landed fish. "You want to spend time with me?" It was a simple question, but I yelled it like an epithet.

"Yeah!" he yelled back. "You've made it clear over and over that you're not attracted to me, so I —"

"Wait, what?" I stopped short, rewound his words in my head. "Who the hell said that? A brick wall would find you attractive."

"*You* say that!" He waved a hand at me. "All the damn time. Whenever I try to flirt with you, you shut it down in, like, two seconds, so I —"

"Wait. That's *flirting*? I thought you were *joking*!" My brain skipped back over all the times he'd propositioned me, all the times I'd turned him down. I thought it was a bit — part of the push-pull that had become our friendship. With the multitudes of women at his beck and call — bendy acrobats, curvy belly dancers — it had never occurred to me that he'd ever been serious.

"No, I wasn't joking. Holy shit, is my game that bad?" Amusement sparked in his eyes now, a ray of sunshine cutting through his indignation.

I shook my head, that same ray of sunshine making a smile flirt with my own lips. The rain still fell around us, getting worse by the second, but our emotional storm was clearing up fast. "That's not flirting, my friend."

"Oh, really." His voice dropped to a dangerously low octave as he moved toward me. I stepped back, then back again, until my back hit the wall of the motorhome. The metal was cold against my back where it pressed my wet costume against my skin. Dex placed one hand on either side of my head, caging me between his arms. I knew I could push at him, break that cage, and he'd let me go. But I didn't want to.

"Dex . . ." My voice was little more than

an exhalation, and if he weren't standing right there, our chests almost touching as we breathed, he wouldn't have heard me.

"What about this?" His voice was a low growl in my ear, and all my nerve endings came alive at the sound of it. He bent toward me, his lips grazing against the shell of my ear. "Am I flirting now?"

I shivered. I was thoroughly soaked from the rain, my clothes and my hair wet and cold against my skin, but all I felt now was heat. Heat from Dex's body, dangerously close to mine. Heat from his breath, hot against my neck. My traitorous body swayed toward him, seeking out more of his heat, and he caught me, one of his arms dropping to the small of my back, his hand pressing, pulling me into him. His breath hitched at the contact, and I felt it all through me.

I had one shred of indignation left, and I used it now. "For God's sake, will you just kiss me already?"

That startled a laugh out of him, and that was what did it. I could never resist that laugh, and when he looked down at me he didn't look like the Ren Faire Lothario anymore. He looked like a man — a very, very attractive man — who wanted to spend time with me. *Me.*

"Yes, ma'am." Those words, in a fake

southern drawl that might have been poking fun at me, was the last thing I heard before his mouth closed over mine, and then I became Someone Who Was Kissed by Dex MacLean.

I had a feeling my life was never going to be the same.

Sixteen

The man made kissing into an art.

That first kiss lasted only seconds, but it felt like hours. His mouth, intense and hot, but also languorous and lazy, explored mine with an enthusiasm that told me that I'd just become his favorite thing to do. Kissing Dex was sinking into an almost-scalding bathtub, making all of your muscles melt in relief. It was the cool side of the pillow, nestled perfectly against your cheek as you slide into a pleasant dream. But it was also holding a lit match to the fuse of a firecracker: that dangerous sizzle that told you that the good stuff was on its way.

I snaked my arms up around his neck, hanging on for dear life as his mouth took mine. The rest of his hair had long since fallen out of its tie, the wet strands tangled and wild and clinging to my fingers. My nails grazed the back of his neck, and he shivered under my hands. His palm flattened on my back, pulling me more firmly against him, and oh damn. Firm was absolutely the correct word to use in this instance. Kilt fabric wasn't particularly thick, but what was growing hard against my lower belly sure as hell was.

A crack of thunder made us jump, breaking what had become an increasingly frantic kiss. Dex turned his head up, squinting at the darkening sky. "We should go inside."

"Uh. Yeah." It took me this long to realize that we were making out against the side of a giant lightning rod as the thunderstorm grew closer. But what a way to go.

We stumbled up the rickety metal steps and into the motorhome just in time, as a flash of lightning lit up the darkened interior, followed immediately by a rolling crash of thunder, longer and louder than anything we'd heard before. Something bumped against my calf, and I looked down to see a black blur as Benedick streaked under the sofa. That was probably for the best; I already had my bedmate for the night.

The weather had very kindly waited for us to get inside, because now all hell broke loose out there. The rain, which had already been falling steadily, came down in sheets, pounding down on the metal shell of our shelter with an almost-deafening roar.

Flashes of lightning lit up the windows so that we didn't need to turn on a single light.

None of that mattered. We didn't need lights. We didn't even need to hear each other. The break we'd taken to dash inside and secure the door behind us had been long enough. Dex hooked two fingers into the top laces of my bodice, pulling me toward him, and I had just enough time to plunge my hands into his soaking-wet hair before his mouth crashed down on mine again. He tasted like rain and his skin was cold, but his mouth was a furnace, lips burning on my skin. Our hands were busy between our bodies, unlacing and unbuckling and pulling at fabric. Soon my bodice slid from my shoulders, and I pushed it down my arms before tugging at his shirt. He helped me with the wet fabric, pulling the garment over his head, letting it drop behind him.

I caught my breath at the body that had just been bared to me. The soaking-wet shirt had given me a preview outside, but the reality was even better than I could have imagined. How did a guy stay this fit from playing guitar and living on beer? I laid a hand flat on his stomach, blazing a trail upward through the hair that furred his chest, feeling the rise and fall of his breath quicken as

I touched him. His heart thumped wildly under my palm and I marveled; I did that to him. I could have looked at him forever, but I made the mistake of glancing up to his face. His dark eyes pierced through me, and my body reacted instantly. Without my bodice on, I stood there in my chemise and skirt; my breasts felt heavy, unsupported, my already overly sensitive nipples pebbling against the cold, wet fabric. If he didn't touch me soon, I was probably going to die.

Thankfully, Dex was there to save my life. His hands came up between us, cupping my breasts through the cold fabric, weighing them gently in his hands, a rough sound tearing from the back of his throat. "Christ, you feel good."

"Right back atcha." My voice was raspy as I swayed toward him. My hand was still flat on his sternum and I leaned in, replacing it with my mouth, laying a kiss in the center of his chest. His sharp intake of breath encouraged me, so I let my mouth explore, tonguing his solid pecs and the flat of his nipples. His hands slid to my waist, fumbling first with my belt, then the drawstring of my skirt. Soon all I had on was that wet chemise that I ached to be rid of, but taking it off would involve stepping away, and I didn't have the strength to do that.

Dex didn't seem inclined to let go of me, either. As my mouth made a thorough exploration of the column of his throat, his hands returned to my breasts again, thumbs skating over my nipples, the rough fabric of my chemise making the sensation unbearable. My cry was muffled against his skin. If he felt this good while we still had most of our clothes on . . .

I tilted my head up to kiss him — there wasn't too much of a height difference between us, so I didn't have to stretch too far onto my toes. He took over immediately, his mouth eager, hungry, and for long seconds I was lost. "Come on," I finally whispered against his lips, dipping my head back behind me. "Bed's back there."

We couldn't let go of each other long enough to undress and get to the bed, and the space we were in was cramped, so we were all reaching arms and banging elbows, kissing and swearing and laughing as we went. There was awkwardness as we removed boots and shoes and long socks before we finally, finally collapsed naked together onto the bed. I'd never pictured a man like Dex downright giggling, and somehow it just made him even sexier. Amusement still sparkled in his eyes as he rolled to his side and reached for me.

261

I wasn't sure what I expected from him. Was he going to climb on top of me and just go for it? Or was he the kind of guy who would take his time? I was going into this with no expectations, and even though I knew there was no happily-ever-after here, I wanted to enjoy this time. And I really, *really* wanted him to be good at this.

I shouldn't have worried. Rather than rolling me under him he laid a hand on my hip, stroking slowly around the curve of my waist and up. My breasts positively ached for him, and he was there to ease the ache, cupping, stroking. The pads of his fingertips were rough, guitar player's hands, awakening my already-sensitive skin.

"You're beautiful." His voice was low, whiskey and smoke, and I felt it in a tingle up my spine.

"I bet you say that to all the lawyers." It was a terrible joke, but he smiled anyway as he leaned in, hovering over me. His thumb circled one stiff nipple with intent, and the gasp that came from deep inside of me was cut off when his tongue replaced his thumb, circling, suckling, biting. For the longest of moments I couldn't breathe. All I could do was feel, every nerve ending alive under his hands and his mouth, and when his body settled over mine I welcomed his weight with a moan that came from the tips of my toes. I let my thighs spread, cradling his hips like I was welcoming him home. I'd never craved anyone this much in my life, and even as I tilted my hips up toward his, a thrill of apprehension went through me at how intensely I felt at this moment. Then another thrill, a worse thrill, went through me, because . . . shit.

"Wait," I said, though my body continued to roll against his. How could someone else's skin feel so good? I had skin, it didn't feel this good. "Wait." I kissed him again because I couldn't not. "Protection," I finally managed to choke out. "We don't have . . . I'm not on . . . we need . . ." Sure, I was pretty carried away and couldn't complete a sentence, but I hadn't lost my head completely.

But he didn't seem bothered. "Oh, yeah. Hold up." He levered himself up with one hand, pressing his hips harder into mine, making my bones dissolve even more under him. His other hand came up beside my head, but instead of reaching for me, he slapped at the wall just above me. The wall popped open, revealing a storage hatch I'd never noticed. He fished inside and came back with a fistful of condoms, which he dropped next to the pillow.

"Damn." I tilted my head up to peer at the storage hatch. "That's convenient."

"Sure is."

I trailed my fingers through the foil packets by my head. "Quite a few here. Is that a comment on your stamina?"

He laughed, and then ducked his head as though surprised to be laughing in bed. "Hey, I'm up for it if you are."

I took up one of the condoms, pressing the wrapper against his chest like a bargain struck. "Let's start with one and see how we do."

He took the hint, rolling away from me and suiting up while I watched, my eyes lingering, my mouth watering. I was about to have this guy, and I couldn't wait.

His gaze flicked to mine, his eyes burning with promise. "You sure about this?"

I'd never been more sure of anything. I rolled to my side, reaching for his hip. "C'mere."

His smile was full of wicked intent as he crawled up my body, and I fell back against the pillows in delicious surrender. "Careful," I said as he hooked one of my legs around his hip, opening me even more to him. "I'm not bendy like your little acrobats, remember?"

"You're gonna do just fine." There was an

intent focus in his dark eyes that hadn't been there before, and a new kind of shiver went through me. Playtime was over. The tip of him brushed against my center in a hot glance that stole the last of my breath. If this man wasn't inside of me in the next five seconds, I wasn't going to be responsible for my actions.

He must have gotten the message because he reached down, guiding himself, circling me, teasing me one last time before starting that slow push inside. I felt him everywhere, that long stretch as I closed around him. His breath released in a shaky exhale as our hips met and I tilted myself up, wanting more of him even though I already had it all.

"Shit." He dipped his head down, mouth on my neck. "You feel . . ." He rocked once, slowly. Then twice, even more slowly. Even through the latex I felt the heat of his cock, the slow slide, the way he felt absolutely perfect against me, inside me. I never wanted this to end.

"You too." I leaned my head back, pressing on the pillow, giving him more of my skin. More of everything I had. It was all his. And he was all mine. I stroked up his back, muscles rippling under my fingers, and when I scratched lightly with my nails his whole body jerked, pushing harder inside me while he gasped.

"Damn." He pressed his hips forward in another slow rock. This boy was taking his time, and it was going to kill me.

"Too much?" I cradled the back of his neck in my hands.

He laughed — a low rumble that I felt all through me — and shook his head. Strands of his hair danced over my skin, stoking the fire inside me. "Do it again."

"You like that kind of thing, huh?" I grazed my teeth over his earlobe, giving it a nibble then a firmer bite. Combined with a well-timed rake down his back, the touch made him shiver against me, his hands gripping my hips so tightly I could feel the indentations his fingertips were sure to leave in my skin.

I wasn't aware of a whole lot after that. His skin hot against mine, all cold from the rain was forgotten as he drove into me with a steady rhythm. His mouth took mine just as urgently; I felt utterly consumed by this man. My body under his hand was another instrument he'd mastered, and he was enjoying showing me how well he could play.

"Shit." I reached behind me, my fingernails scrabbling at the wall by the pillow, grasping for anything to hold on to as the world continued to spiral away from me. The sensations inside me continued to build; I knew it wouldn't be much longer.

Dex knew it too. With a roll of his hips he stopped, buried firmly inside of me, eliciting a gasp from me and a groan from deep in his chest. He reached for my hands, encircling my wrists one by one to bring my hands around his neck. "Me." His voice was strained. "Hold on to me. I've got you."

I clutched his shoulders, warm and solid under my hands, and his hands slid down, mapping the dip of my waist and swell of my hips. Before I knew what he was doing he was up on his knees, bringing me with him, urging my legs around his hips. Our bodies rocked together as he began to thrust again. I clung to him, and he anchored me with a strong hand on the small of my back. His other hand reached in, finding my clit, stroking hard.

"I've got you," he said again. And with that reassurance, I fell, every muscle trembling, every cell coming apart under him, around him, against him. My nails dug into his shoulders, and the one rational part of my brain that was still online knew I was leaving marks on him and was glad of it. I wanted him to remember this. Remember me.

With one final cry I broke apart, shuddering around him, and the answering tension in his body told me he wasn't far behind. His long, low groan against the side of my neck carried me through the aftershocks.

Outside, the thunderstorm raged on, but in here we were sated. After dealing with the condom we sank down into the bed again, Dex pulling me across his chest like the warmest blanket. I laid my head on his chest, listening to the steady thump of his heart as his rough fingertips trailed up and down the length of my spine. Our legs tangled together as though they'd been longtime companions.

I'd always enjoyed sex, but this was another level. I was hooked on Dex, and I could already tell that withdrawals were going to be a bitch.

Soon, too soon, he stirred underneath me.

"That was a good first round."

"First round?" What the hell? I was ready to fall asleep.

"Yep. Nice little quickie after work. Come on." He sat up, moving me to do the same. "Shower, something to eat, then back to bed."

I laughed as he slid out of the bed and moved to the minuscule bathroom in the motorhome. "In there? There's no way we'll both fit." But I leaned back on my elbows and enjoyed the view.

He threw that wicked smile of his over his shoulder. "We'll figure it out."

SEVENTEEN

We did not figure it out.

Sure, we tried, but the laws of physics simply did not allow us both to occupy the world's smallest shower. There was a lot of laughing as we eventually took turns getting clean and dressed in dry clothes, raiding the fridge for snacks to get us through the night since neither of us had thought about dinner. We'd been hungry for other things.

The thunderstorm outside had calmed down, thinning to a steady rain that pattered against the shell of the motorhome. We sat on the sofa, safe and warm inside, my legs across Dex's knees and Benedick in my lap.

I popped a grape in my mouth and chewed slowly, studying the cut of Dex's cheekbones in the minimal light.

"Why'd you say that?" My voice was soft. "About Frederick?" I barely wanted to bring it up. But whatever was happening between us, I didn't want any more lies going forward.

"How'd you find out?" He shook the mostly empty potato chip bag, which could have been a distraction, but when he glanced up at me, he met my eyes squarely. No hiding. That was a good sign.

"I saw Frederick at pub sing yesterday. He was watching Patrick perform." My lips quirked up in a smile. "It was pretty easy to figure out from there."

"Fuck." The word was small, quiet, and I could barely hear it over the rain. "Yeah. Of course you'd talk to him."

The look of defeat on his face hurt my heart. This wasn't the way I was used to Dex looking. "Why'd you lie?" I asked again.

He shook his head, staring into that potato chip bag as though it might have the answers. "I don't know," he said to the bag. "It's not . . . that's not me, you know? I don't lie about stuff. I don't need to." He heaved a big sigh. "I'm so stupid."

"Hey." Defensiveness rose in me. The way he threw it out there like that told me it wasn't the first time he'd been called that. "You're not stupid."

He sighed again. "Stupid thing to do, though." When I didn't respond he looked up at me. Good: we were back to direct eye contact. "I don't know," he said again. "Probably because I know you'd rather hang out with Freddy. He's fun. He's cute."

"He doesn't play for my team," I reminded him, and he answered with a half smile.

"It's not about that, though, is it? You and Freddy, you're friends. I don't . . . I'm not friends with chicks."

I pulled another couple of grapes off the stem. "You could start by not calling them chicks."

"Yeah, that's probably right." He was silent for a moment while a distant roll of thunder rumbled outside. "It's just . . . that's not why I'm there, you know? Delilah doesn't want me there to *hang.*" He said the word like it tasted sour. "We're not streaming cooking shows or whatever the hell. She doesn't care about the music I play. To her I'm . . . I dunno. I'm a dick with a person attached that she doesn't care about."

"Awww. Poor little fuckboy." But I poked him in the ribs with my toes to show I was kidding. He caught my foot in his hand and gave it a squeeze.

"I mean it." His gaze went inward as he massaged my instep. "Like, remember when Josh hurt his ankle? I was with Delilah that night. She never mentioned it." He shook his head. "I'm not part of her life like that. Chicks — *girls* — like her just want to bang."

"And you don't?" I raised my eyebrows, because no way was I going to let him wiggle out of at least half the blame.

"Well, yeah. I do too. Or I did." His sigh sounded like it came from his toes. "But you and me, it feels different. We talk about stuff. You ask me what I think. People don't ask me what I think."

"Daniel does," I reminded him. "Just the other day, he was asking you about venues to book for you guys."

"Yeah." That memory produced a little more of a smile: three-quarters this time. "That's new. And don't get me wrong . . ." He ran a hand up my leg, pushing the skirt of my sundress out of the way to cup the curve of my calf in his palm. "Banging with you is pretty great."

"Glad to hear it." I crunched on another grape.

"But we do this too."

"This? Eating the last of the potato chips?" I leaned over, waking up the cat and earning a feline glare for my trouble. "Did you eat the last of the chips?" I took the bag and peered inside. Nothing but crumbs.

Bastard.

"That too. But I mean this." He gestured between us, encompassing the way we sat together on the sofa. "Talking. And just, like . . . being."

I wanted to laugh. I wanted to say something snarky, like *that's called a relationship.* But there was true vulnerability on his face, and I couldn't laugh at that. I had a feeling he didn't drop that bravado of his very often. Dex was used to being naked with his body, but his emotions, his soul . . . that was another story. I recognized the moment as rare, and I didn't want to squander it.

But also, I didn't want to give what was happening between us a name. Especially one as fraught with meaning as *relationship.* I was here for another few weeks, until we left this Faire and went to Willow Creek. That was my stop. Maybe one reason he felt so comfortable with me was because this — whatever this was — had an automatic end date. Just like his "girl at every Faire" hookups, it was all over when the Faire moved on.

So instead I laid my head on the back of the sofa. Benedick purred in my lap, and when I scritched him on his neck his purrs increased in volume, his front paws getting in the action with some biscuit-making. Dex was still stroking up and down my leg, pushing my dress a tiny bit higher with each pass, and the feel of his rough fingertips on my skin made me want to join the cat in some purring of my own.

"I like just being with you," I finally said, my voice sleepy from the sex and the snacks and the generally contented feeling that warmed my soul. "Delilah's missing out."

A chuckle rumbled out of his chest, and I watched as he ducked his head with a smile. A shy smile. A real one.

A tiny voice in the back of my head whispered that it was going to be hard to let this one go. I told that voice to shut the hell up.

Several hours and a couple of condoms later, I awoke to early morning sunlight streaming into the motorhome. Alone.

Blinking in sleepy confusion, I pulled the sheets up my very naked body. Either I'd had an extremely active dream that involved me losing my pajamas, or Dex had gotten up already. The sounds of outside were alarmingly close, then I spied the flowered curtains moving gently. The windows were open.

After splashing some water on my face and slipping back into last night's sundress, I spied a takeout cup of coffee on the small kitchen counter, the sip hole still plugged with a plastic stick. I took a fortifying sip to chase away some of the cobwebs in my brain. But as I slid my feet into my cheap flip-flops, I frowned in the direction of the sofa. The pillow was practically folded in half, and the blanket was heaped in a ball at one end of the sofa. Why did it look like that? I distinctly remembered moving both to the dinette table last night when we'd had snacks on the sofa.

The sound of voices outside broke into my thoughts. Alarmed, I glanced over at the clock on the microwave. I'd really slept in; the rest of the band must already be here. I grabbed my coffee and headed to the door.

Outside, the campground was dotted with puddles, the only remaining evidence of the violent storm the night before. Dex sat on the picnic table, balancing his guitar on one jean-clad knee. His T-shirt was loose and his sneakers were untied. Todd stood next to him, sipping from a travel mug, but their conversation was drowned out by the sound of Daniel's truck, splashing through puddles on the way to our campsite.

"Morning." Dex raised his coffee — a twin for my own takeout cup — to me, and my body hummed at the sound of his voice. That voice had growled in my ear enough last night that I was going full Pavlov now.

But he gave nothing away. It was like I'd stepped into an alternate universe, where Dex and I hadn't slept together last night. Where we were just roommates who kept their distance.

So that was the way he wanted to play it. It stung a little, but okay. I could do that.

"Hey." My voice was as breezy as this sunny morning. Then I turned away from him to greet Stacey, who had just alighted from Daniel's truck. It was Monday morning, and we had stuff to do.

But that pillow and blanket didn't leave my mind all day. Obviously Dex had deliberately messed them up, so anyone who came inside the motorhome would think that he'd slept on the sofa, just like always. Except it was sloppy; until now he'd always folded the blanket — maybe not well, but he'd folded it. The blanket always lay on top of the pillow in a neat little stack.

He wanted it to be obvious. He didn't want anyone to know that we'd slept together.

I wanted to roll my eyes. What a high school way to behave. And if we were in high school, I might have been offended. I might have wondered what was wrong with me that he'd want to hide what had happened between us. But I wasn't in high school. I was a thirty-seven-year-old woman who was too old for that shit. I wasn't going to let him get under my skin.

And a good thing too, because Dex barely spoke to me all day. If I was at the picnic table with my tarot cards he was over by the chairs, talking to one of his brothers. If I was near the chairs, getting a drink out of the cooler, he suddenly had to fetch something from inside the motorhome. It was almost comic, and I even tested it, sitting down next to him at the picnic table when he was eating. He practically looked right through me before deciding that he didn't really want that sandwich after all.

Two could play at that game. Sure, I was a little hurt — who wouldn't be? But I was mostly annoyed. So when the day was over and everyone left for the night, I didn't pay attention to him, either. I'd already gone inside and was curled up on the bed in the back of the motorhome, sipping tea from a travel mug and reading. Benedick had gotten plenty of cuddle time from Stacey that day, so he was asleep on my feet. I kept my eyes on my e-reader and did my best not to react when the motorhome rocked a fraction, telegraphing that Dex was climbing the metal stairs to come inside.

The door to the mini-fridge opened, followed by the clink of bottles. "Want a beer?" Dex asked, as though that wasn't the first full sentence he'd said to me all day.

"Nope." I didn't look up from my book. It was getting to the good part. "I'm good."

The fridge closed, and he popped the cap off the bottle. "You okay?"

"Mmm-hmm." I clicked to the next page as a shadow fell over my e-reader. Dex leaned in the small doorway, filling up most of the space. Bottle abandoned somewhere behind him, his hands were empty, shoved into the front pockets of his jeans. His uncertain expression looked foreign on his face.

"You don't look okay," he said. "You look kinda pissed."

Was he really going to play it like this? Fine. I put down my e-reader and met his eyes squarely. "I'm not pissed. Disappointed, maybe, but not pissed." Okay, maybe I was a little pissed.

"Disappointed?" He crossed his arms. "What did I do?"

"I just wish . . ." A lump came to my throat, and I coughed it down. I was not going to let this guy get to me. Nope. I was going to be an adult. "We should have talked about it earlier, you know? That you didn't want anyone to know what had happened last night."

"What? That's not . . ." He frowned, but I wasn't done speaking.

"I get it, you know. I'm not a kid. If it's better for . . . I don't know, your reputation or whatever, to not tell anyone that we'd slept together, that's totally fine. But give a girl a heads-up, that's all I'm saying."

His eyes widened. "You think I didn't want anyone to know?"

I scoffed. "I mean, it was obvious from the way you very much didn't speak to me all day. Not to mention that . . ." I threw my arm out, pointing behind him toward the sofa. "You never leave it that messy. That was deliberate."

"Of course it was deliberate!" He threw up his hands in exasperation. "It wasn't for me, you weirdo. It was for you."

"Me?"

"Yeah." He must have sensed the shift in my mood because he took another step forward (the only step there was room to take) and sat gingerly on the side of the bed, not far from my hip. Benedick blinked at the movement but went back to sleep. "Last night was . . . I thought I was pretty clear about how great last night was."

"I thought you were too," I said.

"You know me," he said. "I don't care who knows what I've been doing. But you . . ." He reached out a tentative hand, and I let him touch a lock of my hair, tuck it behind my ear. "You seem like the type of person who would want to keep a guy like me a secret."

Words failed me. While I gaped at him and tried to summon a thought, he continued. "You know, you're all educated — college and law school and all that." His fingertips traced the shell of my ear as he spoke, his eyes following the movement, studying my face like it was the most fascinating thing he'd ever seen. "You go out with hotshot lawyers and shit usually, right? You're not going to want to be seen with a guy like me."

I banished that thought with a *pfft*. "Lawyers are boring, believe me." I leaned toward him, catching his gaze. "You think I'm that shallow? That I need someone's résumé to know if they're worth caring about? You've met my cousin Mitch, right? One of the best people I know?" While I talked his touch skimmed down my jaw to my throat, and his eyes darkened as I swallowed under his hand. "That's why you did all that today?" I chided, my voice barely above a whisper. "Avoiding me, not talking to me . . ."

"Yeah." His voice was hoarse, barely there. "I thought I was doing the right thing."

I shook my head. "It was the absolute wrong thing." I pulled back the quilt I was under, scooting back in the bed to give him more room. "Get over here."

He didn't need any further prompting, crawling into the bed and over me. I sank down underneath him, into the pillows, and let his arms cage me in. I tugged his shirt out of the waistband of his jeans before sliding my hands underneath, enjoying the feel of warm skin over tight muscle. He growled, a sound I felt against my hands as much as heard, as I pushed his shirt higher and higher up his chest until he reached one hand behind his neck, gripping the shirt and pulling it off.

"No more secrets." I popped the button on his jeans and teased my fingers beneath the waistband. "If you want me to ride you like a pony onstage during pub sing, that's the burden I'll bear."

"That'll fill up the tip basket." He grinned down as he tugged at my tank top, pulling it over my head and down my arms.

"Whatever I can do to help pay my way around here." I slid a hand down the front of his jeans, finding my target right away — it was a large target. He caught his breath as my hand curled around him, then his chest emptied in a deflating sigh. His head dropped as I stroked slowly, all the way down and then back up.

"That might be . . . a little . . . too public." He tried to get the words out but I'd started stroking in earnest, rendering him breathless. He held himself up on arms that shook, his hips rocking, pushing against my hand. "Ah, God. Lu, you better cut it out. I haven't even started on you yet."

I wanted to keep going. I loved seeing this look on his face, absolutely wrecked, knowing I was putting it there. But I slowed my strokes and settled instead for pushing his jeans down his hips. He kicked them off and then reached for me.

"Fuckin' yoga pants." He pulled on the stretchy waistband, getting one side down to expose my left hip bone. "Get this shit off." Together we wrestled them off; the e-reader went flying and the cat relocated for a more stable sleeping spot. Which was fine; we weren't planning on sleeping anytime soon.

Eighteen

Things were a lot different after that.

We weren't teenagers. It wasn't necessary to hang all over each other to say *Look, everyone! We're having sex!* But the message was clear. It was clear in the way he went on his coffee run a little later in the morning, getting back after everyone else had arrived for the day. It was clear in the way he handed me my coffee, kissing me on top of my head as he did so. Many pairs of eyebrows went up that first time, but no one asked for clarification, and we didn't offer any. We just smiled at each other and went on with our morning. He had songs to rehearse, and I had . . . well, I had tarot cards to learn. Only one of those tasks was an actual job.

I should have turned my attention back to my to-do lists. The days were flying by, and I'd be in Willow Creek before I knew it. Back to real life. I had a new career to figure out and plans to make. But none of those things seemed to matter when music was the background of my day, when the sun was shining, and I had a gorgeous guitar player smiling at me from across the way.

No one said anything about Dex and me, and I wasn't sure if he was relieved or disappointed.

That all changed on Thursday night. The guys had a show, and Daniel went with them. Stacey and I had a girls' night; the first one we'd had since I'd come on board.

"Why didn't we do this earlier?" Stacey laid her head on the back of the sofa with a happy sigh. She had a sheet mask over her face, which made her look a little like a horror movie villain. Those things were relaxing as hell and made the skin glow, but they were not attractive while being worn.

"I don't know, but I'm glad we're doing it now." I sat cross-legged on the floor, halfway done painting Stacey's toes bright pink. My own toes were wine red and almost dry. I was waiting until I was done with Stacey's pedicure before applying my own sheet mask, so we could look like horror movie killers together. Was there any better way for women to bond?

"We should have done it at the hotel." She leaned over to peek at her toes, but her mask slipped; she had to tilt her head back quick to keep the paper from sliding off her face. "You've got to be getting sick of this motorhome."

"Nah. It's actually kind of nice. I'm thinking about getting a tiny home once this is all over." Truth be told, I was getting used to the cramped quarters. My condo back home now seemed like a palace — who needs two whole bedrooms anyway? I was going to be reassessing a lot once I got back to reality.

Toes done and sheet mask applied, we semireclined together on the sofa, a companionable silence stretched out between us. But not for long.

"So." Stacey's gaze was still directed up at the ceiling to keep the sheet mask on her face. "You and . . . uh . . . Dex?"

I smiled, then immediately reached up to smooth my own mask back into place. "Yep."

Her sigh came from somewhere deep in her chest. "Be careful, okay? I don't want to harsh your mellow or whatever, but he's bad news."

She'd said that before. "He is?" I kept my voice neutral, but my heart rate sped up. "That's right, he said you two had some history. Is there something —"

But before I could finish the sentence, Stacey sat up. "He told you about us?" She peeled the sheet mask from her face, tossing the soggy paper to the dinette table. Even as she massaged the supposedly calming serum into her skin, emotion blazed in her eyes. I wasn't used to seeing Stacey like this. She was the most cheerful person I'd ever met.

I sat up too, removing my own mask even though it wasn't quite time yet. Some things were more important than moisturizing. "No," I said carefully. "He said it wasn't his story to tell. And I didn't think it was any of my business." I smoothed the leftover serum over my face and down my throat.

"Oh." My words banked some of the fire in her eyes, and she sat back again. "He said that?" Off my nod, she looked down at her nails, picking at a cuticle. We hadn't gotten to our fingernails yet; those were next. But apparently this talk was happening first.

Finally, she sighed again. "So Dex and I had a . . . a thing." From the way her cheeks colored when she said it, and the way she didn't quite meet my eyes, I knew exactly what kind of thing she was talking about.

My eyes flew wide. "A thing?" I repeated. "That's . . ." I searched for a word that didn't sound judgy. She'd been with two guys who were not only cousins, but worked and lived together? That had to be awkward.

"Complicated." She finished my sentence with a weak laugh. "It's a long story. You know how Dex hooks up just, like, all the time?"

I nodded. "A girl at every Faire?"

"Exactly. Well, for a couple years, every time he came through Willow Creek, I was the girl. And don't get me wrong, it was fun. Nothing wrong with no-strings hook-ups, right?"

"Absolutely." I kept my voice neutral. Was this a warning? Was she letting me know that Dex wasn't in it for the long haul with me? Because I didn't have any expectations here.

"Except one day I wanted more." She winced. "Okay, maybe I'd had a lot of wine, and I was feeling particularly lonely, but . . ." Another deep sigh. I didn't like it when Stacey looked this uncertain. This sad. She shouldn't look like that. "So I messaged him. You know, slid into his DMs."

"Oh boy." I sucked in a sympathetic breath. DMs on too much wine? That never ended well.

"Right? I know. Terrible idea. But then he messaged me back! Which, amazing, right?"

"Yeah." But my brow furrowed. I'd hardly

ever seen Dex with his phone out. He didn't seem like much of a social media guy.

"So for a while we're messaging back and forth. It goes to emails, then texts, and it's all so . . ." Her sigh this time was happy at the memory. "It's great. It's romantic. It's . . ."

"Wait." I held up a hand. "Romantic? Dex? You've met the guy, right?"

"That's the thing. It wasn't Dex. It was Daniel."

"Daniel?" I sat up.

"Yep. He got the first message and thought I'd sent it to him."

"But you were in Dex's DMs." Daniel liked control, but that seemed over the top even for him. Dex couldn't have his own social media accounts?

"I was in the *band's* DMs." She shook her head. "Too much wine, remember? By the time he realized I thought he was Dex the whole time, he didn't know how to tell me I had the wrong guy. But the thing was, I had the *right* guy. All this time, I was falling for the guy I was messaging. It didn't matter what he looked like anymore."

"But that's . . ." I gestured in outrage, too mad to come up with actual words. "He was catfishing you. Weren't you pissed?"

She sighed. "I was. And maybe I should

have been angrier about it. If he'd been out to deceive me from the start I would have been. But it was an honest mistake, at least at first. I wasn't exactly clear in my first message. Plus . . ." She blinked hard. "He got me through some hard stuff during that time. There was a health scare with my mom and he . . ."

"Oh, no! Is she okay?"

Stacey waved a hand. "She's fine. But at the time, it was one of the scariest days ever. And Daniel, while he was pretending to be Dex, got me through that. I think that's one of the reasons I forgave him so easily."

I nodded slowly. "I get it. I think. But . . . how does this make Dex bad news? Was he in on it the whole time? Was he lying to you too?" Something inside of me blazed with indignance on her behalf. Hadn't Dex just lied to me recently? He'd told me he wasn't a liar by habit, but isn't that something a liar would say?

"No. He didn't really know about it."

"So it was all Daniel? Why are you mad at Dex about it, then?"

She gave a tiny laugh. "I told you it was complicated. Apparently when Daniel realized I'd meant to message Dex, he told him. So he could answer me, you know? But Dex told Daniel to handle it. Handle me. Like I was a groupie who was getting too close."

I nodded with a grimace. That was harsh, for sure. But it sounded like something Dex would say. He wasn't a relationship kind of guy.

While I was thinking, Stacey had dug her phone out of her blue leather backpack. After a little scrolling and tapping, she passed the phone to me. It was a screenshot from an email that read, **Oh, and too bad, Anastasia. You can't give me a name that feels like music in my mouth and not expect me to revel in it. The name suits you.**

I raised my eyes. "Anastasia? That's your name?"

She nodded with a laugh. "That went over great in first grade."

"I bet." I handed her the phone back, and she swiped to another screenshot, handing it back. **Tell me what I'm missing about small-town life. Besides you. Which, let's face it, might be enough to convince me.**

"Stuff like that," she said while I read. "Those were the kinds of emails Daniel sent me."

"Nice. But . . ." I cocked my head at her as I handed the phone back. "You couldn't tell this wasn't Dex? There's no way in hell he'd talk like this."

"I know that now!" Her voice was defensive. "But we hadn't done a whole lot of . . . uh . . . talking back then. Most of our time together was . . ."

"Nonverbal?" I suggested. I raised an eyebrow. "Horizontal?"

She sputtered out a laugh. "Something like that."

"So . . ." I went over everything she'd said, summing it up like a closing argument, with Dex MacLean as my client. "Dex never lied to you about who he is, or what he's after. He didn't misrepresent himself in any way, right? But you're still saying he's bad news."

Stacey gaped at me for a moment, closing her eyes in a slow blink, then clicked her phone off. "Yeah," she finally said. "Maybe I've been holding a grudge, huh?"

"I think that you really love Daniel," I said as gently as I could. "And he really loves you too. So maybe it was easier to take all the weirdness over how you two got together and push it on Dex. I have a feeling no one around here expects much from Dex, so it's easy to put the blame there."

"Wow." The word was a forceful exhale. Then she gave me a watery smile as she ran her fingertips under her eyes. "Are you sure you're a lawyer? Not a shrink or something?"

"The last few weeks I've sold turkey legs,

worked the tip basket, and taken appointments for fortune-tellers. I have no idea what I am anymore." But as I reached out to Stacey, giving her arm a squeeze, I realized the most important thing I'd become was a friend.

"There you are!"

I had no idea what it was about me that made Sasha think I was untrustworthy, but at the start of every weekend she seemed mildly surprised that I continued to show up. At least she seemed happy about it too.

"Here I am!" I pulled my card table and folding chair from her tent, setting it up in front of their little bower. Another Faire weekend was beginning, and I couldn't wait. With every coming weekend, this whole environment felt more like home than anywhere I'd ever lived. I'd never spent this much time outdoors in my life, and I'd never felt so healthy, so alive.

Of course, some of that could have to do with all the sex I'd been having, which was also more plentiful than I'd ever had in my life. Dex and I had made good use of the limited space in the motorhome, and waking up this morning had been a struggle. Thank God for that boy and his daily coffee runs.

My space all set up, I went back for the large TAROT-PALMISTRY-RUNES sign. My brainstorm for today was to leave that sign up front, near the entrance to Mystics' Glade, so patrons would know we were here. Even though we were doing relatively well, I didn't like that they'd stuck the girls in the back. If I was going to be their de facto office manager, I was going to do the best job I possibly could.

My gambit worked. Our appointments filled up in record time, and while I hated refusing potential clients, I had to start turning people away. Some I pointed in the direction of the tarot card seller's cart, selling them on the idea that they could buy some cards and learn to divine their own futures. The card seller caught my eye from across the way and gave me a wave in thanks.

"You're in a good mood," Summer remarked toward the end of the day, when the sun was starting to dip, taking the edge off the heat of the afternoon.

I shrugged, taking a sip of water. "It's been a good day." They were all good days lately. Maybe I was just sex-drunk, but I didn't care. I knew what I was doing. Dex hadn't promised me forever, and I didn't want it anyway. This was still a vacation, a departure from my real life. It just involved a lot more orgasms lately.

The last patron left ten minutes before pub sing, and it was time to break our stuff down for the day. We were done a little early — I'd be able to catch a ride back with either Dex or Stacey if I got to pub sing before it ended.

"Oh, Lulu, wait." Summer reached for the tie-dye backpack that she kept slung over the back of her chair. It was anachronistic as hell, but no one seemed to care, and I wasn't her boss. She tugged the bag into her lap and dug inside the front pocket. "These are for you."

"For me?" As she held out her hand, I held out mine out of instinct, letting her drop two stones into my palm. One was a rich royal blue, the other a deep golden brown.

"Lapis lazuli," Summer said, as though she were introducing me to friends of hers. "And that one's tiger's-eye. I picked them up from a crystal seller a few stops ago, which was weird at the time, since I already have those stones." She reached for the crystals she wore around her neck, and sure enough I saw a dark blue and golden brown in the mix. "I'd forgotten all about them, but then this morning I found them in the bottom of my bag and realized that they were really for you."

"For me?" I was repeating myself, but I was utterly flummoxed. I flexed my palm, and the rocks rolled in my hand, clicking softly against each other. "How could they be for me? We didn't know each other then."

Summer shrugged. "I don't question these things. When I know, I know. You know?" I wanted to laugh at her phrasing, but having spent a few weeks with Summer now, I understood exactly what she meant.

She continued, pointing at the lapis lazuli. "This one's for finding your truth and figuring out how to express it. Sasha told me about the reading she did for you, and that you have big decisions to make. Lapis is great for that. Self-awareness, right? You need to know what you're about before you know what you want. Lapis is also about communication."

"Communicating with whom?" I imagined myself in my old life, bringing a bright blue crystal into a meeting, and telling Bud Stone that this rock was helping me tell him to fuck off. It would probably go over about as well as throwing my phone in the wench tub had.

"To yourself. To anyone. It's all about truth. Inner, outer, what have you."

"Okay." I took the stone between my fingers and held it up to the late afternoon sun, which made it practically glow dark blue. It really was pretty. "And the tiger's-eye?"

"That one's all about clarity. Grounding. It's going to help you really see the way forward. Take any scattered thoughts you may have and turn them into a plan. An action."

"Damn. I can use that." All that from a little rock? I turned it over in my fingers. It wasn't golden brown the way I originally thought; the stone was made up of striations of brown and gold in all shades, and it practically shimmered as I moved it around, showing me all of its variegations. Those colors sparkling in the sun felt comforting. Felt like home. Like a place I wanted to live. Maybe there was something to this whole crystals thing, because I felt grounded already.

The Louisa of a few months ago would have probably scoffed at a gift like this. Sure, she would have been polite, but rocks, even pretty ones like these? Who cared, right?

But I closed my fist, the two stones firmly inside. "Thanks, Summer." Because while Louisa might have scoffed, Lulu . . . she cared. The Lulu that had spent the past couple weeks studying tarot cards cared. The Lulu that tucked the rocks safely into her belt pouch as she walked up to the front to catch the end of pub sing cared a lot, and saw them for the kind gift they were.

As I got to the outskirts of the front stage, my steps slowed, until I stopped completely in the middle of the lane. Because there, off to the house-left side of the audience, Dex was in conversation with one of the laundry wenches. Because of course he was.

My eyes narrowed, and I tamped down the bile that churned in my stomach. Jealousy was an ugly emotion, I reminded myself as the wench threw back her head and laughed at something Dex said. I concentrated on taking as slow and deep a breath as I could as Dex smiled down at the wench, obviously pleased he had made her laugh. *He never promised you forever, remember. And you never asked for it.*

Once I had taken a few breaths and was sufficiently calmed down, I pasted a carefree smile onto my face and walked over to join them.

"So it really does work?" Dex asked her, just as I got within earshot. "Rotating in and out like that?"

"Oh, it really does!" She nodded enthusiastically. "I mean, you're talking about a much smaller operation, but we can cover so much ground. Something to think about, if you wanted to branch out even more."

Dex chuckled, his eyes flicking up as I approached. His smile widened to include me in it before he turned back to the wench. "Maybe later. I'm thinking one step at a time. Hey." He addressed this last to me, putting an arm out in my direction.

I blinked at that arm for a split second, unsure, then slid my hand into his outstretched one. He tugged me closer to him so that we were standing together. "You know Beansprout, right?" His eyes danced with amusement, knowing full well that I did.

"We've met," I said with a smile.

Beansprout — which I really, *really* hoped was her character's name — laughed. "Jill," she said, extending her hand. She dropped all pretense at character, speaking to me performer to performer. "I think your phone is going to be in our hall of fame."

"So glad I made an impression." That day felt so long ago now. Another person had done that, back in another lifetime. I liked the person I was now. She was a lot more fun.

As Jill left, Dex tugged me closer to him. "I can't believe you were jealous. You thought I was flirting with Beansprout?"

"No," I said quickly. Too quickly, and that got a grin out of him. "You can flirt with whomever you want," I said primly, which only made his grin turn into a laugh.

"Busting out the 'whom.' You must mean business."

I blew out a breath. He had a point; that was a very lawyer thing to say. Not very Lulu at all. I looked across the way, at the belly dancers, who had also been at the last Faire. One of them nudged the other, their eyes on Dex. Delilah the acrobat wasn't too far away and wow, I was right. Jealousy *was* an ugly emotion. The looks on their faces were clear: I was hogging my time with the Ren Faire hottie.

Too damn bad. Instead of stepping away I leaned into him, my head on his shoulder. "You sure you're okay with this?" I asked. "You could be with one of those belly dancers instead of me. Or the acrobat. Pretty sure they've all got moves I don't. Wouldn't that be more fun?" What did I, a lawyer who not only knew how to use "whom" correctly but dropped it into casual conversation, have to offer?

He snorted. "I got news for you, Counselor. You're pretty fun." He slid an arm around my shoulder, his thumb stroking the bare skin of my shoulder. His touch zinged through my blood.

"Yeah?" My voice came out much smaller, much more uncertain, than I'd expected. Those belly dancers must have been doing a number on my self-confidence.

He peered down at me. "You have no idea, do you?"

"About what?" I chanced a glance up at him and was instantly caught in the intense brown of his eyes.

He shook his head. "About you. About how hanging out with you, on the off chance I can make you laugh, is my favorite way to spend a night. The only thing I'd rather do . . ." His voice trailed off as applause broke out for the act onstage. We were both startled back into reality and he blinked as he raised his head, breaking the spell that had been woven between us as we joined the applause out of instinct.

The belly dancers took the stage, but neither of us noticed. Our attention had turned back to each other. "The only thing you'd rather do . . . ?" I couldn't hear my own voice over the merriment around us.

"The only thing I'd rather do than make you laugh . . ." He dipped his head toward mine, his forehead pressed to my temple, his mouth at my ear. ". . . is make you come."

"Oh." All my breath left my body in one sigh. How was everyone at this Faire just carrying on like he hadn't just set my blood on fire? I took a shuddering breath. "You're more than welcome to try." I put as much bravado into those words as I could, even though everything inside of me quivered.

His chuckle was low and dangerous in my ear. "Challenge accepted."

A laugh spilled out of me, and as I looked up at him I saw that same laugh echoed in the sparkle in his eyes. His arm around my shoulders tightened as we turned our attention to the belly dancers, cheering them on and every act afterward, with the promise of tonight lighting up everything inside of me. My hand went to my belt pouch, because now I knew why that tiger's-eye had provoked such a reaction in me. Those shades of brown that had drawn me in, made me feel like I'd come home.

Those were the same shades of brown that were in Dex's eyes.

NINETEEN

They always say that turnabout is fair play. They neglected to mention how much fun it was.

The next weekend was another excruciatingly hot one. No breeze coming from anywhere, no clouds in the sky to break up the sun. The fortune-tellers were thankful for their tents, and I repositioned my table to take advantage of the shade from the nearby trees. But that little bit of shade only did so much, so when there was a break in the action I offered to trek up to the food stalls with the promise of frozen lemonades for all of us.

Walking provided some relief; the breeze from my moving skirts cooled off my legs. While I waved at the vendors and performers who had all become familiar faces in the past few weeks, my mind was on that substandard shower in that little motorhome, waiting for me tonight. Right now a trickle of water would be better than nothing. Only a few more hours now . . .

In my distraction, I didn't notice that I was under siege.

"Make way for the pub crawl!" a voice boomed from the lane behind me, and I jumped, startled, before turning in a whirl of skirts. Sure enough, there was a crowd of people heading in my direction, led by a group of five pirates, one of whom waved a massive green flag with a graphic of an overflowing tankard in the middle.

Oh, God. I'd seen the pub crawl marked on the map for this Faire, but I had never run into them. Then again, I spent the better part of each day tucked away at Mystics' Glade. Clearly employees of the Faire, the pirates leading the pub crawl were followed by a crowd of about twenty-five patrons in various stages of inebriation, wielding cheap souvenir tankards. They were heading in the direction of the food stalls, the same as I was. Or at least the tavern that was set up just outside of it.

I obeyed their shouted command, the same as all patrons and performers in earshot, stepping to the side of the lane as the pirates approached.

"Halt!" One of the pirates threw his arm straight up in the air, and the pub crawl obeyed more or less at once, the patrons in the back grumbling and upending their empty tankards. "What have we here? A fair maiden!" He grinned at me, and I narrowed my eyes in response. What fresh hell was this?

Another of the pirates turned to the crowd behind him, raising his voice. "And what do we do when we see a fair maiden?"

I shot a scowl at the pirate who was still grinning at me. I didn't like where this was going, unless the answer was *give her money and leave her alone.*

Of course I wasn't that lucky. "Woo her!" the partially drunken crowd chorused.

I didn't have time for this. Every minute I was away from Mystics' Glade I pictured my carefully set up system going to hell. In my mind's eye, patrons piled up with no idea of where to go, like automated characters in a bad video game.

But at the core of it, I was a Faire performer. And I was now part of this show. So I had to step up and . . . let myself be wooed. Probably.

I made one last attempt to get out of this. "Don't you dare," I said, sotto voce, to the pirate directly in front of me. He gave me a laugh.

"Sorry, miss. Those are the rules!" He produced a flask from his pocket and offered it to me. "Rum? It makes the wooing go down easier."

"I'm not talking about 'going down' with you, or anyone." But I took the flask as he boomed out a laugh at my response. I was parched, and all the performers carried water. It was nice of this guy to share.

As I uncapped the flask, wiping the opening with my sleeve (because that was going to make it so much more sanitary), one of the patrons stumbled forward to lots of prodding and cheering from the group. He was young and tall, with that kind of gangly frame that would fill out by the time he was out of college. His baseball cap had fraternity letters on it, blond curls spilling around the edges, and there was a very good chance the beer in his hand had been procured with a fake ID.

For a moment there was silence, as he looked down at me (down my dress, most likely) with an uncertain expression. "Uhhh."

"Yes, sirrah?" I cocked an eyebrow and took a swig from the flask, and *what the hell*? It burned like fire. Like, well, like rum. I couldn't be mad; the pirate had said as such when he'd offered it to me. My fault for not believing him. I called upon my own college experience, only choking a little as I forced down the shot.

"Go on." One of the pirates prodded the college kid. "Remember, it's your job on this pub crawl to woo any fair maiden that we come across."

"Any fair maiden?" I raised my eyebrows at the pirate, expressing faux outrage. "So I am one of many?" I planted a fist on my hip.

"But certainly the fairest!" he protested. "I don't offer my rum to just anyone."

"I'd hope not." I took another swig, prepared this time. The alcohol helped me get into character as a random wench about to be wooed. But this kid needed to get a move on; I needed to get back to my station.

The college kid sighed, trying to look bored, but there was a pink of embarrassment in his expression. Then he abruptly dropped to one knee in front of me, one hand over his heart, his other arm stretching out toward me, tankard still gripped in his hand. "My lady!" he proclaimed in the worst English accent I had ever heard. I suspected it was fueled by beer. "Thy beauty is like the most delicate flower. Thy smile is like the sun. Also, I am totally impressed by the way thee . . . uh, thou . . . no, thee . . . doth do shots. That's really awesome too."

I pressed my lips together hard, but there was no way I was keeping a straight face through all of that. My shoulders quaked with laughter, and all around us the pirates and patrons laughed too. Not in mockery, but sharing in the absurdity of the situation.

"Well, milady?" The pirate took his flask back from me, tucking it into one of the cavernous pockets of his loose trousers. "Have you been sufficiently wooed?"

"Um." I swallowed hard against the laugh that threatened to bubble up, turning it into my sunniest smile instead. "Yes, sir," I finally managed. "I daresay I have."

A cheer went up from the inebriated crowd, making even the pirates laugh. But then a chant started. "Kiss her! Kiss her!" I turned alarmed eyes toward the pirate I'd shared a drink with, and he made a placating gesture toward me. *Don't worry,* the gesture said. And he was right. The frat bro, still on one knee in front of me, simply tugged my hand closer, planting a drunken kiss on the back of my hand. Yeah, okay. That was fine.

As the cheering increased, I heard someone behind me clear his throat. Loudly.

"You call that a kiss?"

The cheering died, cut off like a switch had been flipped. The college kid dropped my hand, scrambling to his feet. I turned to see Dex standing in the middle of the lane, his arms folded across his chest. With his well-worn kilt, his hair bundled back from his face, and his glowering expression, he looked like a medieval miscreant come to rob us all. Of our cash, our virtue — it was all the same to this guy.

I took the opportunity to surreptitiously wipe the back of my hand on my skirt — that had been a sloppy kiss — as I took a step toward Dex. "You think you could do better?" My chest felt tight with the laughter I suppressed. Was this what it was like to be a Renaissance Faire performer, to be in character at all times? I could handle it if it meant flirting with Dex.

"I'd certainly hope so." His voice was a growl — that growl that he knew did things to me — as he raised an eyebrow. Before I could say anything more, he closed the space between us and slid an arm around my waist. His other hand caressed my cheek, and I had just enough time to see the spark of amusement in his eyes before he bent to me, his mouth closing confidently over mine.

His mouth was a warm welcome, and it didn't take long for me to forget we were performing in front of a crowd. I braced myself with my hands flat on his chest, clinging to the linen of his loosely laced shirt while he slid his hand into my hair, messing up my braid. He cupped the back of my head to better control the kiss.

Cheers from the pub crawl crowd devolved into wolf whistles by the time we eased apart. I looked up into Dex's laughing eyes, and he grinned back at me, planting a quick final kiss on my forehead.

The pirate leading the pub crawl clapped his hands once in finality. "Many thanks for the demonstration, good sir! But now, my companions are thirsty. What say you?" He turned back to the crowd and raised his hands. "To the pub!"

"Aye!" they more or less chorused, some waving their empty tankards in emphasis. The pirate wielding the green flag hoisted it high, and the group was off, the lead pirate offering a fist bump to Dex as they passed one another.

"Damn. I wanna work at a Renaissance Faire if that's what you get to do all day," one of the pub crawl patrons said as they filed by.

Finally alone — or alone as we could be in the middle of the lanes in front of God and everyone — I turned back to Dex. "What are you doing here?"

He shrugged. "Between shows. It's my wandering-around time. Which was what I was doing till I saw some teenager hitting on my girl."

"Hey." My heart skidded over the words "my girl," but I did my best to not let anything show on my face. "He was doing an okay job."

Dex snorted. "Dude was wearing cargo shorts."

"Awww." I fussed with the laces of his shirt, making sure everything lay straight. "You're so cute when you're jealous."

He huffed and narrowed his eyes at me, but the whole situation was so absurd that we both just laughed. "Yeah, okay, whatever." He slung an arm around my shoulders, a gesture that clearly said *mine.* "You headed back to the fortune-tellers?"

I shook my head. "Food stalls. Mostly for some drinks."

"It is wicked hot today." He nodded wisely. "I'll walk you over there."

"You don't have to," I protested, but not very much, as he steered us up the lane, a hand firmly on the small of my back, making sure that we kept a good distance behind the pub crawl. No more wooing was going to happen while he was around.

■ ■ ■ ■

It felt like we'd just gotten here, yet it somehow also felt like I'd lived my entire life at that campground and in the lanes of this Faire here in the Blue Ridge Mountains. But all of a sudden it was the last weekend.

The energy was different that final weekend. The performers, vendors, everyone who helped bring this Faire to life was this odd combination of melancholy that this one was ending, and excited to move on to the next location.

On the last day of the Faire I got to Mystics' Glade a little early, intending to soak in every last moment. At her cart, the tarot seller was settled in her camp chair, sipping at her coffee like usual, but large plastic boxes were stacked at her feet, ready to pack away her wares at the end of the day. I didn't want to think about the end of the day yet.

She started to stand at my approach, to wait on me like a patron, but I waved her off. "Please sit," I said. "It's too early."

She chuckled in response. "How are the cards treating you?"

"Good," I answered, not even considering how the Louisa of a couple months ago would have reacted to a question like that. I looked at the different decks she had on offer with more experienced eyes now. The Rider-Waite deck I'd chosen before had been a good purchase at the time, their illustrations matching those in the books I'd bought to learn to read them. But now I studied the wild variations on these other decks with fascination. How could the messages be the same, when the pictures looked so different? I picked up one deck, smaller than the one I already owned, and flipped it over to see the examples of art that were displayed on the back.

"How do you decide?" I had intended to muse this to myself, but I had spoken louder than I'd intended, because the vendor laughed kindly at my question.

"It's all instinct." She stood up then and looked over her selections along with me. "It's like art, and what provokes a feeling inside of you. If you respond to the art, you might bond well with the deck."

"Hmm." I put the boxed deck down and went back to studying. "But I already have a deck. Why would I need a second one?"

"So many reasons. People say some decks are kinder than others. I've heard readers say that they use one deck when they want a blunt answer to a question. But it could be less woo-woo than that." She shrugged. "Some people like the art. It's seventy-eight pieces of art to carry in your pocket, right?"

"Good point." Just then I spied a deck with a fluffy tuxedo cat on the front of the box. He looked just like Benedick. It was a tarot deck made up entirely of cats, and the idea of that was positively delightful. Hadn't I just wondered why I would ever need more than one deck? Yet I picked this deck up and hugged it to my chest. "This one." Benedick had been nothing but comfort to me since I'd joined up with the Kilts, so the idea of him helping me with my tarot readings after I left filled me with joy.

"See? There you go. It spoke to you." She took my proffered money and peeled off a bill, handing it back to me. "Rennie discount," she said. "I should have done that before."

I wanted to protest, but I just thanked her and stashed the cash back in my belt pouch. My fingers brushed against my lapis and tiger's-eye, which I had started carrying with me all the time, even during the week. Crystal or placebo, they did make me feel better.

"Where are you off to next?" I asked as she straightened up her display to cover the hole left by my purchase.

"Oh, this little Faire up in Maryland. Small town called Willow Creek. They've had a Faire going for about ten, fifteen years now. It's not huge, but it's solid. Four weeks. It's a nice little stop."

A thrill went through me. "Oh! I'm going there too!"

"You are?" She glanced up at me sharply. "I didn't think they did that one." She waved a hand across the glade, and I glanced over my shoulder to where my fortune-tellers were getting set up.

"They don't. But I'm not traveling with them. I'm with the Dueling Kilts. The musicians?"

"Ahhhhh." She drew that word out for a few syllables. "I bet they're a good time. At least one of them is." She raised her eyebrows at me significantly.

Wow. Was there anyone who didn't know about Dex's reputation? A flush crept up the back of my neck, and I really hoped it didn't show. But my skin was relatively fair, even with all this time spent out in the sun, so I was probably screwed there. "No comment," I said primly, and she roared with laughter.

"I'll see you there, then? You can let me know how those new cards treat you." She settled back into her camp chair and picked up her coffee. "Maybe talk to your girls over there about them. I bet they have opinions. All readers do."

I laughed at the sarcasm in her tone. "I'll do that." My eyes were on the box of cards I'd just purchased as I made my way to the fortune-tellers' tents.

"Oooh." Summer's whole face lit up as I opened the box and broke the seal, peeling the plastic away. "New cards!"

Sasha grinned. "Is that your second deck? Already?"

"Don't judge me." I tipped the cards into my hands, shuffling slowly through them. Cats in all sizes and colors, in various arrangements. I flipped quickly through the minor arcana cards — the cups and pentacles, swords and wands — pausing on the major arcana ones to study them a little more closely. Every illustration made me smile. Every illustration made me feel the way I felt when Benedick chose to sleep on my head or curl up in my lap. These cards brought such a balm to my soul that tears prickled at my eyes, like emotion looking for an outlet. Now what the card seller said made sense; these cards were comforting. I had a feeling they would be kind to me.

"We'd never judge you. Are you kidding?" Sasha looked over my shoulder at the cards.

"Those are the cutest! Give it time; we're going to have to give you your own tent soon so you can read cards with us."

My breath caught at the notion. She talked like I wasn't almost done with all of this. Like I wasn't about to head back to the life of pantsuits and sensible shoes. A life where I didn't get to sleep in Dex's arms every night. I'd started to understand Todd a little better these past few days. Being apart from someone who made me feel this alive was going to suck. I was going to have to let Dex live his life while I lived mine. But how?

Nope. Not time to think about that yet. "Unlikely." My voice was sharp as I turned my attention back to the cards, tapping them together into a neat stack before sliding them back into their box. "It takes me forever just to do a three-card spread. I turn one card over, and then I'm flipping through the book for ten minutes to find out what it means. By then I've forgotten if the card is past, present, or future." I wasn't exaggerating. The tarot cards fascinated me, but I didn't have any kind of knack when it came to reading them.

Sasha nodded in understanding. "It does take time. But stick with it; you'll get there. Then you can branch out to bigger spreads

317

that go into more detail."

That made sense. "The books I got have some of those in the back. Twelve cards and all that? That's a little much for me now."

Summer blew a raspberry. "Don't listen to Sasha. She does it wrong."

"I do not!" But this was obviously an old argument, since Sasha was grinning as she put her hands on her hips. "The spreads are there for a reason, you know. The cards like order."

"*Your* cards like order." Summer shook her head in mock sorrow. "Boring."

"Knock it off, kids," Sage said with a tolerant smile. She nestled her blue flower crown into her dark hair. "Nobody wants to see fortune-tellers bickering."

"I do," I chimed in with a grin. That earned me a swat on the shoulder from Sage and a laugh from the other two.

"Listen," Summer said when the laughter had died down. "Grab me at the end of the day, okay? I'll give you a *real* reading, in honor of our last day here." She shot a narrowed-eyed look at Sasha, who rolled her eyes.

"Deal," I said.

I fully expected her to forget her offer. I wouldn't have blamed her a bit. I may have not taken this gig seriously when I first started working with them, but now I could see that it wasn't just flipping cards and making shit up. This was work, and they put care and attention and effort into every reading they did. Sage frowned over the runes like she was working out a foreign language, and after every tarot reading Summer leaned back in her chair, slumping her shoulders like she was exhausted. By the end of the day all three of them were drained, the way I used to feel after spending hours in front of the computer drafting summary judgment motions. The last thing I would have wanted to do after that was write one for someone else.

Besides, it was the last day of Faire. There were more important things on everyone's mind, like breaking down the tents and getting everything packed away for the next stop.

So I didn't intend to hold Summer to her word. At the end of the day, I folded up my table for the last time and then helped Sage break down her stuff. We stacked the tables and chairs together, then while Sage went off to get the car, I went into Summer's tent to help her with her stuff.

But she hadn't broken down yet. Inside, her table and chairs were still set up. A square purple cloth covered the table diagonally, so that the four points of the cloth fell over the edges. Gold accents in the cloth glinted in the late afternoon sun that streamed into the tent. "There you are!" Excitement sparkled in her eyes. "Come on, let's read ya!"

TWENTY

"Are you sure you have time?" I looked back outside to where everything but the tents was broken down.

Sasha glanced over to see what we were up to. "Good luck," she said to me with a pointed look. "That girl is nothing but chaos." But she also shook her head good-naturedly. "I'll get the other tents down."

"Thank you!" Summer called. She waved me to the seat opposite her and reached for the stack of tarot cards at her right hand.

"So Sasha and I have very different approaches to our readings." She shuffled the deck while she talked. "She's a traditionalist. She lives and dies by her spreads, and goes by the literal meanings every time, because to her that's what the cards are about."

"Hold up." I peered closer at the cards in her hands as she shuffled. "Those . . . those cards don't match."

"They don't!" she confirmed gleefully. Placing the stack facedown by her left hand, she spread them out in an arc across the table. The deck I had been working with — hell, even the deck I got today — all had the same picture on the back, like a deck of playing cards did. But the cards on Summer's table were a jumble of colors and patterns. Some of the backs were the same, but they were scattered here and there throughout. Some cards had gilded edges; some were a little bigger than the rest, while others were a little smaller.

"This is my patchwork deck," Summer said. "I've been building it for a while now. I had this big collection of decks that I was getting tired of hauling around, but I didn't want to get rid of them because certain cards in each deck really resonated with me. So I started mixing them together — the Magician from this deck, the Hanged Man from that deck, you know? — so all the cards I worked with gave me the same feeling. Some cards in here aren't really cards. Pieces of art that I had made into cards, or cut down to size so they'd fit in. Right now, there's a hundred and seventeen cards in this deck instead of the normal seventy-eight." She leaned in to whisper to me. "Sasha thinks I've lost it, honestly, but it works for me."

"Okay, but . . ." I watched as she shuffled the cards some more. A hundred and seventeen was a lot of cards, and watching her handle them was mesmerizing. She'd grab a handful, shuffle them together, then add a few from the stack still on the table. Then take half the cards in her hand and swap them with the cards on the table and shuffle again. "What about the meanings?" I asked. "How can you look up meanings of cards that aren't really cards?"

"I don't." She stopped and shook her head, negating what she'd just said. "That's not true. When I first started working with the cards, I learned their meanings, just like Sasha does now. And I use them, most of the time. But the strict meanings don't always apply." She tapped her temple. "So much of reading the cards is about instinct. It's not just about rote translation. That takes the magic out of it.

"But where Sasha and I really disagree is with using spreads. She likes everything all neat and tidy, every card in its place." She shook her head. "The cards let me know when they're part of the reading. You'll see."

Before I could say anything further, she plunked the oversize stack of cards on the table between us. "Cut into three piles, then stack 'em back up again. What kind of reading do you want to concentrate on? Love? Career? General life questions?"

"Yes, yes, and yes?" The cards felt foreign, and they were warm from being in Summer's hands, but as I cut the deck I felt comfort emanating from them. Like I was right where I was supposed to be in that moment. I'd been around these women long enough to know when to trust that feeling.

Summer laughed at my answer. "You got it." She shuffled the deck once more, talking while she did so. "Got a guy at home? A girl? A they/them?"

"Nobody," I confirmed. "I've got nobody at home." My voice was light, but the answer sat heavy in my chest — the knowledge that we were about to leave this place and head for Willow Creek. Soon I'd be leaving Dex behind, and there was nobody waiting for me. Not even a cat to hog my pillow.

She flipped the first card over: the Ace of Wands. "Very funny," she said to the card, then flipped a few more in quick succession.

"What's funny?" I tried to remember what the card meant but my mind was blank.

"No, this is good." She glanced up to me with a quick smile. "Aces are about beginnings, and every so often I get an ace as the very first card, and I'm like, yes! I know! This is the beginning of the reading!" The next card she turned over was the Ace of Cups. "See?" She shook her head with a laugh. Then she tapped a finger on the card. "I like this, though. You said nobody's at home, but something's on its way. An important relationship. Probably romantic, maybe not. But keep your heart open, okay? Just in case."

My mind went to Dex immediately, of course. But we were a good time, not a long time. Not a relationship, I reminded myself almost daily. Not something built to last. But what if we could be? Was I being too hasty, just assuming we were going to end when we got to Willow Creek? My heart thumped at the possibility, and Dex's dark eyes and wicked smile echoed in my brain while Summer kept flipping cards.

"Oh, damn. Okay, this is something you gotta stop." She paused on the Devil. This card was from a deck painted in all dark colors, like an ominous storm on the horizon. "You're spending too much energy living up to people's expectations. Or worse, living down to them. Letting that make your decisions for you." She raised her head, her clear blue eyes staring straight into mine.

"The Devil's come up three times now, so . . ."

"Three times?" I looked closer at the cards. "How many Devils do you have in there?"

She grinned. "Five. Nine Deaths, six Lovers, and three Fools. Point is, the cards really want to make sure you get this message. Which makes sense — you've got that energy all over you."

"I don't doubt it." Hadn't I been living the life my parents wanted for me, not the life I wanted for my own? Living up to their expectations . . . and come to think of it, hadn't Dex been living *down* to people's expectations? I seemed to be the only one in his life who saw that he was capable of more. Maybe that was why the energy was so thick — this message was for him too.

But Summer was already moving on. "Another ace, this time swords . . . a business breakthrough on the horizon. Aces are beginnings, remember? Might be a good time to think about starting a business. Gah, more swords . . . King of Swords. Ooof." She gave me a knowing glance. "You've been making your decisions with your head, haven't you, as opposed to your heart? Too much thinking, not enough feeling. Hopefully this summer is giving you a different perspective. Trust your gut. Page of Cups . . . a younger lover? Love that for you," she said with a smirk while I sat up a little straighter. The back of my neck tingled. I was a few years older than Dex.

The next card she stopped on wasn't a card at all. A small illustration showing figures on a road that stretched out toward the horizon. Behind them was a murky forest of dark trees and overgrown vines. "Out of the woods," she murmured, setting it aside. "That's good. You've been lost for a long time. Since way before you threw your phone out. But that's all changed. Or it's changing. Either way, you're moving in the right direction." A couple more flips and she paused on the High Priestess card. "There's something you need to remember. Someone? Something or someone, but of huge significance."

"Like something I've forgotten?" I leaned forward to examine the woman on her throne, a scroll in her lap.

She frowned at the card, as though the woman in the illustration could answer the question. "Not forgotten, so much as something that's not in the forefront of your mind. It'll show up — they'll show up — when the time is right, though. Don't worry." Some more flips, and her smile turned wicked. "Okay, they really want me to talk about relationships right now. See . . . Two of Cups. There's attraction, there's awakening, there's a connection happening. Look at these two with their beer goggles on! But . . . oh no! Two of Swords! You're denying your feelings, Lulu, don't do that!"

"I'm not . . . denying . . ." Was I? But she wasn't listening.

"Three of Cups . . . so many cups for you, I love it. You have deep friendships, a sense of community, you love and are loved. And the best cup of all, in my opinion: Nine of Cups. Look at that smug guy! What a great card to end with. You've got exciting things coming. Make sure you not only celebrate your achievements, but appreciate them." She leaned back in her chair, the reading apparently over. She was silent for a long moment, running her fingers over the cards she'd laid out. "You put on such a positive face," she finally said quietly. "But I can tell you've had a shit time. Don't worry, okay? You are coming out of the dark, and the future is so bright." She laid a hand on the card she'd set aside, the one of the silhouetted figures on the road, and slid it across the table toward me. "Here. Take this with you. It'll help you remember."

"But don't you need this?"

She waved a hand. "Cards come and go. That's all part of it. I'll probably drop into a thrift store in a couple weeks and find a handful of old tarot cards for fifty cents. One of them will give me that feeling on the back of my neck, and I'll have a hundred and seventeen again."

I wanted to protest, but I couldn't take my eyes off the card. Off the blazing sunset the figures were walking toward. Or was it sunrise? "Thank you," I said instead.

It didn't take long for Summer to pack her stuff away and break down her tent. Then it was time for a round of hugs as we said goodbye. After all my weekends with them, my time with them was suddenly over. I'd been anticipating this for a while, but now I wasn't ready. These three had become my family. But their path now went one way, and mine went another.

"Will you be at the Maryland Ren Fest?" Sage asked. "It's not far from the Willow Creek one."

"I'm really not sure," I said. "I'll try to." But we both knew I didn't mean it. By the time the big Faire in Maryland started, I'd be back home in my condo, picking up the pieces of my former life and trying to piece together a new one.

Sage gave me another hug, this one so

long and maternal that tears sprang to my eyes. Mom hadn't hugged me like this since the day I'd gotten into the National Honor Society in high school. The last time I hadn't disappointed her. Then Sage held my face between her hands, like a grandmother about to impart wisdom even though she had maybe ten years on me at the most.

"You've got a lot ahead of you, but don't worry. And whatever you do . . ." Her voice was deadpan, her face giving nothing away. "Get a waterproof case for your phone."

I couldn't help but laugh. "I promise."

It was a lot of information to take back to the campsite with me. Thankfully it was a quiet night there too; the weather was perfect, and the firepit blazed. I sat outside under the twinkle of the awning lights, listening to the fire pop and crackle while Stacey made s'mores and Dex and Daniel idly argued with Todd and Frederick about who had seen the drunkest patron that day.

Later that night, as the fire died down and it was almost time for bed, I found myself studying the card that Summer had given me, half dozing, half dreaming.

"What's that?" Dex leaned over my shoulder to look at the card in my hand.

I tilted it toward him so he could see it

better. "Summer gave it to me after she read my cards this afternoon."

"Oh yeah? What did she tell you? You about to be rich and famous, Counselor?"

I snorted. "Doubt it. But she had some encouraging things to say about my path going forward. About maybe starting a business, which I'd been thinking about doing anyway. Something about relationships. A younger man. Stuff like that." I held my breath as those last words hung between us. We'd never given what was happening between us a name, and we'd certainly never discussed the potential for anything after I left the Faire. But the cards had made me wonder, and wondering had made me bold.

"Wow," he finally said. "Sounds like you have a lot to look forward to." His voice was flippant, and I got the message right away. There was nothing here to wonder about. I glanced up at him, but he wasn't looking at me; he was gazing at the few remaining embers of the fire as they winked out. He was smiling, but it was tight, like it didn't quite fit his face.

I rushed to keep the conversation moving, to recover from the awkwardness of asking for something I had no right to. "She said other stuff too. About leading with my heart instead of my head . . ."

"She may have a point there," he broke in. The smile on his face was still small, but this time it was genuine. "You do think an awful lot."

I pushed lightly on his shoulder, and he chuckled and wrapped an arm around me. "How I've gone through some bad stuff, but the future is looking bright." I held up the card. "She gave me this so I'd remember."

"Sounds like that was the important part, then." He stood up then, moving to the fire, pouring water on the remaining embers. He came back to me, offering a hand. "Come on. Bedtime."

Was I disappointed, as I let him pull me to my feet and take me to bed? Maybe a little. But I certainly wasn't going to turn him down. We didn't have much longer left, and I was going to enjoy every minute.

The future looked bright, Summer had said. That future just didn't involve Dex.

The closer it got to time to leave for Willow Creek, the more excited Stacey became.

"Going home!" she sang as we started packing things away in the motorhome for the trip to Maryland. Everyone was at the campsite; Frederick had returned to the fold since Patrick had moved on to the next

332

Faire. He gladly took the sofa in the motor-home, with the caveat that Dex and I not subject him to anything that would make him feel like a voyeur. This easy acceptance of Dex and me as a couple felt at odds with the knowledge that things between us were coming to an end. Then again, a relationship with an expiration date was Dex's specialty, after all. I'd been wrong to expect anything more than that. It wasn't fair to either of us.

Determined not to dwell on it, I focused on Stacey's excitement instead. It was infectious, but I noticed that not everyone was affected.

"Come on, Danny," Dex said one evening. "Aren't you stoked to be going to Willow Creek?" His grin said that he knew the answer to that question, and that it wasn't good.

Stacey giggled, her arm through Daniel's. "Oh, leave him alone." Her smile toward Dex was good-natured, friendlier than I'd seen her address him before. "You know how he gets."

Dex shook his head. "You have got to get over that, man."

"Get over what?" I glanced from Dex to Daniel. There was something going on here; there was a tension in Daniel that had nothing to do with schedules.

Dex leaned over to me, bumping his shoulder against mine, as if about to impart a secret. "He's scared of Stacey's mom."

"He is *not*!" But Stacey's laugh negated any seriousness about the statement.

Daniel clucked his tongue. "It's a long story."

"Wow," I deadpanned. "That's not a denial."

That brought a round of laughter, except from Daniel. It was hard to tell in the dark, but it sure looked like his cheeks were flushed.

"We stay with Stacey's parents while we're in Willow Creek," Frederick explained when Daniel didn't speak up.

"And while we're at the Maryland Ren Fest," Todd said. "So a little over three months, all told."

"That's a long time for y'all, isn't it?" After living this life with them, I couldn't comprehend staying anywhere for more than four to six weeks. Three months had to feel like an eternity.

Todd nodded. "It works out great. They have room in the backyard for the motorhome, so we can store it there. But there's plenty of guest rooms, so we all get to sleep in a real bed."

I gave a low whistle. "Luxury."

"I'm in Stacey's old room," Dex added with a vigorous nod. "I'm still mad she got rid of the pink canopy bed."

"I told you, I was a teenager when I had that!" Stacey giggled again, and this time I noticed the smile that passed between the two of them. Looked like Stacey was putting in the work of moving on from their weird situation. Good for her. "After college, I lived over the garage," she continued. "Daniel and I sleep up there."

"And Mrs. Lindholm makes us breakfast every morning," Todd added. "It's great. I don't know what Daniel's problem is."

"That's because you're not the one sleeping with her daughter," Frederick supplied, and the group all dissolved into laughter again. This time Daniel joined in.

"I have a fear of thin walls, okay?" He finally defended himself. "I can't help it. It's just . . . it's a thing."

"That does seem like a problem." I shared an amused glance with Dex, but I felt the enormity of the situation between us like a thick wall of plexiglass. When we got to Willow Creek, I'd be staying with Mitch and April while Dex would be with the others at Stacey's house. No more sharing the motorhome. No more us.

I laid my head on Dex's shoulder, and he put an arm around me, tugging me close. Neither of us spoke, letting the conversation continue around us. I wasn't ready for this to be over, but I didn't have a choice. Dex had made that clear. What was between us was finite, and time marched on. I had no right to ask for more.

TWENTY-ONE

Daniel wasn't kidding about being afraid of Stacey's mother. He'd tried to stall the trip up to Maryland by booking the band for Wednesday night at the local Irish bar, but when they realized they'd accidentally double-booked, the gig was canceled. So we'd packed up and started the caravan from the mountains of western Virginia to the rolling hills in Maryland on Tuesday, reaching our destination in the evening just as dusk began to streak the sky.

Once the motor home was safely parked in Stacey's backyard, I pulled out my stuff. An alarming amount of stuff — I'd accumulated a lot more than what had fit in my one weekender bag back in May. But skirts and bodices and chemises took up a lot more room than pantsuits. As I tossed my bags in the trunk of Dex's Challenger — he was running me across town to Mitch's house — Stacey approached, my laptop bag slung over her shoulder.

"Here you go." She handed me the leather bag and a slip of paper. "You've earned it back. And that's my phone number — text me when you're back online, okay?"

"Of course." I hefted the bag onto my shoulder. Had it always been this heavy? And I'd carried it around every day? When I'd handed it over to Stacey all those weeks ago, it had been like handing over a limb. I'd felt the loss so keenly back then. I'd expected to be relieved to get it back. Eager to restart my life. But I felt neither of those things. The laptop felt like a relic of an old life — one I wasn't sure I missed.

The silence between Dex and me was heavy as he drove me to Mitch's house. At a stoplight he reached for my hand, holding tightly, and I squeezed back with everything I had. But when the light turned green, he dropped it without a word. When I cleared my throat, he threw a sharp glance my way, expecting me to speak. But I had nothing to say, and neither did he, until he killed the engine in the driveway. Mitch was waiting for us on the front porch. Illuminated in the porch light, he looked like a caricature of a stern father, but he broke into a smile when he saw us.

"Malone!" Dex grinned at him as he got

out of the car, all good cheer and bro-like attitude. They clasped hands and hugged like dudes: bringing it in with a sharp clap on each other's backs.

"How's it going, man?" Mitch threw him a grin and didn't wait for an answer before turning his attention to me as I got out of the car.

"There she is." I was barely upright before he caught me up in a hug that lifted me off my feet.

"Hey, big guy." I closed my eyes and buried my head in his shoulder, fighting hard against a sob that came out of nowhere. I'd come home. Friends come and go in this life, but there really was nothing like family. Someone who'd known you since you were a kid, who loved you down to the core. That shit was rare, and I had it in my cousin.

Mitch set me down and took hold of me by the shoulders, stooping a little to peer into my eyes. "How you doing?"

I dashed the tears from my cheeks — why was I crying? — and managed a smile. "Good," I said. "I'm good." And I meant it.

"You look good. Rested." He shook his head with a frown. "You should have done this ages ago."

"What, torpedoed my career and run off to join the Renaissance Faire?"

"Exactly." He looked over at Dex then, who'd popped the trunk on the car and was setting my bags in the driveway. "She behave herself?"

"Yeah." Dex coughed into his fist, but he rallied quick. "She was . . . uh. She was good."

My first instinct was to smirk and say something filled with innuendo, but Mitch was taking my bags into the house, leaving me with Dex in the driveway. The night was growing dark, and I couldn't see him too well in the light that came from the front porch. And here came that silence again. I didn't know what to say, and apparently neither did he.

I finally broke the silence. "Thanks. For the ride. For . . ."

"Yeah," he said quickly. "No problem." He looked to the open front door, where light from inside spilled out through the screen door onto the porch, then back at me. His hands were shoved in his front pockets and he rocked on his heels. We'd somehow turned into two of the most awkward teenagers you ever saw.

Finally I blew out a breath. "This is dumb. You're here for a while. I'm sure I'm here for a while. We're going to run into each other."

His eyes lit up. "Sure. Yeah. Of course! It's not like you're leaving tomorrow or anything." A cloud of uncertainty flitted across his face. "Right?"

"Right." I nodded firmly. "I'll be around. I'll probably even stop by the Faire. You know, see Mitch in action." I gestured behind me toward the house.

"Good. That's good. Yeah, you should come by and see us. You never see our show anymore." A joke: this was good. Maybe we could salvage this awkwardness.

"As long as you play 'Whiskey in the Jar' for me."

"Always do." His smile was crooked, and he rocked forward on his toes as though he were going to lean in toward me, but another glance toward the front door changed his mind. "Anyway." He gestured toward the car. "I should get back."

"Yeah." I fell back a step, fighting to not let disappointment show on my face. Apparently, it was one thing for us to be a couple in the confines of the Renaissance Faire, but we were back in the real world. Kissing me goodbye in my cousin's driveway was out of the question.

I waved lamely as he backed his car down to the street, and then stood rooted to the spot until his taillights faded in the distance.

I recognized this moment; it felt the same as when I'd pitched my phone in the laundry wenches' tub. I was about to exit one life and begin another. As scary and uncertain as it had been to go on the road with Stacey, Daniel, Dex, and the rest, somehow coming off the road felt scarier.

But it was time. I picked up my laptop case and headed into the house. Time to say goodbye to the Ren Faire and go back to real life.

I should have known better.

No sooner had I closed the front door behind me than Mitch gave me another hug. "Thank God you're here." His dramatic sigh of relief stirred my hair.

"Thanks for letting me stay," I said. "You're right, I need some time to figure out what I'm doing next. I —"

"No. I mean, yeah, of course. Stay as long as you want. Mi guest room es su guest room. But I really need your help with something."

"Of course," I said immediately. "Anything you need." Wasn't that the least I could do?

His smile was wide, and oh no. What had I just agreed to? He clapped his hands together in finality as the water running in the kitchen turned off. "Awesome. I'll call Simon and —"

"No." We both turned at the voice in the doorway. Mitch's girlfriend, April, leaned in the archway that separated the dining room from the living room, wiping her hands on a kitchen towel. "Mitch, she just got here. For God's sake, let her take a breath before you start in on her."

"I'm not starting in!" He held up defensive hands. "But it's already Tuesday night. Faire starts on Saturday, so we're gonna need to —" But he fell silent at the look in her narrowed eyes. "Ugh. Fine." He turned back to me. "Lu, you want a beer or something?"

I looked from him to April and back again. "I have a feeling I'm gonna need one."

"C'mere." April tossed the towel over her shoulder and reached an arm out to me, sliding it across my shoulders in a sideways hug. "I've got some of that craft cider you like in the fridge. Come in and sit down."

"Bless you." I followed her into the tidy kitchen. The lights in here cast a warm glow on the freshly wiped-down counters, and the dishwasher hummed its way through its cycle. A small dinette set that I recognized from Mitch's old apartment was tucked into one corner. Next to it, an elderly black-and-white dog snoozed in a plush dog bed. I knew how he felt; it was cozy in here.

I got two ciders out of the fridge while April took glasses out of a nearby green cabinet.

"Are you hungry?" April slid a glass across the kitchen island toward me. "There's leftovers in the fridge. Or we have plenty of cold cuts if you'd like a sandwich."

I shook my head as I popped the lids on the ciders, sticking the bottle opener back onto the door of the fridge. "I'm good. More tired than anything. We were on the road most of the day."

"I can't even imagine. Mitch said you were living in a motorhome the past couple months? Like, with a little kitchen and everything?" We took our drinks over to the dinette table. April took the chair next to the dog, running the toes of one foot over his back. He didn't wake up.

I nodded. "It took some getting used to, but it wasn't that bad." My mind chose that moment to play a flashback of that little kitchen. Dex had bent me over that kitchen counter, his hands flat on my back, trailing up and down my spine while he thrust into me, his voice and his cock both thick with passion. *So good . . . God, Lulu, you feel so fucking good . . .*

I cleared my throat and took a cooling sip

of my drink. "Cute dog."

That was a good subject change. April smiled down at him. "Murray's a good boy. He's an old man, so he spends a lot of time sleeping. But he's great to hang out with if you're reading or watching TV."

"Then we'll definitely be buddies." Murray snorted in his sleep, and April and I shared a smile. "Thanks again for letting me stay. Are you sure you're okay with it? I feel like Mitch kind of forced me on you."

April tsked at me. "Don't be silly, Lulu. You're family." She raised her glass to me, and I raised mine back in a grateful salute. "Speaking of family, Grandma Malone's doing fine. We've talked to her every Saturday morning since you've been gone."

I practically slumped to the counter in relief. "Thank you. I mean, they can take care of themselves, I have no doubt, but —"

"Grandparents are fragile. Especially once they get up there in age. I get it." April nodded. "But everything's good there. We thought we'd call on Friday this week, since you'll be here too. Not to mention, Faire starting on Saturday . . . things get busy around here on the weekends."

"Perfect." I took another sip from my glass. I couldn't wait to talk to Grandma again.

"She's pretty great," April said. "I haven't spent much time with her yet, but she seems to be good with Mitch and me being together."

I tsked at her. "Of course she is. You're family." Hadn't she just said the same thing to me?

April's gaze went to the table, and her hands turned her glass around in a revolution or two. "I appreciate that." She raised her eyebrows at me, cracking a smile. "She's also very excited about some photos of men in kilts you seem to have promised her. I think she's a little jealous of your travels."

I groaned, my head falling back on my neck, but I couldn't help but laugh at the thought. "I'll tell her all about it on Friday."

"She misses you." April held up a defensive hand as I groaned again. "I'm not trying to guilt you. Just . . . it seems like you're really close with her."

"We are." My condo was about an hour away from my grandparents' house, and even though I called as much as I could, I didn't visit them nearly enough. Maybe part of this new life I was building could build in more time with them too.

April and I sat in companionable silence for a few minutes while the dishwasher did its thing and Murray snored at our feet —

two sounds that should be combined and put on one of those relaxation apps. I slowly drank my cider and let contentment seep into my bones. It had been a long day. A long summer.

"What do you need to do next?" April asked. "Do you need any help with anything?"

Right. Plans. I sat up a little straighter. "Good question. I'll fire up my laptop tomorrow, start checking out some recruitment websites. Get a new phone soon. I guess that's a good place to start."

She raised her eyebrows. "I'm impressed. You didn't start looking for work while you were away? You really did unplug."

I gave a thin laugh. "Stacey let me update my résumé, but then she took my laptop away from me for the rest of the trip. She wasn't going to risk the wrath of Mitch."

April snorted. "God forbid."

Speak of the devil, Mitch appeared in the kitchen, rummaging around in the fridge before joining us at the table with his beer. "Now?" He turned puppy dog eyes to April. "Now can I ask her?"

April was able to meet his eyes squarely for roughly three seconds before giving a short laugh and shaking her head. "Fine. I assume you already called Simon?"

"Yep." Now he turned the puppy dog eyes to me. "You know how we do the human chess match every year, right?"

"Yes?" I answered carefully. "People on a field that's made to look like a chessboard, right? All kinds of fights going on?" I'd seen this last summer when I'd brought my grandparents to the Faire. Grandma had loved watching Mitch pretend to fight. Grandpa had wondered how he didn't hurt himself with his giant sword.

"Exactly. We've been rehearsing the fights all summer, that's going great. But we lost a couple of our pawns."

"Your . . . pawns." Maybe it was the cider going to my head, but this was a ridiculous conversation.

"Two of the pawns," April confirmed with a nod. "You know, like, the chess pieces? They don't do much, just move up a square or two."

"I'm familiar." I was terrible at chess, but I at least knew that much.

"Yeah," Mitch continued like this was a perfectly normal conversation. "Erin and Suzanne, two of our high school kids. Apparently, their parents decided to schedule a trip to see their grandparents in California this summer and they leave tomorrow. Tomorrow!" Disgust was clear in his voice;

how dare anyone consider anything more important than this Faire he helped put on every year.

April laid a hand on his arm. "Different people have different priorities," she said, for what was probably the fourth time this week.

"No, I get it and that's fine! But when did they tell me? Last week." He shook his head. "It's like they didn't connect the fact that they were going off on this trip with being gone the first weekend of Faire. So now . . ."

"Now you're down two pawns." I nodded as the picture snapped into focus, crystal clear. "You need me to be a pawn in the chess match."

He clasped his hands together, like he was praying. "Just for this weekend, I promise! They'll be back for the rest of Faire." Here came the puppy dog eyes again. "I know you have a lot to do, and whatever help you need during the week, I am there. You know I'm there."

"I know." I shrugged. "Sure, why not."

"Awesome! Thank you, thank you so much. You have no idea . . ."

"Yes, thank you," April said, as Mitch strode out of the room, pulling his phone out of his pocket. "He's been begging me all week to do it, even though I told him

349

there's no way in hell."

"Are you sure? I mean, he did say they need two pawns."

"Nope." April shook her head firmly. "You doing it gets me off the hook. And Mitch. It's Simon's job to find the second one."

"Who's Simon?"

"My brother-in-law. He's married to my sister, Emily."

"Oh, okay." I was pretty sure I'd met her last summer, but I'd been interrupted by a buzzing phone a lot then too. Memories of that day that didn't involve Mitch or my grandparents were sketchy.

"Simon runs the whole Faire, so technically all of it's his job, but Mitch helps out where he can. If nothing else, Simon can probably wrangle Emily into doing it." She finished her cider off and set down the glass while out toward the front of the house the front door opened and closed.

"Hey, did Lulu get here yet?"

"In here," April called. Her smile warmed as the newcomer appeared in the doorway. "You remember my daughter, Caitlin."

"I do. Hey, Caitlin." I turned in my chair to greet April's daughter. Almost nineteen and home from college for the summer, she looked just like her mother. Though her curly brown hair was a little less tamed, she shared the same dark blue eyes as April. We'd met over the holidays when she and April had joined the Malone clan for Christmas dinner, and we'd hit it off pretty quick. She was a nice kid.

She greeted me with a cheerful wave, leaning in the doorway. "Hey. So are you doing the pawn thing?"

I laughed at the terminology. "I guess I am."

"Oh, thank God." She slumped against the doorway in exaggerated relief. "I was about to be drafted."

"Hey, you could still do it." Mitch nudged her shoulder as he came into the kitchen, sticking his phone into his back pocket. "Simon hasn't found a second yet." He settled himself against the kitchen island. It was getting a little crowded in here, but this was the kind of kitchen you wanted to hang out in. The soul of the home.

Caitlin made a *pfft* sound. "I'm busy enough," she said. "I'm doing three sets with the Gilded Lilies. Three! Do you know how much singing that is?"

"No, but I bet you're gonna tell me." Mitch grinned as he leaned his elbows on the counter.

Caitlin's attempt at outrage was belied by her smile. "It's a lot!"

Mitch clucked his tongue in mock sympathy. "No one appreciates you."

"Oh, shut up." But she was laughing as she moved to the fridge for a bottle of water, bumping Mitch with her shoulder as she went. I covered my smile with my hand as I met April's eyes. I'd wondered how Mitch was going to deal with being a de facto stepfather when he and April moved in together. I should have known he'd handle Caitlin much like he handled the younger cousins in our family. More fun uncle and less authoritarian.

Sure enough, the true authoritarian spoke up. "This family is providing exactly one pawn, and Lulu's got that covered." April turned to me as she stood. "Come on, let me show you to the guest room. I'm sure you'd like to get settled."

The guest room was ginormous. Probably not by normal standards: it was a cozy room, barely big enough for the full-size bed and dresser. But after two months of the crowded closeness of living in a motorhome, the room was like a palace. And it was all mine.

The meager possessions I'd amassed during my time away barely filled up three dresser drawers. I left the two decks of tarot cards on top of the dresser, the tiger's-eye and lapis stones set carefully beside them, and the little faux tarot card/art print balanced on top of the decks. I already missed my fortune-tellers and wasn't quite ready for that part of my life to be over.

My collection of period garb hung safely in the closet, making it all much easier to access than when it was all stashed away in duffel bags. Which was fortunate, since apparently the Renaissance Faire wasn't done with me yet. Tomorrow Mitch and I would be going over what it meant to be a pawn in a human chess match, so real life could wait a few more days.

The small guest bed was barely long enough for me, but it felt luxurious. I had a sheet *and* blankets, all to myself, with no cat to fight me for the pillow. No kilted guitar player hogging the covers and throwing his leg over mine when we slept. This was normal life, I reminded myself. I should be glad to be back.

And I was. But I also keenly felt what I left behind. And I was thankful that my vacation wasn't quite over.

TWENTY-TWO

I knelt in the grass, a pawn on a white square of the chess field. One hand was wrapped around a long wooden staff, its point stuck in the grass next to me, my weapon at the ready. My long green skirts puddled around me, and the new boots I'd bought that morning pinched my feet. But I maintained a stern expression. A warrior's pose, even. After all, I may have just been a pawn, but I was ready for battle.

Next to me, one of my fellow pawns sighed. "This is bullshit."

"Shhh." My lips quivered as I suppressed a laugh. I glanced over at April, who knelt on a green square. She was dressed in a similar style to me, but her dress was red, with a green and blue plaid sash. A quiver of arrows was buckled to her back with leather straps, and she wore a longbow diagonally across her body. She'd tried to fire some of those arrows last night in the backyard. It hadn't gone well. Thankfully, her weapon was just for show.

April glanced over at me, her expression tight. "I'm going to kill Emily," she said. "Too busy doing other things to be in the chess match, my ass. This is her way of making me participate."

"She's the worst," I deadpanned. I knew April better than her sister, so by default I was on April's side.

"I swear, if Mitch makes one joke about me being on my knees, he's sleeping in the garage for a month."

Now I couldn't hold in my laugh. "He wouldn't dare."

One of the other pawns shushed us, loudly, and I remembered that we were theoretically performing. We exchanged surreptitious eye rolls but fell silent as the chess match began.

The field was full of people portraying the pieces on the chessboard, and the benches that ringed the chessboard were full of even more people — patrons here to see the performance. April and I were white pawns, and as Mitch played the white knight, he was behind us somewhere. Which was good because I would have trouble keeping a straight face otherwise.

Everything went exactly as Mitch had described. There were two cast members in garb who "played" the chess game, directing the pieces where to go. The "game" was planned out in advance, and my role was simple: I would be the second white piece to move, forward one square. That was it. After everything I'd done for the past couple months, this was a piece of cake.

My turn came, and I stood up, doing my best to walk with a soldier's purpose toward my assigned square. The other pieces on my side cheered like I'd scored a victory. I kept my face stony, channeling my inner warrior, and lifted my staff in salute. After that my main part in the match was over. Now all I had to do was scurry to the sides of the board when it was time for one piece to fight another for a square, and cheer for the white side. I remembered that part well enough from being a spectator, but it sure felt different from this side of the chessboard.

It was a lot of scurrying — out and back, out and back. After the third time, I started getting winded wearing this outfit.

"No one told me there'd be running involved," I panted as April and I collapsed next to each other in the grass on the sidelines, attempting to catch our breath while on the field a kid from our side in an ersatz

Robin Hood outfit battled a pirate in black leather.

"No shit. Where is he?" April craned her neck, looking around. "I'm going to kill him."

"You two having fun?" As if on cue, Mitch appeared, crouching down behind us, the point of his enormous sword buried in the grass. It wasn't his turn to fight yet, and he spoke quietly enough to us that he didn't have to use his ridiculous accent.

"You said this was only for one weekend, right?" April threw a narrow-eyed glance over her shoulder at him.

He nodded. "The other girls will be back next week. Hey, at least you didn't have to learn a fight or anything." He chucked April under the chin. "Have to say, babe, you're looking good out there."

April's eyes stayed narrowed. "Thanks." Her voice was flat.

Then Mitch made a poor life choice. "Yeah. On your knees like that, I can see clear down your —"

"Oh, look, time to go!" I grabbed April's arm and hauled her bodily to her feet and back to our places.

"Told ya," she muttered. "Garage. One month minimum."

After the match ended and the white side

was declared the winner, April stalked up to the pirate in black leather, who was off on the sidelines, shrugging on a red leather vest.

"You better be grateful." She poked him in the chest, and he fell back a step, his eyes wide.

"Oh, trust me, milady, I am more grateful than you can ever imagine." His smile made me wonder if he was flirting with her — didn't he know she was with Mitch? — but when he placed his left hand flat on his chest I caught the glint of a gold ring. Ah. Not flirting, then. He made his way over to me, April walking beside him with her arms crossed.

"Louisa, I presume?" The pirate held a hand out to me, his hazel kohl-lined eyes twinkling, his smile just as flirtatious as it had been with April.

I placed my hand in his, giving it a squeeze. "May as well call me Lulu. Everyone else does."

His grip was firm, squeezing for a moment before letting go. "Simon Graham," he said, dropping the accent and the flirty pirate personality like a mask falling from his face. "Listen, thanks again for stepping in. Both of you. We were really in a bind here, and —"

358

I heard Stacey's high-pitched squeal from behind me just before she all but tackled me with a hug. "Look at you two! Performing in the chess match!"

"You were amazing!" Another woman came trotting behind her. She wore a blue dress over a white chemise and a crown of red roses in her dark curly hair. "I had a hard time believing it wasn't real."

"Don't give me that shit, Emily." But April accepted the hug from her younger sister — now that they stood together the family resemblance was striking. Those two and Caitlin: the genetics were strong in that family.

"Oh, come on." She grinned at April. "You had fun. Admit it."

"I will not."

"You both did such a great job!" Stacey moved to April — her turn for a tackle-hug.

April's smile was tolerant as she accepted the enthusiastic embrace. "Don't get too excited," she said. "I moved exactly one square and then sat there until the end."

"Exactly," I said. "It wasn't like it was hard."

"Still looked good out there." The voice at my ear sent a spark down my spine. I turned my head to see Dex right there, at my left shoulder, and my insides went all mushy. It had only been four days since I'd seen him, but after spending so long in such close proximity it seemed like forever.

As our eyes met, his softened as his gaze darted over my face. Maybe he missed me too. "Hey." It was a breath of a word.

"Hey." I seemed to have lost my voice as well. How could I have ever denounced kilts? Because Dex looked mouthwatering in his.

"Looking good, Counselor." He slid an arm around my corseted waist, tugging me closer to him. "Adding performer to your résumé?"

"Why not?" I embraced him too, my hand flat on his back. I'd missed this. Missed him. Ugh, this was bad news. I pushed down those feelings and kept things light, the way I knew he liked them. "I thought I might go see if they need help at the joust next."

He laughed. God, I wished he hadn't laughed. It was making it very difficult to remember that things between us were all but over. "Those knights won't know what hit 'em." He touched his forehead to mine, an intimate gesture that wasn't a kiss, but also wasn't something I was going to do to Simon, whom I'd just met.

"You watched the chess match, huh?" My voice had gone all husky against my will.

"Sure did. Stacey said you were in it. You think I was going to miss that?"

My heart thumped as I took in his expression. He seemed genuinely pleased to see me. Genuinely pleased to have his arm around me. There was something very real about all this.

"What are you up to now?" His voice was low and dangerous, as though suggesting we should slip behind a nearby stage for a quickie. For the life of me I couldn't say why that would be a bad idea.

I licked my lips, and his eyes tracked the movement. "I have another chess match later this afternoon, but I'm free till then. What's up?"

"Come on. We've got a show in twenty minutes. Your turn to see me perform."

I tsked at him as we started toward their stage. "I've seen your show plenty of times."

"Yeah, but not lately. You were too busy with those witchcraft people."

"Fortune-tellers," I corrected.

"Close enough."

We bantered as we walked, Dex's arm around my shoulders and mine around his back, and as we skirted the edge of the chess field I caught Mitch's expression. He looked stunned, only blinking when April tugged on his arm. He turned his head to talk to

Stacey, but I was too far away to hear their conversation.

I had a feeling I was going to get an earful later. The idea of it was hilarious. I was five years older than Mitch; what was he going to say to me?

"What the hell are you doing with Dex MacLean?"

Mitch had managed to hold it in the rest of the day; he hadn't said a word to me during the second chess match, and had even kept up small talk in his truck on the way home. But once April had gone into their bedroom to shower, and Caitlin — whose voice was indeed raspy from singing in her a cappella quintet all day — was doing the same in the hall bathroom, that left Mitch and me alone in the kitchen.

At least he'd handed me a bottle of water before he started in on me.

"Nothing." I took the cap off the bottle and drank about half of it in one go. It was hot out there, and I never drank enough water during the day.

He frowned, leaning against the kitchen counter with his own bottle of water. "I mean, I like the guy, but as far as seeing him with my cousin . . . You know that guy is bad news, right?"

"For God's sake, not you too." I thumped the plastic bottle onto the counter. "Are you talking about what happened with him and Stacey?"

"Oh." Mitch blinked. "You know about that?"

"I traveled with these people for two months. There's not a lot about them I don't know."

"Good. Then you know that he —"

"I know that he went out and picked up coffee for the two of us before Faire every morning," I shot back. I could feel a rant coming on and I didn't try to stop it. My blood was hot, and I'd had enough Dex slander for one summer. "I know that he loves his family more than just about anything. I know that he has a great sense of humor, and I know that I've really liked getting to know him."

I sighed and leaned on the kitchen island, picking up my water again. "I know that he doesn't do relationships, and I know that once I'm back to my old life I'll probably never see him again." I took a long swig of water, swallowing hard at the lump that had suddenly appeared in my throat. "I also know that his family doesn't expect much from him, but there's more to him than they give him credit for." I stared hard at Mitch.

"I dunno. Maybe you know what that's like."

We had a staring contest there at the kitchen island, my cousin and me. I knew he caught my meaning: he and Dex had some things in common. In a family of over-achievers, myself included until very recently, Mitch was the black sheep. The one grandchild without an advanced degree. The gym teacher. The meathead, if you asked my asshole brothers.

Mitch was the one to blink first. "Okay. Just . . . I don't want to see you get hurt. He and Stacey . . ."

"What happened between him and Stacey wasn't his fault," I said softly. "Sometimes two people aren't right for each other. Doesn't make him not right for anyone."

He closed his eyes and sighed, his head dropping in a nod. "Okay." He came around the island and wrapped an arm around me, pulling me close. "Okay," he said into my hair. "I'm sorry."

"It's okay." I hugged him back, but not for long. "Let go of me." I pushed ineffectually at him. "You've been outside all day. You're all sweaty and you stink."

But I should have known better; that only turned his embrace into a bear hug while I struggled and giggled.

"Ahhh, you're probably right." He let me go with a kiss on top of my head.

"Of course I'm right. You smell terrible."

"That too." He gave me a punch on the shoulder. "I'm going to go barge in on April's shower. She loves when I do that."

I laughed and finished my water before heading to my room. I unlaced and tugged myself out of the layers of my costume, leaving only my chemise for the run across the hall when it was my turn for the shower. While I waited I picked up the stones on the dresser. The lapis and tiger's-eye flashed blue and brown in the lamplight as they clicked together in my palm.

"Speaking my truth," I said softly to the stones. I was getting good at that.

Twenty-Three

I'd put it off long enough.

I spent the full weekend at the Faire, a place that had become as much like home as my grandparents' house. But on Monday morning I poured myself a very large cup of coffee and took it out onto April's back deck. Murray followed me, wandering out into the backyard for a prolonged sniff session, followed by a morning snooze in the sunshine. Mitch had gone to the gym early, and when he came back we were going out to get me a new phone. But I had some time, so I settled myself at the round wrought-iron table and fired up my laptop.

And then I waited, while it did roughly four hundred rounds of updates. It had been a while since I'd had it on, after all. But that was fine; I was in no real hurry to get back to real life.

After logging into my personal email, I spent most of that first cup of coffee deleting spam emails. It took a second cup of coffee for me to tweak my résumé and upload it to the three business networking sites I had signed up for back in the day. One of those sites had a handy looking-for-work icon that I could attach to my profile picture. I was reluctant to do that — it would make everything too official — but I put on my big-girl panties and clicked OK. There. I was officially back in the world and looking to connect.

I wasn't excited about it at all.

Getting a new phone was fun, at least. It was blue and had twice as much storage and a better screen than my old one. The salesman assured me that once I activated it, all the data from my old phone would be saved. I wasn't sure how much of that data I wanted; I was most likely in for an afternoon of deleting contacts and old texts.

"You sure you don't want a better case for that?" Mitch asked as we got back to the house. "I dunno, maybe something waterproof?"

"Very funny," I tossed over my shoulder on the way to my room.

It took some time for the phone to activate, but once it did it was just like the old one, down to the wallpaper image of me on graduation day, receiving my law degree.

Opening up the text message app was like cracking open a time capsule of unpleasantness; I wasted no time in deleting all the messages, even the unread ones. It was clean slate time.

My voicemails were just as bad. There were weeks of new voice messages, which apparently only stopped when the voicemail box filled up. There were three from my mother, which I deleted with only a slight wince, and the rest were from the law office. A few from the main number, and more that were from Bud Stone's direct line. Those all went in the trash too — I wasn't going to need any of those. I felt queasy as I deleted them, but once I emptied the trash, clearing the messages for good, the queasiness went away.

The first thing I did was text Stacey. **Back online! I promise to keep this phone safe from water damage.** I added a couple of droplet emojis for good measure. After hitting Send I added her to my contacts. That felt good — more friends in my contact list, fewer work commitments.

My phone chirped almost immediately, and I scooped it up, impressed. Stacey must have been right by her phone. But it wasn't a text from Stacey; it was a notification from one of the networking sites I'd updated this morning. **Imogen Dunbrowski wants to connect with you. Click here to . . .**

Shit. I dropped the phone onto the bed before I did something stupid like open that notification. Imogen Dunbrowski, the only woman whose name was on the building of the firm I'd just quit. The one person there I'd admired and wanted to emulate, but had never managed to work with. Why was she contacting me? Had this been Bud Stone's next move after I failed to answer his voice mails — send her after me? And why now, two months later?

After a cleansing breath, I opened the notification. I clicked on it, bringing up her profile on the networking site. **Imogen Dunbrowski, Founding Partner, The Dunbrowski Group. P.A.**

That was new. It only took a couple quick Google searches to find out what had happened while I was gone. My old firm of Stone, Prince, Rogers & Dunbrowski was Stone, Prince & Rogers now, and Imogen had struck out on her own. Damn. Good for her.

In that case . . . I clicked Connect on the request and pulled up her new firm's website on my laptop for a little recon. Five minutes later my new phone rang, and my stomach leapt into my throat. It was still only Monday . . . things were happening faster than I wanted them to.

"Louisa Malone." Oh, God. I sounded like a lawyer again. I hated it. Should I run a bath and throw this phone away too?

"Louisa. Imogen Dunbrowski here."

"Hi," I tried to say, but my throat had completely closed up. I cleared my throat and tried again. "Hi, Ms. Dunbrowski. What can I do for you?"

"Call me Imogen, please." Her chuckle on the other end lowered my blood pressure a few points. "That was quite the disappearing act you pulled. I tried calling you after you . . . ah, quit. But your phone went right to voicemail."

"Yeah. I'm sure it did." I mentally replayed every conversation I had ever had with Imogen. It was a short list, most of them taking place at the annual holiday party in fifteen-second increments.

"I left you a couple voicemails, but when I didn't hear back I figured you weren't interested. But then I saw your profile on the networking site, and that you hadn't updated it. I sent you a friend request there, but of course didn't hear back on that, either."

"Yeah. I've been . . . I've been off-grid for a little bit." I winced as I said it. It sounded better than *I ran off to join the Renaissance Faire,* but not by much.

She chuckled. "That's what I figured. Now that you're back, I thought maybe it was time to try you again." She cleared her throat. "I'll get right to the point. Bud Stone is an ass. I'd been planning to open my own firm for months, and when you got back from that deposition in North Carolina, I was going to ask if you wanted to come with me."

"With you?" I repeated dumbly. My nervous energy got the best of me and I started pacing my room, phone stuck to my ear. I scooped up the lapis and tiger's-eye stones from my dresser, to have something to fidget with.

"That's right. I'd tried to claim you from the start, you know. I thought you'd be a great asset to our contracts section, but those dicks in litigation got you first. And apparently you're so good at what you do that they wouldn't let you go."

"Really." I'd thought that after doing that one project for her, she'd been so unimpressed that she'd never brought me on anything else after that. This was a total shift in perspective.

"Tell me, Louisa. Why did you get into law? Do you like litigation?"

371

"God, no." I shifted the stones in my hand, looking down at them as they clicked together. Grounding. Clarity. Truth. I wasn't sure what I was going to say when I started speaking, but then words started pouring out. "When I was in college, a developer tried to take my grandparents' house. The family house we've had for generations. They got a good lawyer and fought it, and that's why they still have their home. All I could think was: How many elderly people out there don't have good lawyers? That's why I decided to go to law school. I wanted to be that good lawyer for other people's grandparents."

Imogen was silent for a long moment, and I clutched the stones harder. This was the truth, one that I'd never told anyone at the firm. Maybe I should have. But I'd been so busy trying to impress everyone, to make partner, that I'd forgotten what had brought me there from the start.

"I think you'll be a great fit here," she said. "I want to develop a full-service, boutique firm, focusing on client development and loyalty instead of billing them to death. I'll be honest: the money won't be what the partners are making at Stone, Prince & Rogers. But —"

"I was never going to be partner there

anyway," I interrupted, too excited to let her finish her sentence. I set down the stones and took up one of the tarot decks, tucking my phone between my ear and shoulder so I could shuffle the cards, working off some more of this energy. "I love that idea. Are you planning to focus on elder law?"

"Elder law, estate planning . . . maybe some real estate. I have some relationships with real estate agents and title agencies. Have you done work in either of those areas?"

"I haven't." My heart sank as I said it, but I couldn't lie. I sat down on the edge of the bed and let the cards drop down beside me. Oh well. It had been a good thought.

But Imogen didn't care. "Eh, that's fine. Bud always said you were an extremely quick study. I bet I can get you up to speed in no time, if that's something you're interested in doing."

"I am. I really am."

"Perfect. Are you back in town?"

"Not yet." That was the question, wasn't it? Technically I could go home tomorrow. Mitch would be happy to drive me. But I wasn't ready. Even with this job offer that had all but fallen into my lap, there was so much here I wasn't ready to say goodbye to. So many people I wasn't ready to say goodbye to. The MacLeans and Stacey were here through the end of October; there was no way I could stall that long. But there were only three more weekends of the Willow Creek Renaissance Faire. "I'm out of town helping family." Technically that wasn't a lie — hadn't I bailed Mitch out by playing a pawn over the weekend? "But I should be back around the end of August." Okay, more like mid-August, but nothing wrong with giving myself a buffer. I was going to need some time to mentally transition back to real life and the workforce after all this.

"Why don't we call it September. You can start after Labor Day. I'll be in touch with details in the meantime. We could even get a start on you working remotely if you want. How does that sound?"

How could I answer that? "It sounds amazing. Thank you so much, Ms. Dunbrowski. This is —"

"Louisa, didn't I just tell you to call me Imogen?" Her voice was dry, but I could detect the humor underneath.

I smiled back. "Then you can call me Lulu." Because this new direction in my career wasn't Louisa's doing. Speaking my truth, guided by tarot cards and crystals? It was all Lulu.

I hung up in a daze. Had that just happened? I dropped the phone to the bed, where it jostled the deck of tarot cards next to me. Cards started sliding off the stack, and one landed faceup. The King of Wands. The third card from that very first reading Sasha had done for me: the card that denoted my future. An older figure in my life, to do with business. A mentor.

"I'll be damned," I said aloud. That described Imogen Dunbrowski to a T, didn't it? Masculine energy, my ass. The future was female.

My phone beeped, and I groaned. I wasn't sure how much more life-changing news I could take in one day. But this was a text from Stacey, which had arrived while I was on the phone. **Welcome back to the land of the connected! We're going to Jackson's this afternoon for happy hour. You in? I miss you!**

I smiled. Okay, maybe having my phone back wasn't so bad after all. My eyes were glued on the word *we*. I was a thirty-seven-year-old woman; I was going to play it cool. But damn if I didn't hope that Dex was part of that *we*. If I only had three more weeks with him, I didn't want to waste a minute of it.

■ ■ ■ ■

"You have a new job?" Stacey squealed. "Just like that?"

"Just like that!" Her enthusiasm was contagious, and I found myself laughing.

"I have to say . . ." Mitch slid a draft cider in front of me, and another in front of April. He knew how to take care of us. "I really thought you'd have a harder time. Like, I dunno. Take longer than ten minutes to get a job." He peered at me. "And you're sure it's not the same old bullshit?"

I nodded firmly. "It's not the same old bullshit. I promise."

"Hey, Mitch!" someone called from across the bar. "Karaoke's starting, you in?"

"Hell yeah, I am!" He looked around the table, eyebrows raised. "Who else?" He pointed around the table, to a general chorus of denial.

Simon shook his head firmly. "No, thank you." He took a sip of his beer and leaned back in his chair, one arm slung over the back of his wife's chair.

Emily, for her part, snorted at the thought. "Nope, we're out." She clinked her beer glass against Simon's.

"Absolutely not." April shut down that notion immediately, and I shook my head with a grin when Mitch pointed at me.

"No way in hell," Todd said.

Frederick backed him up. "Gonna let you amateurs handle it for a while."

Mitch shook his head in disgust. "None of you are any fun." And he was off, threading his way through the crowd.

Next to me, April took a sip of her cider. "As long as it's not 'Mr. Brightside.' "

"It better not be." Emily gave a mock shudder from across the table. Then she addressed me. "Sorry, Lulu. Your cousin isn't the best singer."

I didn't mind a little bit of Mitch slander. "Don't I know it." I flipped open the menu. "Do we need to get another round before happy hour ends?" My cider might get a little warm, but I was willing to make the sacrifice for happy hour prices.

Emily shook her head. "Happy hour never ends here. That's what's great about this place." She looked pointedly around the place. It was dingy, furnished in a dark wood aesthetic that said 1970s dive bar. The kind of place that seemed to have a layer of smoke in the rafters even though nobody had smoked a cigarette inside in years.

"Point taken. How about the food? What's good here?" I glanced around the table, noticing I was the only one with a menu open. Was I the only one who needed one?

April shrugged. "Basically everything. Pizza's good, so are the burgers. Mozzarella sticks are a must, if you're into that sort of thing."

"Who the hell isn't into fried cheese?" I clucked my tongue. "Monsters, that's who."

It was a typical night out at a dive bar with a group of friends. Mitch and his karaoke buddies entertained us with classic rock standards, and everyone moved around our pushed-together tables as conversations ebbed and flowed. It took way too long to find myself sitting near Dex.

"There you are." He plopped his bacon cheeseburger and half-eaten fries in their plastic basket onto the table across from me, then plopped himself into the chair. "You been avoiding me?"

"Of course not." I wanted to reach across the table for his hand. I craved the touch of his skin more than the fried cheese in front of me. My heart trembled like a giddy schoolgirl, but I popped the rest of a mozzarella stick in my mouth and tried to keep my cool. "How is life at Casa Lindholm?"

"Different." He gave me a lopsided smile. "The bed's real big without you, though."

"Funny," I said. "I was thinking the same

thing the other night."

"Oh, yeah?" His eyes lit up, and his smile was that perfect mix of wicked and genuine that I didn't know what to think.

"Of course. Between you stealing the covers and Benedick hogging the pillow, it's been weird to have a bed all to myself."

Dex snorted at that, reaching across to my mozzarella sticks and helping himself to one. "So." He took a bite. "New job, huh?" His expression was neutral. Almost too neutral. Too uninterested.

"Yep." I reached for a mozzarella stick of my own, but I'd lost my appetite. I settled for peeling off the breading, letting it sprinkle back onto the plate.

"And it's what you want to do?" He carefully took a bite of his cheeseburger.

"Yeah. It's . . ." I sighed. How to explain it? "It's what I've always wanted to do."

"On your terms? The way you wanted?"

My eyes flew to his. He'd remembered that talk of ours that night. He'd actually listened. "Just call me Molly. And/or Jenny."

"Good." He nodded while a small smile played around his mouth. "That's really good." An awkward silence settled over us. This was the right move for me, we both knew that. But I was still going to miss what I was leaving behind.

"When do you go?" He looked over my shoulder as he asked the question, feigning complete disinterest. But I was on to him.

"I thought I'd stick around a couple more weeks." I dropped the denuded stick of cheese back onto my plate. "Till the end of this Faire. Just in case those jousters need me."

"I knew you hadn't gotten enough yet." His easy smile was back as he looked at me again.

Now there was a double entendre. I raised an eyebrow. "Enough of what, exactly?"

"This life. Once you're part of it, it doesn't like to let you go." His eyes remained trained on me, and I wasn't sure if he was really talking about Faire life, or himself. Which was more reluctant to let me go? "You should definitely come to Faire this weekend," he said again, reaching for his burger. "We could hang out."

"Hang out? Why, Declan MacLean, are you asking me out on a date?" I put on my best terrible southern accent and fluttered my eyelashes. I thought he was going to choke on his bite of bacon cheeseburger; he pressed the back of his wrist to his mouth to hold in both the food and his laugh. The denial I was expecting, though, never came. Instead his eyes sparkled with merriment as he chewed and swallowed.

"Maybe." He dragged a french fry through the ketchup on his plate and offered it to me. "Would that be so bad?"

The fry was perfect. Crisp and salty with the sweet tang of ketchup. I licked my lips and smiled. "You know, it wouldn't be bad at all."

TWENTY-FOUR

The next morning after coffee, breakfast, and a quick meditation over the morning's tarot cards, I opened my laptop to a flurry of emails from Imogen Dunbrowski. Apparently my new job was starting early.

I was just putting on a new pot of coffee, ready for another lazy morning on the back deck with Murray, when the doorbell rang. Dex leaned against the doorjamb, guitar slung across his back.

"What are you doing here?" But I opened the door wide, gesturing him in.

"Told you last night. I missed you." His arm slid around my waist as I closed the door behind him, turning to press me against the door. I caught the flash of his smile as he bent to kiss me. I was trapped against his body, but I wasn't going to complain. Not when his mouth was urgent against mine, soft and searching, and his hand fisted itself in my hair. There was nowhere else in the world I wanted to be than in this man's kiss.

But this wasn't the time or place. I reluctantly pushed at his shoulder until he stepped back a fraction, giving me space. "We're not alone," I said.

"No?" His eyebrows went up. "April's at work, right? And Mitch's truck isn't outside. I assume he's at the gym."

I nodded. "He is. He'll be back any minute, though. But Caitlin's here too. And I don't —"

"Who?"

"April's daughter. She's home from college for the summer."

Dex's eyes widened. "April has a daughter?"

"She sure does!" A chipper voice called from the kitchen. I looked over Dex's shoulder to see Caitlin passing through. She hoisted a coffee mug. "Thanks for making more coffee, Lulu! And I didn't see any of this." She gestured from Dex to me and back again as she headed for her room. We both watched her go, then Dex turned to me with a grin.

"I like her."

"Me too. But I also don't want to traumatize her with a live sex show."

"Eh." Dex waved a dismissive hand.

"She's in college. I bet she's seen worse."

He wasn't wrong. I cupped his cheek in my hand, leaning in for one more kiss. I hated to admit I was itching to get to Imogen's emails, but with Dex here I could handle a change in plans. "I have some work I was going to do this morning, but I could always blow it off if you . . ."

"Nah." Dex shook his head. "I figured you did, so I brought work too." He gestured at the guitar on his back. "I have a couple songs I'm trying to tweak, get ready to share with the guys. Okay if we work together?"

My smile widened; it was more than okay. "Want some coffee?"

"I thought you'd never ask."

We spent the better part of the day on the back deck. Murray joined us for his regular nap in the sun, and Mitch dropped by for a conversation that was only slightly awkward and contained a minimal amount of glaring. He was coming around on the whole Dex-and-me thing, if slowly. While Dex took over a lounge chair, working his way through a handful of melodies, I turned to my laptop and Imogen's emails.

There was a lot to review: new hire paperwork, business plans, brainstorms about where she wanted to take her small firm. Three case files to get up to speed on drafting estate planning documents. I wasn't used to feeling this good about work, but reading through it all was a joy. She was building exactly the kind of law firm I wanted to work for, and I closed each email eager to start this new chapter of my life.

It was a warm summer day, there was a cool breeze taking away the worst of the heat, and there was a gorgeous man enjoying the day with me. While I worked, he was working too. He kept coming back to one song, playing it over and over, in slightly different keys and tempos, until he was happy with it.

"I really like that one," I said, my voice dreamy from the heat of the day and the music. He glanced up from his guitar and smiled.

"Me too. I'm thinking it'll be a good one for Frederick to sing." He ran through a few notes again, humming along in a higher register than he usually sang, and I could see what he meant. "We'll need to work on it for a little bit, but I'm hoping we can try it out at the Maryland Ren Fest."

"Oh, that's soon," I said. "Just a few weeks. I can't wait to . . ." The words died in my throat. At the beginning of that sentence, I'd forgotten that I wasn't that Lulu anymore. I wasn't going with them to the next stop. Or any more stops after that. The silence that lingered between us told me that for a moment, he'd forgotten too.

"Hey." His voice was soft. "C'mere." He set his guitar aside and held out a hand. I closed my laptop and obeyed, sliding my hand into his. He pulled gently, settling me sideways into his lap on the lounge chair. It was awkward and I was sure we were going to tip, but it was worth the risk.

I relaxed into the circle of his arms as his lips brushed my temple. "So much going on in there," he said, tapping a gentle finger on my forehead. "How'd you get to be so smart?"

My lips lifted in a smile. "Years and years of practice. A shit-ton of student loans." I turned my head to claim a kiss. "How'd you get to be so good at the guitar?"

"Same. No student loans, though."

"Eh. They're overrated." I felt his laugh more than I heard it: the soft rumble in his chest, his smile against my mouth.

Then he drew a breath, pressing his forehead against mine. "You sure you have to go?" The words were whispered, like a confession he didn't want to make, and it stopped my heart.

"Dex . . ." I took a shaking breath. "You know this isn't my life. I'm just a ride-along here." The only thing giving me the strength to walk away from this — from him — was that we both understood it to be finite. I wasn't going to ask Dex to quit the band and come with me, and he wasn't going to ask me to stay. That would mean one of us giving up our life, the thing that gave us purpose, to stay together, and that wasn't right. As much fun as it had been to hang out with Ren Faire musicians and fortune-tellers, this life was his, not mine.

"Yeah. I know." His voice was thick, and he cleared his throat before continuing. "I know this was all a vacation for you." His arms tightened around me, pressing my head to his shoulder. "Forget I said anything."

"Okay." But could I?

"Oh, hey." Dex straightened up, and so did I. We were both desperate for a subject change. "Did I tell you that Michele is coming? She'll be here this weekend."

"Michele?" My mind drew a blank for a long moment before the penny dropped. "Oh! Todd's Michele?"

He nodded. "He's been kinda grumpy again. Hopefully getting him laid will cheer him up."

"He hasn't seemed that bad lately." I frowned, trying to remember. I'd been tied up with the chess match last weekend, and with Dex last night at Jackson's, so I hadn't seen Todd much this past week.

"You don't have to live with the guy," he said solemnly. But when I looked at him, humor danced in his eyes. "Nah, I'm glad she's coming down. They have stuff to talk about."

There he was, looking serious again. But before I could ask what was up he kissed me, his mouth urgent against mine, and I let him make me forget what I was going to say. Wasn't important anyway.

Michele was indeed there by the weekend, but Dex really buried the lede. Because not only was she there at the afternoon show when I dropped by it on Saturday, but there was an entire row in the front taken up by nothing but MacLeans. The DNA was strong in that family: lots of tall gingers and shorter brunettes, cheering and heckling as soon as the Dueling Kilts took the stage.

"Welcome back." I nudged her shoulder as we both leaned against the merch table at the side of the stage.

Michele grinned. "Lulu, right? Good to see you again. Todd been behaving himself?"

I clucked my tongue. "Like you even have to ask." I couldn't imagine anyone more loyal. Just then, Daniel emerged from the backstage area, pausing at the merch table to drop a kiss onto the top of Stacey's head. She smiled all over and gave his hand a fond squeeze as he moved on. Hmm. Maybe loyalty was part of the MacLean DNA too.

I turned back to Michele. "So did you bring all these . . ." I waved a hand toward the rowdy front row. ". . . with you?" There sure were a lot of them, like a family reunion converging on the Willow Creek Faire.

"Sort of." She shrugged. "More like it worked out that way."

"They're good people," Stacey said, and Michele nodded in agreement. "Come hang out with us at the house this week, if you have a chance."

I looked at her with horror. "They're *all* staying with you?" How many bedrooms did Stacey's childhood home have?

A laugh bubbled out of her. "God, no. They're in a couple of vacation rentals the next town over. But my mom loves to entertain, so there's going to be at least one cookout while they're here."

"Nice." I relaxed against the table, bracing myself with my hands behind my back. Something pricked at my brain; something I wasn't noticing. But it was too nice a day, and Dex had just smiled at me as he swung into "Whiskey in the Jar," so I decided to give it a rest.

If there was one thing the visiting Mac-Leans were, they were loud. So after my favorite song was over, I waved goodbye to Stacey and Michele and set off down the lanes. I hadn't seen too much of the Faire the weekend before, what with being in it and all, and it had been a long time since I'd been at a Faire without working it. Time to explore.

It was a hot summer day without any rain in the forecast, and I was grateful for the liberal amount of sunscreen I'd put on that day. I munched on a funnel cake and wandered around, my skirts brushing the ground and my boots kicking up dust — I may not have been working, but I was still in costume. The lanes at this small Faire wound through the trees, and it seemed there was something to see at every clearing. Vendors were set up along the sides of the lanes, their tents and wares bright pops of color against the green and brown of the trees. Snatches of music came at me from all sides, and off in the distance was the clash of steel and cheers from a large crowd. Yep, that was the joust.

The layout reminded me so much of our

last stop at the Blue Ridge Faire that it didn't take long for me to become home-sick for it. I missed my fortune-tellers. I missed the excitement of the patrons lining up to get their cards and palms read. I missed the rattle of the runes. But this was a school fund-raiser, I reminded myself. Maybe there was a prickly school board member who was against that kind of thing. Wouldn't be the first time.

But then I turned a corner, finding myself near the front stage. This was probably where pub sing happened at the end of the day — it was nicely situated not far from the front gate. There was a handy tavern nearby that was doing a brisk business on this hot day, staffed by volunteers in red T-shirts. I took the opportunity to duck into the shade of its canopy — sunscreen didn't last all day, after all. I bought a bottle of water and sipped on it slowly, when what I really wanted to do was dump it down my cleavage. When I emerged from the tavern again, I saw the most welcome sight: a ven-dor's cart that looked like a traveling wagon. I knew that wagon, and even from this dis-tance I knew that it sold tarot cards. My steps picked up speed as I headed over there.

"There you are!" The seller looked pleased

to see me. "How are things going?"

"Well, this morning I drew the Sun card, so you tell me." The card had filled me with optimism, and I'd known as soon as I'd looked at it that it was going to be a good day.

She laughed, throwing her head back. "That sounds pretty damn good to me. So everything is going the way it should, then, huh? That's great — let that energy flow from you to everyone you meet." She regarded me for a minute, looking me up and down like I was a grandchild she hadn't seen in years and was about to remark on how much I'd grown. "You're a long way from that lady that threw her phone in the laundry wench tub."

I covered my eyes with a hand. "That's going to follow me forever, isn't it?"

"Not forever. Just until someone else does something more interesting."

I shook my head ruefully as I walked away. Nothing like leaving the legacy of being Lulu the Phone Girl to the folks on the Renaissance Faire circuit. I should have been embarrassed, but instead I was oddly pleased. The business-oriented, parent-pleasing Louisa wouldn't have left any mark at all. If that same Louisa was returning to being an attorney now that would be a problem. But I was Lulu now, twenty-four/ seven. I had a feeling that I would be leaving more marks going forward.

After two months of traveling with the Dueling Kilts, it felt foreign to be away from them. It was ridiculous, since I could see them whenever I wanted, and Dex came to spend time with me at Mitch's house more often than not. But I was nostalgic for those nights around the firepit and falling asleep to the murmur of voices on the other side of the motorhome wall. So when Stacey told me they were having a get-together at the Lindholm house on Tuesday night, I jumped at the invitation.

The Lindholm backyard had been transformed into its own private campsite. The motorhome sat parked in a back corner, dark and unneeded, while we gathered on the covered patio. A firepit blazed merrily in the backyard, providing additional seating on the stone benches around it.

I looked for Dex the second I got there, and to my delight he was looking for me too, greeting me with a kiss and a bottle of water. "How dehydrated did you get today?"

He knew me a little too well. "I'll have you know that I drank plenty of water." Okay, maybe two bottles of water wasn't "plenty," but I wasn't going to tell him that.

While we sipped at our drinks, he gave me the lay of the land, pointing out each family member with his beer bottle and giving me a condensed version of their life story. I had no prayer of keeping up or remembering a single name out of the throng, but I did my best to nod along and look like I was retaining what he said.

Until he got to the tall kid talking to Todd. "And that's Seamus. Remember him? He's the one that plays fiddle."

"That's Seamus?" I looked closer at the teenager, all long arms and legs, a nose that looked a little too large for his face. He would be absolutely devastating once puberty was done with him. But for now . . . "Oh my god, he's an infant."

Dex raised an eyebrow. "I wasn't the one asking if he was cute."

"Ugh. I take it back."

He laughed and slid an arm around my shoulders, tugging me into a sideways hug with a kiss on my temple. I loved that little gesture of possession; I'd come to notice that he did it when he wanted to show that we were connected, whether it was to others around us or just to the two of us. I nestled my head into the crook of his neck and let myself enjoy the feel of his arm around me. How had he become my safe space? And how was I going to let him go?

I already knew that the MacLeans were a musical family, and now that there were more of them I was able to see just how far that went. It didn't take long for Seamus to break out his fiddle, and he and Todd played gorgeous duets around the fire. Soon, Frederick accompanied them on his drum, and while I was talking to Stacey I heard guitar chords start up. I looked up, and over at the other side of the fire I spotted Dex sitting next to another cousin, this one even younger than Seamus. They both balanced guitars on their knees, and as Dex demonstrated a chord, the kid mimicked him. No melodies were coming from the two of them, the way that Todd and Seamus played together. This was start and stop, start and stop, then stop for a while as Dex slowed down what he was doing so his younger cousin could catch up.

I was mesmerized watching the two of them. This was a side of Dex that I'd never seen. He was patient; when the kid got frustrated he stopped everything, making jokes until the frustration cleared away and they were both laughing. I would have never imagined this from the Ren Faire Lothario I had met at the beginning of the summer.

"They're talking about letting Seamus sit in on the show this weekend." Stacey raised her eyebrows over her hard lemonade.

I raised my own eyebrows back. "Really? So it'll be a quartet?"

"No. A trio." She imbued that last word with meaning. "They want to see if he can handle Todd's spot. Todd asked him to come down with Michele, so it sounds like it's been in the works for a little bit." She shook her head, her forehead suddenly pinched with worry. "I'm not sure what it means for us, you know, long-term. But I guess we'll see."

"Oh." I sat with that for a long moment. It had been a while since anyone had talked about Todd leaving the band. But with Michele here and talk of Seamus subbing in for Todd, maybe it was actually going to happen. "At least the band isn't breaking up?"

"True." She saluted me with her bottle. "There's always a bright side, right? Anyway . . ." I could practically see her forcing the cheer back onto her face. "I'm sure it'll be fine. It'll all work out."

"Of course it will." I slid an arm around her shoulders, and she leaned into my offered comfort. It was nice to be able to do that: give back the comfort she had given me all those weeks ago.

But I needed comfort too, and toward the end of the night I found Dex near the cooler.

"Hey, what's up?" He looked startled as I snaked my arms around him.

"Nothing." But my tight grip said otherwise, and he put his beer down on a nearby table to give me his full attention.

"Hey," he said again, his voice lower. "Lu. What's wrong?"

I snuggled in closer. "I just need to feel you. Just for a minute."

He didn't argue. "Okay. I got you." I snuggled in closer as he planted one kiss after another in my hair, on my temple. His heart thumped against mine, and I let its reassuring beat calm my racing thoughts. His hands were flat on my back, rubbing in slow circles that had nothing to do with sex and everything to do with comfort.

It occurred to me then that it hadn't been about sex for a while. In fact, we hadn't been intimate since we got to Willow Creek. The Dex I'd met at the beginning of the summer wouldn't have stood for that; he would have found someone new by now. But this Dex seemed content to hold me, in front of my cousin and his family, like we were something real. Something that was going to last.

That was, of course, impossible. But I held him with everything I had. Because it wasn't long now: that future without the two of us together. It was getting closer by the minute, and I felt the passage of each of those minutes.

At the first show on Saturday, I held my breath as Frederick and Dex took the stage with Seamus, and a sideways glance at Daniel and Stacey told me that they were as tense as I was; Daniel's jaw was set so hard I was worried he'd crack a molar, and Stacey gripped the merch table with fingers that turned white from the effort. But none of us had to worry; while he didn't have the smooth patter down that Todd had developed from years of performing with his brothers, Seamus certainly had the skills to make the music flow effortlessly, his fiddle blending in seamlessly with Dex's guitar and Frederick's drum. A couple numbers in, I could see Daniel visibly relax; he bent down and murmured something in Stacey's ear, and she nodded vigorously in agreement.

The two of them looking less tense made me feel the same. And I couldn't help but think that something was shifting, changing with the band. I could only hope that it would be a good change as far as Dex was concerned. Because as supportive as he was of my future, I couldn't help but feel the same for his. If we weren't going to be moving forward together, I wanted to leave here knowing he was going to be happy.

Otherwise, what was the damn point?

TWENTY-FIVE

Maybe I should have stuck with the fortune-tellers; turned out I knew my shit. When I'd sensed that something was shifting within the band, I'd been dead-on.

The bomb dropped on Wednesday night, in one of the big booths at Jackson's. We'd gathered for happy hour, and Todd and Michele in particular looked happier than usual. It only took one look at the diamond on Michele's left hand to find out why. I thought Stacey was going to vibrate out of her skin with happiness, and a quick glance around showed that everyone shared in the excitement. This kind of news would have fallen flat on Dex a few months ago, but now a smile lit up his eyes, and he bent to hug his sister-in-law-to-be with a tenderness that made my heart swell.

"Big news, huh?" He took the seat next to me, nudging himself as close as our chairs would allow.

"I'll say." I tilted my head and looked at him closer. "Why aren't you more upset about it?"

He looked surprised at the question, but before he could speak, Frederick did.

"Wait." Frederick leaned back in his chair after examining Michele's ring. "What does this mean as far as everything? The band? The future?"

"Yeah." Stacey's face fell a fraction. "Todd, does this mean you're quitting? I mean, Seamus did a great job and all, but I don't know if he's quite at your level yet."

"Maybe not yet." Todd looked happy to agree with Stacey. "But he will be. And it's not like I'm leaving for good."

She blinked. "You're not?"

"No. We talked it out." His gaze went to Michele, and they shared a look that was pure heart eyes. "We've got some work to do, but Seamus is going to join the band part-time. He'll cover the shows we do that are down south — especially through the spring and summer — and then I'll join up with you when the shows are closer to home."

"Then he's only on the road a few months a year, a month or two at a time. Closer to home, so I can see him during the week." Michele beamed as she hugged his arm.

"That's so much more manageable."

Todd nodded. "Seamus and I will rotate in and out."

Rotate. My mind skidded on that word. I'd used the exact word to Dex, and he'd used it when talking to the laundry wench about their business model. This was Dex's idea. No wonder he wasn't upset about it. He was in on it. My heart rate sped up as I looked at him in wonder. But Dex didn't meet my eyes. His attention was trained on both Todd and Daniel. The latter nodded.

"That's the plan. Kind of like how the laundry wenches have different casts that cover different Faires, but with the same material. Who knows, maybe we could branch out like that too if we get ambitious. We could cover more ground. But anyway, that's one reason Seamus and his parents came down when Michele did."

Stacey gaped at them. "You two planned this?" Her voice was delighted.

No, I wanted to say. *No, this wasn't their plan. This was Dex's plan. Dex's idea.* The edges of my vision grew red as Daniel nodded in confirmation, while Dex picked up his beer and took an overly casual swig. He didn't seem to care that Daniel was taking credit for his work. For his thoughts.

But I cared. I dug my nails into Dex's

arm. "What the hell's going on?" I hissed out the words, just loud enough for him to hear.

Dex winced and put down his beer before removing my hand from his arm, threading our fingers together. "It's fine."

"It's not fine!" I sounded like an angry snake. "This was your idea, and you're okay with them taking over?"

"Sure." He shrugged. "It's all gonna work out. That's the important thing."

"But . . ."

Meanwhile, Todd was still talking. "There's details to figure out. But that's the general idea. I think it's going to work out great."

Everyone seemed to agree, but I seethed. It didn't matter that two months ago I saw Dex as nothing more than a fuckboy without a brain in his head. How dare his family treat him like that too. So when Daniel got up to fetch another round of drinks, I followed under the pretense of helping.

I barely made it out of earshot. "What the fuck are you doing?"

Daniel blinked. "Excuse me?" His voice was sharp, and his eyes were sharper.

It was a delicate balance, talking loud enough to be heard over the bad karaoke but not yelling so that they heard me back at the table. But I did my best. "This whole new 'business model.' " My use of air quotes was stellar. "I know that wasn't your idea. It wasn't Todd's idea. It's —"

"Dex's. I know." Glasses of beer started to arrive, and Daniel slid them across the bar in front of the two of us. "He and I talked about it back in Virginia. Then I went to Todd with it, and —"

"Then why didn't you say so? Back there." I threw my arm out, gesturing toward the table.

"Because he said not to." Daniel threw up his hands in frustration, and in that moment he looked so much like his cousin, even though he looked nothing like his cousin. "He said it would sound better coming from me, which . . ."

". . . is ironic?" I raised my eyebrows. "Stacey filled me in on how you two got together."

Daniel's laughter was a short bark, unexpected. "You're not wrong about that. But I think he meant because I'm the business-minded one around here. A plan from him wouldn't sound like a serious plan." He sighed. "Look, all that's important to him is that the band stays together and keeps playing. That's the most important thing in his life. He doesn't care how it happens, and who gets credit for what."

Something in my chest dropped at that. *The most important thing in his life . . .* Those words were like mental Windex, wiping the clutter from my mind, leaving everything clear. No more what-ifs about the future. No more wishing. It wasn't going to change anything. I was a temporary presence in Dex's life, and my time here was done.

What was I doing here? Why was I sitting at that table with Stacey and Michele like I was a permanent part of this group? I was on my way out the door, and Dex was ready to close it behind me.

"You're right." It was hard to breathe around my heart, which had grown too big and was beating too hard. "You know what, I should . . ."

"Hey." Daniel stooped a little, his eyes concerned as I put my palm to my forehead. "You okay? Do you need to sit down?"

"No," I choked out. God, I felt like an idiot. I just wanted to leave.

"Come on." He touched my arm. "Don't worry about the drinks, I'll get them. Let's get you back to the table."

"No." My voice was higher this time, louder. "I'm gonna . . . I need to go."

I fled the bar like a chickenshit, but I needed to get outside before the sob I knew was coming escaped from my throat. I barely made it, the door banging behind me and drowning out the broken sound I made.

This was what sucked. I was in love with Dex. And he had no room for that kind of thing in his life.

I paced around the front of the parking lot, my breath evening out as I calmed down. Finally I stood in the parking lot, my hands on my hips as I stared straight up into the sky. Night had fallen and the stars were out. I counted fifty-seven of them before I felt halfway normal again. And with that came clarity of thought: I didn't have a ride home.

Just then the door to Jackson's opened behind me. Golden light spilled out to where I stood, along with music and a general murmur of voices. The light and sound cut off abruptly as the door banged shut, and I closed my eyes. Measured footfalls walked toward me, and I didn't even need to look. I knew it was Dex before he even spoke.

"You okay? Daniel said you needed some air. What's up?"

"Nothing," I choked out, which sounded super convincing. I took out my phone, scrolling for a rideshare app. "I just need to get home."

He paused for a beat, long enough for me

to realize he wasn't going to argue for me to stay. "Need a ride?"

I should have said no. I had an Uber account. I should get my own ride. Pull off this Band-Aid and get started on the rest of my life without him. But I made the mistake of looking at him. Those kind dark eyes. That smile, the one that revealed a dimple in one cheek, covered by that week's growth of beard. I was helpless against both of those things. Helpless against him.

"Sure." My voice was still thick with tears, and I hoped the darkness covered my runaway mascara. "I'd love a ride."

We never talked much when we were in his car, and tonight was no exception. The Challenger's engine was loud enough for the both of us, though, and when he pulled into the driveway and turned the car off, the silence was momentarily deafening.

Finally he broke the silence. "Daniel said you were pissed." His voice was low, even. Giving nothing away.

I couldn't help but snort. "That's putting it mildly."

"About me." Now he turned to look at me, his expression puzzled.

"Well, yeah." I was confused by his confusion. "Why wouldn't I be? You did the legwork on that whole thing, and Daniel got to sit back and take all the credit."

"That's not how that works, though. That's not how *we* work. Remember? I'm not the one who makes the plans. I'm the one who plays the guitar and —"

"— And looks pretty. I remember." I sighed and looked at my hands. None of this was any of my business anymore. If it ever had been. "I just wish . . ." I sighed again, because this was it, wasn't it? Cards on the table time. I was never going to get this chance again. "I wish they saw you like I do. You have so much more to give than that."

It was Dex's turn to sigh; his head fell back to hit the headrest of his seat. "What's the point? I tried, Lulu. I tried to be the guy you want me to be. And I like that guy. But you're still leaving."

Those words hit like a dart, and I teared up from the sting. "That's not fair," I whispered harshly into the dark. "My life isn't here. This life is yours."

"I know. That's not what . . ." He shook his head with an inarticulate sound of frustration. "I see how happy you are, doing what you do. If you gave all that up for me, you wouldn't be the woman I . . ." His breath caught, and mine did too. I knew what he wasn't saying, but the words hung there unspoken between us.

"I want you to be happy too," I said. "Everything's all set with the band, so you don't have anything to worry about. And now that I'm gone, life can get back to normal for you."

"Normal?"

I nodded. "I bet those belly dancers and acrobats miss you." I tried to keep my voice light, but it was hard to do when tears clogged my throat. "Whoever gets you next is going to be very lucky. But you already know that, of course." The idea of him taking someone else to bed made me sick, but I swallowed hard against the feeling. I knew who he was, and it wasn't fair for me to expect him to change.

Dex's sigh came from deep in his chest. "I don't know. That's not . . ." He shook his head. "I'm not sure I'm that guy anymore." His voice trailed off, and when I glanced over at him he was staring hard at the front porch light, blinking hard. "I wish your life and mine weren't so far apart."

"Yeah." My voice was harsh. "Me too. But I can't ask you to come with me. That's not your life."

"No. And you can't stay here anymore, either. That's not yours." He blinked hard, and it could have been the shine from the porch light, but his eyes looked wet. "I knew this was coming. But I guess I didn't want to think about it. Because if I thought about it . . ." His hand covered mine, threading our fingers together and holding on for dear life.

As we lapsed into silence, I felt a crater open up between the two of us. Maybe it had always been there. Maybe it had been a small crack that had been easy to jump back and forth over, as we bickered and flirted our way through this summer. But that crack had widened, inch by inch, until we could no longer jump across. It was time for me to turn down my road, away from Dex, and let him continue down his life's path.

We weren't Todd and Michele. There was no teenage cousin ready to take up the mantle for Dex. And even if there was, he didn't want that. He'd made that clear long ago, and Daniel made it even clearer tonight. *The most important thing in his life . . .* Music. Not me. I couldn't force that. And if I could, would Dex be the man I loved?

"I've never felt this way." Dex's voice was rough now, harsh with emotion. "You and me. It stopped being about sex a long time ago."

"Pretty good sex, though." I smiled around

410

an errant tear, and he was surprised into a soft laugh, nodding in agreement.

"I'm really going to miss feeling like this."

"Me too." I clutched his hand, then clutching became pulling. His seat belt unclicked and then mine followed. I reached for him, or maybe he reached for me. Our kiss started out frantic: lips and tongues and teeth; but soon his mouth gentled against mine. One kiss blurred into another, tasting like the salt of tears as we sought to memorize each other. My fingers threaded through his hair like coming home, just as it was time to leave. I was never going to forget this. Forget him. Forget us.

Finally the kiss came to an end, his lips nipping against mine once, twice. He pressed his forehead against mine as our breaths mingled and calmed.

"I know there's still one more weekend, but this feels like goodbye." His voice was choked, and his hands tightened in my hair, determined to hold me to him as long as possible. The rest of our relationship was now measured in moments, and I felt those moments tick by like a doomsday clock.

"I think it is." My voice was tiny, barely audible over our breathing. I wound a strand of his hair around my fingers, wishing I could keep us linked. The doomsday clock ticked another moment closer to midnight.

He leaned in one more time, his kiss hard, final. When we parted he pressed his lips together, as if holding on to the way I tasted. My shattered heart was reflected in his eyes, but his smile was full of encouragement.

"Good luck, Counselor," he whispered. "I'll miss you."

"I'll miss you too."

Pushing open that car door was the hardest thing I've ever had to do. Walking away from him was the second hardest. But I forced myself to put one foot in front of the other, toward the front porch light. As I touched the front doorknob, the engine of the Challenger fired up behind me. I didn't turn around as Dex backed down the driveway and out of my life. The doomsday clock hit midnight. We were over.

TWENTY-SIX

The living room windows were dark, so I let myself in as quietly as I could, easing the door closed behind me. It was a weeknight, and April got up early for work. Mitch was probably already in bed too since he went to the gym at an ungodly hour of the morning. It was a relief to have the house to myself; I'd been holding back tears for a while now, and I felt like a dam about to burst.

But I wasn't alone. While the living room was dark, the kitchen blazed with light. Caitlin sat at the kitchen island, scrolling through her phone with her earbuds in. She glanced up at my approach and offered me a half smile, taking out one of her earbuds.

"You okay?"

I'd never really talked to April's daughter one on one, even though I'd been here for a couple weeks now. I took a shaking breath to say sure, everything was fine, all of those polite things you say when someone you don't really know asks if you're okay. But to my surprise, I said, "No. Not really." I was still holding the tears at bay, but one or two had leaked out from the corners of my eyes.

She put down her phone and got up, heading for the fridge. "You want some ice cream?" After getting a carton out of the freezer, she moved to the silverware drawer, coming back with two spoons. I couldn't help but smile at the kind gesture.

"Sure." How could I refuse? I sat down next to her and attacked the carton with the proffered spoon. Chocolate chocolate chip may not put my broken heart back together, but it would help get me through tonight.

We each ate a spoonful or two in silence before Caitlin spoke again. "Did you two break up?"

"How did you know?"

She shrugged. "His car was in the driveway for a long time. So either you were making out or breaking up. And people usually look happier when they've been making out."

I choked on my bite of ice cream; she was astute. Once I'd recovered I shot her a sideways smile. "You're not wrong." I studied the chocolate chips that studded the ice cream, planning my next bite. "Yeah. We broke up."

"Ugh." She made a disgusted noise. "Did you dump him? He probably deserved it."

I had to smile at this show of feminine solidarity. "No, I didn't dump him. And he didn't dump me, either. It was more like . . ." I dug in the carton for another bite of ice cream. "More like our time was up. He has to go his way, and I have to go mine. And the shitty thing is that our ways aren't in the same direction. So we can't be together anymore."

Caitlin nodded slowly, as though she understood, and maybe she did. I hadn't anticipated hashing out the details of Dex and me breaking up with an eighteen-year-old that I barely knew. But maybe she was the best possible person to talk to right now. She wasn't going to be mad at Dex like Mitch probably would be, and she wasn't going to aggressively try to cheer me up, like Stacey might. She just listened.

"My roommate was in a long-distance relationship," she finally said, stabbing at the ice cream with her spoon. "When she first got to college, they talked for hours every day. To the point that she wouldn't go out with us or do anything around campus. She was in class, or she was on a video chat with him. She spent the whole first semester that way. But I think it was too much for them.

They broke up over Christmas."

I clucked my tongue. "I'm sorry." Maybe this validation, that long-distance relationships didn't work out, was what I needed to hear.

"She was better after that, though. It was like she was afraid of doing anything new when she was still with him. Like if she made new friends or went out to new places without him it was threatening their relationship. But once she was single she could . . . I don't know. She could live her life. Like what you just said, about life going in separate directions. And it's no one's fault."

"It's no one's fault," I agreed. "It's just life." But the tears had been held back enough, and despite my best efforts, when I blinked a tear hit my cheek, then another.

Caitlin nodded, carefully not meeting my eyes, her mouth working on a bite of ice cream. "Still sucks, though."

"That it does," I agreed. "Welcome to being an adult. A lot of it sucks."

Her sigh was belabored. "Great."

On Saturday I went to Faire one last time. My costume pieces were already packed away, so I wore a sundress and my favorite purple Converse. I had no reason to be

416

there; everything there was to possibly do at a Renaissance Faire I had done and seen, eaten and drank. But this had been my life for the past few months, and it felt wrong to just skip town without saying goodbye.

April and I split one last funnel cake, and we almost immediately regretted the choice as we shook the remnants of powdered sugar from our clothing. I visited the tarot card seller, giving her a hug and asking her to pass along my goodbyes to the fortune-tellers when they met up at the next stop. We took our seats on benches at the very front of the chess match, cheering on (okay, heckling) Mitch as he threatened his opponents with his claymore, and Simon as he fought valiantly with his pirate's rapier.

"We were better pawns than those guys," April muttered to me as the show came to an end and we moved on.

"Be sure and tell Mitch that," I said. "I bet he'll have no problem putting you on the cast for next year."

She gave a mock shudder that looked very real. "No way in hell."

While April had advised against it, we followed the signs to the Marlowe Stage, where the Dueling Kilts were about to start their second show of the day. Things were over with Dex, sure, but technically we were still friends. I didn't know where that left me with the rest of the band, though. They'd become a second family to me these past few months, but would that feeling last now that I was leaving?

I shouldn't have bothered worrying. Stacey's hug was just as genuine as ever. She grasped my shoulders and peered into my eyes. "Are you okay?"

"Yeah." I forced a smile on my face; I was not going to cry at a Renaissance Faire. No way in hell, to quote April. "But thank you for everything. I'd be in a much different place now if it wasn't for you."

Her *awww* sound was muffled against my shoulder as she hugged me again. "I'm so sorry you're leaving," she said. "I admit, I was kind of hoping you'd stick around. We could have done pumpkin spice latte season together."

Perplexed, I looked from her to April, who nodded sagely. "She's very into her PSLs."

Now the *Pumpk!nSp!ce* Wi-Fi password made sense. "You have my number," I said. "Call me anytime. I promise to take better care of this phone."

That earned me a giggle. "You better!"

My next goodbye came from Daniel, who touched my shoulder when Stacey and I broke apart and she'd turned her attention back to the merchandise table and approaching patrons. "Hey." His voice was as soft and direct as it always was. "Listen, I'm sorry about the other night. I didn't . . ."

"No." I wouldn't let him finish that sentence. "Please don't be sorry. That was all me. I can be kind of a bitch when I think people I love are threatened." I realized almost immediately what I'd said, but screw it. Sure, we weren't together anymore, but it didn't change the way that I felt. I hadn't been able to tell Dex; someone in the family may as well know.

Daniel's smile was sympathetic. "I know what you mean." He glanced up at the stage, then back down to me again. "It was great having you along with us."

"Thanks." I stretched up on my toes to give him a hug. I wasn't a hundred percent sure that Daniel was a hugger, but I was so he had to suffer through it. To my surprise he hugged me back.

"If you ever have another breakdown, you know where to go." He adjusted his baseball cap as we separated.

I snorted. "I'll keep that in mind."

A round of applause went up then, bringing my attention to the stage, where the show had started. Dex started it the way he always did, greeting the audience, encouraging light drinking and heavy flirtation. The patter was as familiar by now as my own heartbeat, and I was so focused on this last look at Dex that at first I didn't even notice the rest of the stage. But when I did . . .

"Seamus seems to be working out, huh?" I directed the question over my shoulder in the general direction of Stacey and Daniel. Both nodded.

"He's going to play the rest of this Faire," Daniel said. "Work out the kinks. Then he and Todd will switch off over at the Maryland Ren Fest. After that show we're going straight home for the holidays. Todd wants to do some intense rehearsals with him over the winter, so the kid is up to speed."

"That makes sense." Of course Todd wouldn't just ditch the band. This was such good news.

"And we're going to have to hammer out the schedule, make sure everyone's happy with it." His brow was furrowed with worry, but I knew Daniel by now. Aside from Stacey, schedules were his favorite thing. "But I think it'll work out."

"That's fantastic." As we spoke I spotted Todd in the audience, about halfway back. He was leaning forward, elbows on his knees, watching the stage intently: the look of a man who would have plenty of notes for Seamus after the show. Michele had an arm threaded through Todd's, her head resting on his shoulder. They'd figured out their relationship, and while it may not be the most conventional, it worked for them.

I was thrilled for them. I was sad for me.

I let myself look at the stage one more time. Flanked by Seamus — an actual teenager — and Frederick — who basically looked like one, Dex looked older, even more rugged than usual. I didn't want him to know I was there, but between songs about midway through the set, his gaze wandered over toward the merch table. I saw it in his face when he spotted me. But he was a professional; he didn't stop the show or say a word. I raised my hand in a wave and his answering smile was soft. We'd already said goodbye; there were no more words to say.

His smile, his whole face, blurred as I found myself blinking back tears, and April hooked her arm around mine.

"C'mon." Her voice was kind. "Let's get out of here."

I didn't trust myself to speak. I blinked until my vision cleared, then I let her lead me away from the stage and back to the lane. We didn't make any more stops on the way to the car. It was time to say goodbye to this life for good. It was almost time to go home, and I had to finish packing.

Mitch was quiet on the drive to Virginia on Monday, which was unlike him. But then again, he'd spent the past few weekends as a brawling Scotsman. The man wasn't twenty-five anymore; maybe he was just tired. Or pouting: we'd fought good-naturedly over the music as he'd pulled out of the neighborhood, until I ended the argument by claiming the aux cord.

Then again, I'd been quiet too. After all, I had a lot to think about. Just a few short months ago I'd said goodbye to one life and thrown myself headlong into a new one. And now here I was, doing it all over again. I couldn't get my head around how I could be so excited for my new life and career, yet so sad to be leaving behind the life I'd made with the Faire.

Finally, I cleared my throat. "You were right."

"I know." Mitch didn't even glance in my direction; he kept his eyes on the road as he took a sip of coffee. But when he nestled his mug in the cup holder he glanced over at me, eyebrows raised. "About what?"

"About this summer. Running away and

joining the Renaissance Faire. It was just what I needed." I leaned my head against the passenger-side window, watching scenery zip past. "It was nice to be Lulu again."

"You don't have to stop being Lulu, you know." Mitch's brow furrowed as he glanced over at me. "That was kind of the point of all this."

"Oh, I know." I let my mind drift back over the past few weeks. Louisa had bashed her head against the glass ceiling for years, in a job where her best was never good enough. Lulu applied her talents to new situations — schmoozing for tips and being an office manager for fortune-tellers. Lulu had laughed more in the past two months than Louisa had in the past two years. Lulu had loved. Lulu had *lived,* while Louisa had only been surviving.

Now it was time to bring Lulu back into my real life. Do some living of my own.

"Anyway." I reached over and patted my cousin on the shoulder, which was like patting a brick wall. "Thanks."

"Don't mention it." He took a sip of coffee and tossed another smile my way. "But can we please listen to something else? Because nineties alternative sucks."

I gasped. "Blasphemy." But I swapped our phones, disconnecting from the playlist of my favorite songs from my college days. Mitch's phone was full of hair metal and other gym-based playlists, so we rocked our way down the highway toward my new life.

TWENTY-SEVEN

My phone rang on the way to work. I wasn't surprised; I was fifteen minutes late and had a client coming in first thing this morning. Not the best first impression to be making.

I tried for a professional tone as I hit the Bluetooth button on my steering wheel, just in case it was my boss. "Louisa Malone."

"Hey, Lulu." My assistant, Cheryl, sounded as chipper as ever. Though I should stop thinking of her as my assistant. She was the receptionist/office manager at the Dunbrowski Group now. Her resignation from Stone, Prince & Rogers, by all reports, had been legendary. "Your nine-thirty is here. Are you on the way?"

I bit back a sigh as I pulled up to a stop sign. "Yep. Sorry. Slight emergency with Grandpa, but I'm almost there." Turned out that disappearing off the face of the earth had consequences. Sure, everything had been left on autopay, but without that big law firm salary my savings had taken a huge hit. The answer had been to put my condo on the market — and in this seller's market it went fast — and move in with the Grandparents Malone. It was a better arrangement than it sounded: they had plenty of room, and I could keep a better eye on them. The only downside was the long-distance commute. I was on the road an hour each way, every day, but I made it work.

But sometimes it meant dealing with mornings like this. Where Grandpa Malone, determined that he could trim his own damn trees at the age of eighty-seven, thank you very much, spent twenty minutes in a fight with the guy I'd hired to take off the dead branches in the oak over the driveway. I'd had to intervene, Grandpa had stomped off into the house, and now I was late for work. I hated being late. I hated Grandpa being pissed off at me. It took almost every minute of the long drive into work to defrazzle myself.

This new life was busy, but it wasn't full, the way this summer had been. I missed those brown eyes and that devilish smile. I missed snatches of music in the background of my life. I missed nights around a firepit. I missed the almost-long-enough bed in the back of an ancient motorhome. I missed a cat on my head and a guitarist in my bed.

Sometimes during these long drives my mind wandered back to my summer at the Renaissance Faire. Long days in the sun, long nights in Dex's arms. My text chain with Stacey these days had grown extensive as she kept me updated on their run at the Maryland Ren Fest. The place itself looked huge, and I found myself yearning to wander the sun-dappled lanes and browse the shops that lined them on either side. She sent photos of everyone: Benedick lounging in the sun, oblivious as always to the show happening around him. The guys smiling at each other as they played, hoisting their tankards high when it was time to toast the audience. There was even a video clip or two, with snatches of songs that evoked so much nostalgia in my heart that they hurt to hear, even as I clicked on them again and again.

I had Dex's number in my phone too. I'd even saved one of the pics Stacey had sent as his contact photo. But I didn't text him, even though I itched to almost every day. We'd been apart for a little over two months now, and my heart was just beginning to scar over. Reaching out to him would only tear the wound open again, benefiting nobody. *Maybe next summer,* I told myself over and over. Maybe next summer I could visit

Willow Creek during Faire season, and I'd be able to face him again with a smile.

I heaved a sigh as I pulled into the parking lot. Time to push all these melancholy thoughts down and start my day. I could be sentimental and sad later — when I didn't have a client waiting.

"Morning, Cheryl!" My greeting died in my throat as I looked around the small — and empty — lobby. Had my nine-thirty given up? I glanced up at the clock: five till ten. Wouldn't blame them a bit.

Cheryl looked up from her desk in the lobby. "Hey! Your nine-thirty is in the conference room. Go put your stuff down, I'll grab you some coffee."

"Thanks." I hurried into my office, shucking my coat as I went. October was blowing in cold this year. It was almost Halloween, and I wouldn't be surprised to see snow any day now. I tossed my coat onto the coatrack and my laptop bag on the little couch under the window. I could set up my laptop for the day after this meeting.

I sat down at my desk to catch my breath and center myself. The client had waited this long, another minute or two wouldn't kill them. This had already been a long day, and it wasn't even ten in the morning. I took a few slow, deliberate breaths, then I opened the right-hand drawer of my desk and reached for my cards. The cat tarot deck lived at home, where I relied on its kinder energy for readings in the evenings or on weekends. Rider-Waite was more straightforward for a day at the office.

I shuffled the deck till it felt right, then flipped a card over, my breath escaping me in a long sigh of relief. The World. The woman on the card was way underdressed for this chilly autumn day, but this card pointed to a sense of fulfillment. To completion.

I took another deep breath and focused on the half-naked woman dancing on the face of the card. "Okay," I said to her. I tapped the card a couple times on its edge before adding her back to the deck and slipping it back into the drawer. I touched the picture on my desk — the framed faux tarot card Summer had given me back at the Blue Ridge Renaissance Faire. Out of the darkness and into the light. All signs were pointing in the right direction; I was where I was supposed to be. Good to know, because sometimes, all I wanted was to chuck everything in a bucket of water and run away again.

I straightened my necklace: the tiger's-eye stone I'd had wrapped in wire and strung on a chain. I told myself that I wore it every day for its grounding properties. But I knew I was wearing it because I missed Dex's eyes. Other parts of him too, sure, but I couldn't wear those on a chain around my neck.

My office door opened and Cheryl sailed inside, a large mug of coffee in her hands.

"Bless you," I said as she handed it to me. "Did you offer one to the client?"

"He didn't want one, just took a water."

"Remind me again, he's new, right?"

Cheryl nodded and handed me his intake folder. "New client, initial meeting. Said something about future planning."

"Got it." He probably meant estate planning — getting a will and other future directives in place. People often got legal jargon wrong, but that was our bread and butter. Easy peasy.

"This one's cute," Cheryl said as I grabbed a fresh legal pad off my desk. "You should date him."

Cheryl said that about almost every widower that came through the door. "This is a place of business," I reminded her dryly. "Not geriatric Tinder." Just because I was living with my grandparents didn't mean I wanted to settle down with someone their age.

I headed for the conference room, juggling the folder and legal pad, along with a pen and my precious mug of coffee. For a Friday, it really felt a lot like a Monday. My mind was already skipping ahead: get through this meeting, then call and check on Grandpa. Pick up Halloween candy on the way home; it was almost that time. It wasn't until I bumped open the conference room door with my hip that I realized I hadn't checked the folder. I didn't even know the client's name. Some attorney I was.

"Good morning!" I pasted a sunny smile on my face, hoping it would cover my many sins. "I'm Louisa Malone. So great to meet you, Mr . . . ." The intake folder and legal pad fell to the table, the pen clattering after them. It was only the death grip on my coffee mug that saved it. That was most decidedly not an elderly widower sitting at the conference room table.

"Hey, Lu." Dex smiled at me like we'd just seen each other yesterday, not over two months ago. His smile widened as he noted my reaction. "Surprise."

"No kidding. What the hell are you . . ." I couldn't even finish the sentence as I nudged the conference room door closed behind me. A million thoughts whirled in my head at once, but none of them co-alesced into a single word.

Dex seemed content to fill the silence. "You look good." He gestured at me. I'd given up my pantsuits, but I had thrown a blazer on over my jeans on this casual Friday. "All professional and shit. Kinda hot. I like it."

That did it. I huffed out a laugh and sat down while my shaking legs could still hold me up. "Thanks." I let my eyes roam over him. "You look good too." I wasn't lying. His dark blue collared shirt was open at the throat, showing just enough skin to remind me how he looked without it. It was tucked into jeans with a wide leather belt, and when he leaned back in his chair he rested one ankle over his knee, showing dark brown leather boots. His dark hair was brushed back from his face, still pulled up into that effortlessly casual bun.

For a few long moments we stared at each other like lovestruck teenagers, before I cleared my throat. "So." I straightened up the folder and legal pad I'd dropped. "What are you doing here? I assume it's not for estate planning."

"Future planning," he corrected. "That's what I told the lady out front. She said you'd be able to help me with that."

"Really." My tone was as dry as the desert. "And what kind of future would that be?"

"Well." He planted both feet on the floor and leaned forward, his forearms on the table like a businessman about to offer a deal. "You may not know this about me, but I'm really good at planning things."

I felt a smile crawl up my face. "Oh, really."

His nod was solemn, but his eyes sparkled with humor. "Yep. It's kind of what I do. Always has been." He grinned at the snort that came out of me. God, I'd missed him. "Anyway," he said. "You remember Patrick?"

I blinked at the non sequitur but nodded. "Frederick's Patrick? The juggling comedian guy?"

Dex nodded. "Did you know he and his partner split up?"

"He and his . . ." Confusion jumbled my thoughts. "He and Frederick were together, though." Was Frederick nothing more than Patrick's side piece? Was Dex here to get a revenge posse together? Because I was ready to ride at dawn for Frederick's honor.

Dex tsked at me. "No, I mean his *performing* partner."

"Oh." I sat back in my chair, revenge fantasies squashed.

"Yeah, we met up with them at the Maryland Ren Fest, and apparently Luke — that's the partner — has had enough or whatever." Dex rolled his eyes, because who could ever have enough of that life? Except for people who didn't want to live full-time in campers. "So they're not doing the act anymore."

"Oh," I said again, because I felt like I should say something. But what did any of that have to do with me?

"Yeah. But here's where it gets interesting. Patrick plays the guitar. Always has. He just started doing this juggling schtick with his college buddy."

I felt like there was something just beyond my comprehension, waiting for me to catch on. But I wasn't there yet. "So . . ."

"So. Maryland Ren Fest ended last weekend, and everyone's going up to Michigan. Remember? Working on the future of the band?"

I nodded, still not clueing in. "Then why are you here?"

He leaned across the table, tapping his finger on the intake folder. "I'm working on the future too. My future. I made an appointment and everything."

"Okay." There was something here that I

434

wasn't getting, but I could play along. Especially if he kept looking at me like that. God, I'd missed him. I pulled my legal pad closer and uncapped my pen. "What do you want in your future?"

There came that smile. The one with the dimple. The one I couldn't resist. "You."

My eyes flew to his, looking for the innuendo, but all I could see in those brown depths was an honesty that broke my heart. "I mean," I said gently, "what do you want to do?"

His smile turned wolfish. "You." And there was the innuendo.

I put down my pen, tried to frown, but my mouth curved in the wrong direction. "Dex." I tried to make my voice disapproving, but it was hard to do around a smile.

"Daniel said he talked to you. Before you left. He told you how I felt. About the band staying together, music and all that."

"Right. That it's the most important thing to you. I remember." I looked down at my legal pad. I didn't need to write that down — it was engraved on my heart already. It still stung.

"Yeah. He's full of shit." At those words, my gaze flew to him, but he was looking at the table too, shaking his head. "Or maybe I'm full of shit. I don't know."

"What?" I didn't like the uncertain look on his face. He looked lost; I hated when he didn't believe in himself. I ached to reach for him, to touch his hand, but touching would lead to other things and I was determined to stay professional. "How so?" I asked gently.

"I tried, you know." His gaze stayed on the table, his fingertips drumming on its shiny wood surface. "To go back to the way things used to be. Be the old Dex. I thought it would be easy. Like going back to normal. But I'm not that guy anymore." He shook his head. "I went to get coffee in the morning, and it was just for me. There was nobody there to talk about the songs I was working on, or even ask me how my day was. I missed that. I missed you. It was like . . . there was this Lulu-shaped space in everything I did."

I caught my breath; I knew exactly what he meant. "Dex . . ."

But he wasn't finished. "I realized that I like my life better when we're together. I like *myself* better when we're together."

I blinked back imminent tears, even as I shook my head. "I miss you too," I said softly. "But I can't go back on the road with you. My life is here. I've been building this . . ." I gestured around the conference room, toward the door that led to the rest of the office. But I couldn't shake what he said, because despite this new life I'd created for myself, I couldn't ignore the Dex-shaped space that nothing else could fill.

"And I want you to keep building it." He reached a hand across the table as though he were going to take mine, but pulled it back before taking a fortifying breath. "But what if I built it with you?"

He wasn't making any sense. "You can't just leave the band. That's your life."

"That's the thing." He shook his head. "You keep talking about my life, and your life. I want *our* life. Like Todd and Michele have."

"Our life?" All I could do was repeat his words. "But . . . we're not Todd and Michele. You don't have a teenage guitarist cousin waiting to take over for you."

"Nope. But we've got a Patrick."

Now the last puzzle piece clicked into place, revealing the larger picture. "Patrick's joining the band." I leaned back in my chair, embarrassed it had taken me this long to catch on. "And you're okay with that? It won't be a family thing anymore."

Dex waved a hand. "He and Freddy are getting pretty serious. So that's close enough as far as I'm concerned. He's already back home with everyone else to get a jump-start on learning the songs. Everyone's there now, with the people they love. Except me. Because you're my person, and you'd gone home."

I sucked in a breath. "You mean you love —"

"Of course I love you." He said it so matter-of-factly. "You love me, right?"

The question was so direct that I was taken aback. This wasn't how declarations of love usually went, but there wasn't much about Dex and me that was normal. "Yes," I said. "I do."

"Good." He kept talking like he hadn't just dropped a bomb in my lap, but his shoulders relaxed a touch, and his smile was easier around the edges. "So what do you think? Ren Faires in the summer and law firms in the winter. Rotate in and out with me?"

How did he make that sound dirty? "Rotate our entire lives?"

"Sure." He gestured at my legal pad. "You were working while you were at Mitch's house, right? Couldn't you work anywhere? Like, say, at a camper during the week when you're not playing with your fortune-tellers and getting wooed by pub crawls."

That sounded like heaven. "Yeah. I . . . I

could." My mind whirled with new ideas as a completely different future began to come together. A future where I was with Dex, but I was also working remotely during the week. Where I could spend the winter with my grandparents, but wear long skirts in the woods in the summertime.

He must have sensed me wavering, because Dex got out of his chair, circling the table toward me. All the oxygen seemed to slip from the room; I couldn't breathe, and the only sound was the tread of his boots as he got closer and closer.

Finally he knelt next to where I sat. "Lulu." He took a deep breath, his eyes dark and serious, fixed on me. "Being without you . . . it's like half of a life. You took the other half with you when you left." His expression was earnest, free of all innuendo. Nothing like that overgrown bad boy who'd eyed me up and down the day we'd met — was this even the same person? "If you miss me like I've missed you . . . what if we stuck them together? Your life for half the year . . ." He held out a hand, palm up. "My life for the other half." His other hand joined the first, palm up. Then he closed his hands, like slapping together a peanut butter and jelly sandwich. Like he was describing something that was just as easy to fit together. "That makes a whole life. For us both."

It was the most ludicrous thing I'd ever heard. Which was why it made sense for us. I bent to him, cupping his cheek, the rasp of his beard against my palm. "You won't get bored?" My voice broke as I tried to find a flaw in this plan. It was too perfect. Too much like exactly what I wanted. "When you're stuck here with me, and not with the band?"

He laid his hand over mine, holding me to him. "Not if I'm with you." He was so honest, so serious, that for a moment I couldn't breathe. The feel of his skin against mine was like the solution to all my problems at once. It was that simple: I missed him; now he was back. He was going to stay with me, and I was going to go with him.

Could it really be that easy? "I think we have a lot to talk about," I said. "And a lot of plans to make." I let my gaze run over his face as I stroked his cheekbone, his eyes falling closed at my touch. "But maybe . . . I think we could figure this out."

Relief spread across his face like a sunrise. "Good." He rose to his feet, pulling me with him, his hand flat on the small of my back. A shiver sped through me as he leaned in, his lips grazing my cheek. "I'm so good at making plans. You have no idea."

"I've heard that about you." My smile widened and I turned my head just enough to catch his mouth with mine. What was intended to be a sweet, friendly kiss got out of control fast. His mouth devoured mine like he'd come home. I was going to walk out of this conference room with whisker burn, and I didn't give a damn.

"So you love me?" I needed to hear it again.

"God, yes." He nibbled on my throat. "How did you not know that? I thought you were supposed to be smart. Lawyer and all."

"Still. A girl likes to hear it."

"Oh." He pulled away to look straight into my eyes. "I love you, Lulu Malone. I'm fuckin' crazy about you. Let's do this."

His words made me giddy; maybe it really was that easy. "Okay."

I gathered my things from the conference room, and once I opened the door we were two professionals finishing a meeting as I walked him to the front door.

"Where are you staying?" I pitched my voice low, though I didn't know why. Cheryl could hear everything; I was going to have a lot of explaining to do.

Dex shrugged. "Hadn't figured that out yet. If this went well, I was hoping to come back to your place." He crooked a smile. "If it didn't, I figured I'd find a hotel somewhere. Crawl into a twelve-pack."

"My place sounds good. Although . . ." I winced apologetically. "How do you feel about grandparents? I'm kind of living with them now."

He cocked his head at me, squinting. "Isn't your grandma the pervy one who's into kilts?"

"Don't worry. I'll protect you."

"You better."

We laughed, but I sobered up quick. "Seriously, though. Did you pack your kilt? Because that'll make Grandma very happy."

He didn't answer me, but his kiss was a smile against my mouth. We still had a lot to hash out, but at the end of it all we were going to turn these two half lives into one whole one. I'd missed him so much, and now he was back. Better yet, we were back. No more separate lives. We were going to travel the same path together from now on.

EPILOGUE

"We almost there?"

I sighed, keeping my eyes on the road. "You know, Grandma, if I wanted someone asking me that every five minutes, I could have had children." She was just as capable of checking the GPS as I was, but one glance over at her showed that she had her lips pressed together to keep from laughing. Yeah, she was just messing with me.

"Dex is a bad influence on you," I said. "I know you miss him, but maybe I shouldn't take you to see him today after all."

She clucked her tongue at me. "Like you're going to turn this car around. He's been gone a month, and I know how much you miss that boy."

Grandma wasn't wrong. After months of sharing a bedroom with me in the Malone family home, Dex had left in late April for North Carolina, linking up with the Dueling Kilts there. Work had kept me here in

Virginia for another month, but that wasn't long at all. It was his turn in the rotation, and I knew he was excited to be back, not only with his family but on the road.

After that October day when he'd surprised me at work, it hadn't taken long for us to hammer out the details of our new life together. Grandma and Grandpa Malone had never met a stranger they couldn't turn into an honorary grandchild, so Dex had practically moved in that first night. After enduring a Malone family Christmas, we'd flown up to Michigan together for a Mac-Lean family New Year celebration. Then, once the Kilts had gone back on the road, he'd come home with me.

I'd worried about him being bored while he was with me, but he put that notion to rest almost immediately. It had taken him exactly three open mic nights to be hired at a local coffee shop, playing four nights a week. The money wasn't great, but he was having fun, and we didn't have rent to pay anyway. Soon after that he discovered the internet. I didn't know that "Hot Guy Teaches You to Play Guitar" was an internet niche that needed filling, but he did it with aplomb, and his follower count grew by the day. So even when he wasn't on the road, he was making music.

On my end, I couldn't have asked for a better outcome. Remote work had never really caught on at my old firm — they preferred their associates to be live and in person, rendering work-life balance an unachievable fairy tale. But Imogen had embraced the concept when I suggested it. She was more interested in spending time in Georgia with her grandchildren than in building a legal empire, so it didn't take long for us to put a plan into place. A plan that involved remote work, video calls, and a dedicated paralegal to handle intake meetings. While one of us would always be in the office, the other would work remotely, accessible via video chat. Turned out rotating in and out wasn't just for members of a Renaissance Faire band. It was the ultimate in work-life balance, and would have never worked at a big law firm.

I'd held down the fort over the winter, while Imogen enjoyed the holidays with her family and took a second honeymoon with her husband. Now we were on the precipice of summer, and it was my turn. Today was the first day of the Blue Ridge Renaissance Faire, and Grandma and I were on our way.

My mom was not a fan of my new lifestyle — part-time attorney and part-time Renaissance Faire follower didn't fit into her tidy impression of a successful life plan — but Mitch was thrilled. He'd offered to meet us here this weekend to celebrate me joining what he called "the family business," even though he made zero dollars doing it. But his baseball team were on its way to State yet again, so it was just Grandma and me today. We'd see him in his kilted glory in Willow Creek later in the summer. After this day with Grandma, I'd spend the next week wrapping things up at work, and then next weekend I'd be back to stay. Dex and I had called dibs on the family motorhome from now until the end of October, and we were going to enjoy every second of cramped, crowded, glorious privacy.

After what felt like years but was only a couple of hours, we bumped across the field that served as parking for the Blue Ridge Renaissance Faire. Walking through the gates felt like triumph. Dex and I were different people who had very different lives, but beneath it all we loved the same things: family and our work. We'd only spent one month apart, committing the rest of our time to fitting in each other's lives, and everything fit. Like puzzle pieces on Grandpa's coffee table.

Grandma consulted the map we'd gotten at the entrance, and I looked over her shoulder to help her navigate, as though I didn't know this place like the back of my hand.

"Are we late?" She consulted her watch, and I shook my head.

"We should be right on time."

And we were. It was the Dueling Kilts' first show of the day, and Stacey had the merchandise table all set up. She greeted my grandmother with a hug while I bent down to give Benedick a belly rub under the table. When I straightened up I saw Frederick on the stage; he threw me a gleeful wave that I returned enthusiastically. My heart rate sped up; Dex was there somewhere. Grandma was right; it had only been a month, but I missed that boy something fierce.

I'd just escorted Grandma to a relatively empty row in the middle when Dex took the stage like it was his birthright, all red kilt, stompy boots, and open-throated shirt. He spotted us almost immediately, and I couldn't keep the grin from my face.

"Hey." Dex's voice rang out loud and clear through his headphone mic. "There's my girl." The show hadn't started yet, so he hopped off the lip of the stage and started toward us, his grin broad.

My heart swelled in my chest at his approach. As he got to us, he swung his guitar around to his back and . . . bent down to hug my grandma. Her throaty chuckle came through on his mic, and the audience joined in the laughter. I couldn't help but smile. He'd certainly gotten close to my grandparents in the past few months, taking over some of the household chores to help them out. Grandpa appreciated that Dex mowed the lawn. Grandma appreciated that he did it wearing a kilt.

Eventually he turned to me, humor dancing in his dark brown eyes. "Hey, babe."

"Hey, yourself." More applause from the audience as he enfolded me in a hug, tight enough to let me know that yeah, he'd missed me too. Ren Faire Lothario no more. "Missed you," he said, low in my ear.

"Missed you too." I cupped his face in my hands after he let go, very aware that he was mic'd up, preventing me from saying anything more in any detail. But we knew each other well enough by now that we could telegraph it with our eyes.

I let a thumb trace his cheekbone through his usual close-trimmed beard. "Have a great show. Play my song for me."

He turned his head to lay a kiss on my palm. "Always." With one last grin at Grandma, he headed back to the stage, where Frederick and Seamus were waiting for him.

"My girl Lulu is here," he said to the audience once he got back onstage. "And she's a big fan of songs about women betraying their men. Not sure what that says about our relationship, but if you know me, you know I don't like to think too hard. So here you go, babe."

I looked over my shoulder at Stacey as the opening notes of "Whiskey in the Jar" floated out among the trees. She was giggling, and beside her Daniel was shaking his head with a smile on his face. I caught his eye, and he raised his head in pleased acknowledgment. I was home, and I was more than excited for this summer to start.

But it hadn't started quite yet. This day was about Grandma, who seemed to be enjoying herself immensely. The show had barely ended before she had the map out again. "Where to next?"

"If you're hungry, we could get you a turkey leg. The pub crawl seems like a lot of walking; we could skip that today. Or I could take you down to Mystics' Glade." I tapped its location on the map, not too far away. "I have some friends I'd love for you to meet. And you can get your palm read. You know, make sure your marriage is going to work out, find out how many kids you're going to have."

On our way out we passed Dex, holding court at the entrance with the tip basket, and he let me pass with a kiss. "You coming back later?"

"Of course I am." I didn't just mean today. He was right about this Renaissance Faire life. Once you were a part of it, it didn't want to let you go.

And I didn't want it to.

ACKNOWLEDGMENTS

This book was a hard one to write, as the "oh, God, we're in a pandemic" panic of 2020 morphed into the "oh, God, this pandemic is never going to end" depression of 2021. Brains were broken, and even easy tasks became difficult. Writing a rom-com set at a Renaissance Faire felt nearly impossible. But nevertheless, I persisted, and I'm so glad I did. Getting to know Dex and Lulu has been a joy, and I hope you love them too.

The biggest thanks go to my agent, Taylor Haggerty, and my editor, Kerry Donovan. Thank you both for being so kind, and more importantly, patient, as I navigated writing this book. I appreciate you believing in me, and assuring me that I could finish this book when returning my advance, changing my name, and running away to live in a cave felt like a better option. Additional thanks and love to Jasmine Brown, Jessica Mangicaro, Mary Baker, and Kristin Cipolla for all their efforts in keeping me on track. And thank you to Colleen Reinhart for my gorgeous purple cover!

Writing simply does not happen without my critique partners, Gwynne Jackson and Vivien Jackson, cheering me on and praising my spelling when there's nothing else nice to say. Thank you for the reassurance that I'm not the worst at this!

This book would not have been written without my sprinting partner, Eva Leigh. Years ago, I read her Blades of the Rose series and was in awe of this immensely talented author. Now, that same author texts me to check in and to do writing sprints. Life comes at you fast!

Special thanks to Alyson Grauer and Drew Mierzejewski for their hospitality at the Bristol Renaissance Faire, including that prime seat at the joust. You're my favorite noble couple!

Special, special thanks to *The Gwendolyn Show* for letting me borrow her character to give Lulu advice at a crucial moment.

This was the first book written in my new residence in Tucson, Arizona, and I'm so grateful to the people and businesses here that have started to make it feel like home. Huge thanks to Mostly Books for their friendly welcome and being such a joy to work with. Shout-out to Cartel Roasting Company, Raging Sage Coffee Roasters, the Starbucks at First and Wetmore, Ren Coffeehouse, and the Barnes & Noble on La Cholla for being there when I needed to get out of the house and write. Additional thanks to Sarah, Sari, Kimberly, Brooke, and Jeanne for putting up with my awkward self! Looking forward to more writing dates with you all.

Finally, I want to say thank you to all of the readers out there. The Bookstagrammers and Booktokers. The cosplayers and merch creators. The love that you show to my books and my characters blows me away, and when it's hard to write I remind myself that I'm writing for you. I'm so thankful for each and every one of you.

ABOUT THE AUTHOR

Jen DeLuca was born and raised near Richmond, Virginia, but now lives in Arizona with her husband and a houseful of rescue pets. She loves latte-flavored lattes, Hokies football, and the Oxford comma. Her novels, *Well Met, Well Played,* and *Well Matched,* were inspired by her time volunteering as a pub wench with her local Renaissance Faire.

CONNECT ONLINE
JenDeLuca.com
Facebook: JenDeLucaBooks
Twitter: Jaydee_Ell

The employees of Thorndike Press hope you have enjoyed this Large Print book. All our Thorndike, Wheeler, and Kennebec Large Print titles are designed for easy reading, and all our books are made to last. Other Thorndike Press Large Print books are available at your library, through selected bookstores, or directly from us.

For information about titles, please call:
(800) 223-1244

or visit our website at:
gale.com/thorndike

To share your comments, please write:

Publisher
Thorndike Press
10 Water St., Suite 310
Waterville, ME 04901